Shadows in Salem
Wicked Tales from the Witch City

A FunDead Publications Anthology

Edited by Amber Newberry

ISBN:0989472620
ISBN-13:9780989472623

This is a work of fiction. Names, characters, businesses, places, events and incidents are either the products of the author's imagination or used in a fictitious manner. Any resemblance to actual persons, living or dead, or actual events is purely coincidental.

We humbly dedicate this book to the Witch City.

CONTENTS

Memento Mori

ACKNOWLEDGMENTS

A huge thank you to Laurie Moran for jumping in for last minute edits and providing moral support throughout this project. She was finally talked into joining the FunDead Publications team, so now we can give her proper acknowledgement for her future endeavors! (Not that we'd go without thanking her for all of her previous contributions!)

We'd also like to extend a "thank you" to Jeff O'Brien, author of the enthralling Bigboobenstein series, for dishing out advice when asked. Your help was monumental.

NOAH'S DOVE
Laurie Moran

Jerusha slid her legs over the edge of the bed and dropped her feet flat on the wide pine floorboards. Moonlight crept in around the drapes, casting shadows across the peaks and valleys of the boards, worn and warped from hundreds of years of footsteps and bitter New England winters. She inhaled the cold night air, holding it in her lungs, and breathing out slowly.

Shit, she thought, *that was a weird one.*

Avoiding creaky boards with practiced skill, she grabbed the cut crystal knob of the door and stepped into the hall. She heard Oliver stir and roll over in the bed as she closed the door. Shaking visions of the nightmare from her head, she stepped into the bathroom and flicked on the light switch. Turning on the tap, she waited for hot water to find its way up through the house in a twisting maze of pipes. She closed her eyes for a moment, crossing her arms across her chest, tucking her hands in the folds of her armpits to combat the chill. She was greeted by flashes of falling feathers, tattered canvas flapping in the wind, and cadaverous gray skin holding lifeless black pupils. She snapped her eyes open. Her reflection in the mirror held those lifeless eyes, inky and vacant. These nightmares were taking their toll. She bent to splash water on her face, and sucked in a sharp breath between her teeth. The water was still ice cold.

Grabbing a hand towel, Jerusha dried her face as she walked down the stairs. She leaned against the kitchen counter, dropping the towel next to the sink, as she gazed out the window at the moon. In the hall, the grandfather clock chimed. *Four*, she thought, *Oliver's flight leaves in six hours.*

His documents and passport were laid out on the kitchen table, his packed bag sat by the back door. She sat at the table, and flipped open the passport. A tear that she hadn't realized she'd wept trickled down her cheek. She brushed it away like a buzzing fly, pushed the passport across the table, and walked toward the door. She grabbed a worn brown canvas jacket off the hook, slipped on a fleece lined pair of suede moccasins, and

1

stepped out onto the porch.

The wind blowing in from the ocean was bitter and salty, so she wrapped Oliver's coat around her, sticking her hands deep into the pockets. The moonlight and streetlights cast opposing shadows across the yard. She walked to the end of the porch nearest the front of the house, looking down the street. Through the frame of the porch, she focused on the gray bark of the witch hazel bush, its twiggy fingers creeping up to the railing. The witch hazel was in bloom; the pale yellow flowers were curled into tight fists to protect themselves from the cold, but in the sun they would furl open like streamers of a discarded party horn. Her mother had loved witch hazel for its contrariness, blooming when most respectable plants had dropped their leaves and gone to seed.

Jerusha leaned against the railing. It was spongy, the wood soft with decay, and paint was peeling off in places. It needed replacing, as did much of the house. The salty wind and hard winters wore away at the historic home. Her family had lived in Salem almost since its incorporation. Her grandfather had loved to tell stories of his hometown, and was particularly fond of one about a doomed ship called Noah's Dove, written by Reverend Cotton Mather, a preacher and notoriously vehement advocate for the witch trials of 1692. In typical Puritan style, the Reverend's story taught fear of the unknown. The ocean was the main way of travel back then, and they held many superstitions about sailing and the sea. *Now, all that the ocean means is higher real estate taxes and a nice view*, she thought.

She stepped down from the porch, and headed toward the water. The street dead-ended at the seawall. She leaned against the cold, smooth rocks. *Much sturdier than the porch railing. My ancestors should have built a stone house*, she thought, and allowed herself a smile.

She had spent her childhood walking the rocky shoreline of the harbor. The first time she left the sea was when she moved away for college. She'd stayed in Chicago after graduation, found a job, and settled in. She was proud that she had established herself in a completely new place. Then her mother got the diagnosis, and Jerusha went home. During the most stressful moments, she would find comfort in breathing the sea air. She hated that it consoled her. She wanted to break free from the town of her ancestors. Yet here she was. At least there was nothing keeping her in Salem now, no one who needed her. *Well, one,* she thought, *but there's no guarantee that he's coming back.*

Oliver had to make the same journey she had: home, and reluctantly. He had to travel over the ocean. *I should tell him about Noah's Dove,* she thought. *It would be a more fitting name for an airplane than a ship, anyway. Ha!* The laugh came out loud, casting a puff of white breath into the air. Jerusha shook her head at herself.

Not long after her mother died, on another walk to clear her thoughts, she'd found herself sitting on the granite steps of Old Town Hall, overlooking the brick plaza. It was late September, but already the Halloween tourists were beginning to filter into town on the weekends. She watched a young woman in the coif and petticoats of colonial costume passing out flyers advertising a reenactment of Bridget Bishop's witch trial. A group of middle aged women, wearing outlandish sequin and tulle adorned pointed witch hats and carrying the bright pink bags of the local novelty t-shirt store, stopped to take a flyer. The Puritan woman implored them to attend the trial, and see that "justice was served." The city was full of anachronisms, caught in a strange time paradox, history mixed with fiction around every corner. Jerusha closed her eyes, imagining the square as she'd seen it in early photographs: lined with stalls selling vegetables, horses pulling carts embellished in proud calligraphy with the names of businesses long gone, men in bowler hats tending the horses. She opened her eyes to the rhythmic beat of shod hooves meeting the ground. A horse and buggy, brought in as an attraction for the tourist season, rumbled over the cobblestones of Front Street.

"Where were you just now?" asked a British accented voice just to her left. Jerusha gasped and turned to find a man sitting a few feet from her on the same step. She pulled her fingers into fists against her sides and drew her body back a few inches. No one had been there just a moment before. His slate gray eyes swirled with confusion, like the ocean before a storm, and then cleared as he broke into a smile. He laughed, a hearty, honest guffaw, and exclaimed, "So sorry to startle you! I thought you knew I was here. You were very lost in that daydream; must have been somewhere wonderful."

Jerusha was instantly disarmed. "I was just thinking about the past," she said.

"Ah, the good old days. I do like a proper reminisce myself. I'm Oliver by the way."

"Jerusha." She held out a hand to shake, but Oliver took the back of it to his lips instead. Jerusha would have thought that move terribly cheesy, and normally would have braced herself for a bad pick-up line, but it seemed so effortless and natural when he did it, that she found it utterly charming instead.

"Jerusha, that's an old fashioned name. I like it. I like a good traditional moniker, and other excellent traditions, like a visit to a pub on a Saturday afternoon. Would you like to join me for a pint? We can commiserate on how things used to be so much better in the old days."

Only two months later she felt like she had known him a lifetime. Oliver had blinked into her life, and fit in like he was always meant to be there. Maybe if she closed her eyes again at just the right moment, he would never leave. She let her lids drape across her eyelids, then open again to the sea.

3

The tide was out, and moonlight glistened off the wet rocks, white with barnacles. Her eyes were drawn to empty space, a blank expanse of sky that caught her by surprise. *Oh, yeah,* she thought, *repairs.* The Friendship, a replica East Indiaman merchant ship that served as a floating museum in the nearby wharf, was dry-docked in Maine for maintenance. The ship had been part of the view since Jerusha was a teenager. The missing masts left an unsettling void in the skyline.

She sensed movement in her peripheral vision, and turned toward it. Two figures were picking their way across the rocky, muddy stretch of beach exposed by the tide. *Drunk college kids? The bars closed hours ago.* The larger figure in black grabbed at the arm of the smaller figure in white, as if to steady itself. She heard a female voice whimper and "No…" echo across the water. The figure in black was forcibly guiding the white clad one, a tight grip on her arm. She stumbled, and her accompanier began to pull her along.

"Shit. Not okay," Jerusha muttered to herself. She slapped at her pockets, looking for her phone. Empty. She'd left it in the house. She glanced over her shoulder back up the street, and then looked again at the figures on the beach. She started running toward them. Jerusha followed the seawall to the side facing the wharf and slung a leg over. She clung to the top of the wall, dangling her legs, stretching them out straight, trying to bridge the distance to the bottom, and then let go, dropping the final few feet onto the slimy rocks below.

She kept a hand on the wall to steady herself on the slick, uneven footing, and swiveled her head to scan the beach. The two figures where nowhere to be seen. Icy salt water soaked her moccasins and wicked up onto her flannel pajamas. *Ugh, what am I doing? I should just go back to the house and call the cops,* she thought. She turned back to the wall. As a kid, she used to scale it daily, often with pockets bulging with sea glass and twisted pieces of bleached driftwood. It suddenly seemed so tall and foreboding in the moonlight. She reached for familiar hand and foot holds, but found nothing but smooth stone with bits of wet seaweed clinging to it. She faced the beach again, scolding herself for being so impulsive. *Cold and wet, and now I have to walk around the block to get home.* She turned to walk up the beach toward Derby Street.

The moon was behind her now, and her shadow cast a dark column across her path. The street was only a dozen yards away, but the warm glow of the streetlights melted into blackness before the water's edge. Jerusha could see the gold eagle perched atop the Customs House glinting in the moonlight, but when she looked down at her feet, she could only see misleading shadows, hiding loose rocks and slick seaweed. She began the careful chore of choosing her footfalls, gingerly putting a foot down to test the stability of her step. The bit of light on the beach ahead grew dim, and then vanished. Cloud cover had crept over the moon. Jerusha stood for a moment, to see if the wind would favor her and move the clouds along. She curled and released her toes, trying to warm her numb feet inside her soaked moccasins.

The clouds refused to release their grip on the moon, and Jerusha resumed her snail's crawl across the beach. A few more carefully placed steps brought her within feet of the grassy patch before the street. *Almost there*, she thought, *I can't wait to get home and take a hot bath*. She took her next step more boldly, and the rock underfoot settled beneath her weight. Her foot slipped sideways off the rock. She threw her arms out to break the fall, and fell face down into the mud.

Jerusha lay on the beach, waiting for her nerves to tell her what she had damaged in the fall. Her right shin ached and throbbed. She rolled over and touched a hand to the spot, wincing. There was a large tear in her pants, and she was sure she was bleeding. Her hands stung, full of little fissures. She brushed the palms together angrily, knocking sand and small rocks from the wounds.

"Fuck. Fuck, fuck!" she shouted in frustration.

The ground beneath her began to rumble, like a large truck was coming down the street. Maybe she could get the driver's attention. She crawled onto the grass, and pulled herself up onto her left leg. She looked for headlights coming down the street, but there was no movement at all. The rumbling grew louder. A flock of gulls squawked overhead, spooked from their night's resting spot, and landing on the roof of the Customs House. Jerusha turned to see what had disturbed the gulls, and realized the rumble was coming from something in the sea.

She scanned the darkness, looking for a large ship, but saw only a wall of black. The clouds unraveled from the moon, and Jerusha could see that the tide was still going out, much further than the normal low water mark. She could see fish-shaped shadows flopping around on rocks that had been underwater only moments before. She stared at them, confused. Her brain felt muddled and her leg throbbed. She could see clouds, a few stars, glints of the moon, but where she expected to find the horizon and specks of light from the houses across the harbor, only strange blackness. The rumble grew louder. There was a moving white edge to the blackness, where it met the sky. She could see it turning and foaming like the crest of a wave. Jerusha stared at it in horror. It was a wave, a giant wave. She turned and ran toward the street, dragging her injured leg along a fast as she could. The rumble was deafening.

The wall of water hit her and knocked the breath out of her lungs. She flailed wildly in the darkness, trying to find the surface. The water was like ink; her lungs burned, screaming for air. She slammed into something solid, smashing the side of her head and shoulder. She flung her arms out, hoping for purchase. The surface was rounded and had regularly spaced vertical ridges. Jerusha wrapped her arms and legs around the column and pulled herself along its length, praying to find the water's surface. She broke through into the night air, gasping and sputtering.

The water thrashed around her, pushing against the building like a raging river. She panted, clinging to the column, salt water blasting her face and stinging her eyes. There was a loud smash as the windows of the building shattered and the water rushed inside. The current yanked at Jerusha, trying to pull her along through the new passage it had made. She closed her eyes, hugged the column, and screamed for help.

Suddenly, the water found its level and began to calm. She looked around and realized she was clinging to one of the columns surrounding the doorway of the old Customs House. Bits of debris popped up from the murk around her: dead fish, a look of shock in their eyes. A white Styrofoam cup with the pink and orange logo of a local coffee chain. A lobster trap, its wood slats broken and mangled. A nearby streetlight hissed and sparked as the seawater found its way into the wiring. She needed to get out of the water.

Her teeth chattered and lips trembled. Her whole body felt numb except for the throbbing pain in her leg. She scanned the water, looking for refuge. The other buildings she could see were submerged nearly to their rooftops. Up seemed the only way out.

She moved around to face the building and reached her fingers an inch up the column, then pulled her legs up as well. A slow crawl, but she crept up until she was completely out of the water. The wind plastered her wet clothes against her skin, and she shivered violently. Without the buoyancy of the water, her limbs struggled to bare her body weight. Her heartbeat thumped in her ears. She had to get up on the portico roof; it was only inches away. She stretched her hands toward the railing at the edge of the roof, and wrapped them around the balusters. Unhooking her legs from the column, she tried to swing them up onto the ledge.

She was so tired. Her body felt like a bag of wet sand hanging beneath her. Her arm muscles screamed. She was overpowered by the urge to close her eyes. *If I can just get up on the roof, I can sleep there,* she thought. Her brain told her muscles to move, but they remained languid. Maybe she could just close her eyes for a moment. She succumbed to sleep, falling into the icy water below.

She woke to a splash of water, a creak of oars, and rhythmic rocking side to side. She was wrapped to her chin in a heavy, rough blanket. Jerusha freed her arms from the cocoon, and pushed herself up onto her elbows. She felt like she'd been in a car wreck. Her head ached, her neck was stiff and sore, and her right leg throbbed with pain. She could make out the dark shapes of two figures in the boat with her. One of them was facing away from Jerusha, holding a light. The other was rowing. Jerusha could see gloved hands moving the oars in the halo of light.

"Hello?" Jerusha swallowed and tested her voice. The nearer figure turned. Holding an old fashioned lantern with a candle and a mirrored reflector inside, was a woman with a wrinkled and sun spotted face. She had a white cap covering her hair and a shawl wrapped about her.

"What happened? Who are you?" Jerusha had a barrage of questions ready. The woman put a finger to her lips and shushed, then pointed over her shoulder.

Jerusha sat up and pulled the blanket back. She glanced down and noticed she was wearing a garment with white sleeves tied closed at the wrist in two neat bows. Someone had changed her clothes. She reached up and found that her hair was pulled back into a close fitting fabric cap as well. Her eyes followed the path of the old woman's index finger, and she stared into the darkness. First she saw nothing, then points of light at regular intervals. Those lights turned into lanterns hung between three masts of a large ship.

"Is that the Friendship?" Jerusha asked, but something in the back of her mind told her that couldn't be right. The woman looked at her quizzically, and then turned away.

Jerusha's tried to organize her thoughts. It seemed so long ago that she had left her house. It should be morning, but it was still dark outside. *Morning... something important was happening in the morning,* she thought.

"Oliver!" she screamed the sudden realization aloud. A stampede of thoughts ran through her head, all of the synapses starting to fire at once.

"The wave! The flood! My house! Oliver was sleeping!" She grabbed the old woman's shoulder, "Please! I have to go look for someone!" The woman took Jerusha's hand, patting it with her own, and then forcibly pushed Jerusha's arm back down to her side, tucked the blanket, around her, and turned away again. Jerusha sat still, shocked into silence.

The skiff arrived at the hull of the ship, pulling up along the starboard side. Someone dropped a rope ladder over the rail and down to the small boat. The old woman embarked first, handing her lantern up to the figure on the deck. The lantern illuminated painted lettering on the hull. The brushstrokes were worn and faded in places, but Jerusha made out the name, "Noah's Dove."

"Is this some kind of joke?" she muttered to herself. The man in the skiff turned and pulled Jerusha to her feet, planting her on the ladder, and several more pairs of strong arms pulled her aboard the ship.

On the deck, there were a dozen other people, most of them obscured in half shadow, standing near the port side rail. She could make out bits of clothing, rough woven cloth in earthy hues, wide brimmed hats casting their faces into darkness. Only two figures were completely visible, standing under lanterns strung to the forward mast, a young man and woman, he dressed all in black and she in white. *The couple from the beach!* Jerusha thought.

The woman was weeping openly. The only sounds were water splashing against the ship, and her soft sniffles and whimpers. Jerusha strode toward the couple.

"I saw you!" she chastised the man in black, "You were hurting her!"

"Come with me," she said to the young woman, "Let's get out of here. You don't need to stay with him." Jerusha reached out her hand to the woman, but she was silent and still.

"If you won't go, I still am. I have to find Oliver." Jerusha turned back to the ladder, intent on taking the skiff and leaving.

Suddenly there was deafening thunder and a bolt of lightning that lit the sky, blinding Jerusha with zigzags of white. She blinked a few times, and when her sight became clear, she was standing next to the man in black. He was holding her hand. She recoiled, pulling her hand away, but then he turned his head and looked at her. Instead of the stranger's face she expected, she found Oliver's, his soft gray eyes filled with sorrow. She tried to ask, "What are we doing here?" but found she had no voice. She began to panic, looking wildly around her for an escape.

The ship, which had seemed aged but seaworthy moments before, now showed decay and rot everywhere. The boards beneath her feet were spongy, the mast above her cracked and splintered. Thunder clapped again, and a bolt of lightning struck the mast. It sizzled and groaned, then caught fire. Jerusha turned to run from it, dragging Oliver behind her. All of the pain in her body seemed to melt away as she ran.

The mast fell, hitting the deck and splitting the boards into a wide crevasse. Sea water bubbled up through the split. Jerusha clung to the rotten deck rail, and turned to make sure Oliver had found purchase as well. He was gone. She let go of the rail and threw herself into the rising water, looking for him. She found his hand and grabbed it, kicking back up to the surface. She looked down to find her fingers wrapped around the bones of a skeletal hand, pulled free from the body at the shoulder. She threw it back into the sea, with resignation at her fate.

Jerusha was alone, and the ocean overtook her. Noah's Dove sank to the bottom of Salem Harbor, and pulled Jerusha into the depths, to join the history on the sea floor.

THE DEVIL'S DANCE
Jonathan D. Nichols

I arrived upon that Massachusetts town the final day of October, 1691, exactly two months past my eighteenth birthday. My mother had passed away due to childbirth complications, and I recently lost my father to scarlet fever. The only outstanding kin I reserved were my aunt and uncle, dwelling in Charles Town. As a traveler passing through, I bore no intention of spending an excess of one night in the village, but like so many times in life, my plans were abruptly changed.

Traversing the road into the settlement, I carried a sack within which comprised all my chattels, receiving the attention of residents who cast their eyes upon me and being renowned as a stranger by all persons.

Determined to attain an accommodation to stay the night, I entered an establishment and happened upon a gentleman standing abreast a young lady whom I believed to be his daughter. She was a beautiful girl approximately the same age as myself, and smiled at me as my gaze drifted towards her. I turned to face the gentleman.

"Excuse me, sir; I would like to inquire where I might find a place to rest my head for the night."

"What is your name, young man?"

I told him.

"The good Lord forbid I deny shelter to a person in need. I will gladly provide you a room and a hot meal for supper this evening."

"Thank you, sir. That is very kind of you."

"Elizabeth, could you please escort this young man to our home and explain to Mrs. Griggs his presence so she can make preparation for an additional guest at dinner tonight?"

"Yes, sir." She smiled at me as she walked past and led the way.

The two of us conversed while we fared our conjoint airing, during which time I ascertained the man with whom I had articulated was, in fact, not her father at all, but rather was brother-in-law to the damsel's grandfather. She was orphaned years prior and taken in as a maidservant to the household.

Midway through our commutation, Elizabeth halted and offered salutations to a quartet of girls, two near the same age as myself, and two in their preteen years. The four of them were spending time with an aged Negro woman. It became apparent these young ladies, to include my accompanier, held the slave woman in deep regard, respecting her as a maiden of high prestige despite the conventional treatment as lower class due to servitude status. I found this to be peculiar.

Elizabeth introduced me to the members of her social circle, and I smiled, addressing each person courteously.

"He just arrived to the village." Elizabeth explained.

"You must join in the celebration tonight," the aged woman said. "We welcome a special guest."

"Oh, yes," Susannah, one of the elder girls responded. "You have to come. You can escort Elizabeth."

Although slightly taken aback at this unexpected invitation, I had already constituted a libidinal attraction towards Elizabeth, and my disposition could not resist such an opportunity.

"At what time?"

"After sundown," Abigail, a younger girl, apprised me.

"We must be leaving," Elizabeth said. "But I will visit with each of you come eventide."

"Goodbye," each of the girls hailed the two of us.

We drifted through the village and soon arrived at Dr. Griggs's home.

"Please do not make mention of the festivity this evening," Elizabeth implored me. "My master and mistress are not aware of its existence, and may find objection to my attendance."

I hesitated in my response to this dubious request, but out of an effort to attain positive favor with Elizabeth, I consented to do as she wished.

Mrs. Griggs sat inside the house, reading from scripture as we entered; it was a beautiful home, large and decorated with elegant pillows, richly colored in blue and green. I could see wooden shelves, shining from being freshly polished, on which rested a number of knick-knacks and paperweights. I could not see each one in detail from where I stood, but several of them appeared to be religious in nature. A painting of Jesus Christ hung on the wall above the unlit fireplace; the eyes of the man stared out, lifelike and almost spooky the way they seemed to look with deep intent. The lady of the house stood immediately upon her observance of an unknown person in her home. She greeted me graciously, and Elizabeth explained to her my attendance. Immediately following the introduction, the girl left me and tended to her duties as a household staff member.

"You must be exhausted," the mistress of the house said. "We have a bed unused on which you may lay and rest until supper."

I followed the woman as she led me to the chamber of which she spoke, where I obtained the much needed interval of repose. Images of my new romantic interest visited my dreams, and when I awoke, she was all I could think about. I felt as if a love spell had been cast upon me, and the only resolution to my plight was to find Elizabeth. Wandering the house, I discovered the kitchen, in which the girl labored on the dinner meal.

"Could I offer you some assistance?"

"Oh, no sir." She looked at me and smiled. "I would be chastised for allowing a guest to do such a thing."

I remained where I stood, observing her as she performed the obligatory responsibilities, not wishing to leave the young woman's presence. She looked up every now and again, taking note of my prolonged lingering.

"I dreamt of you as I slept."

"Was it a good dream?"

"Yes." Lowering my voice, I continued. "At what time should I call on you this evening?"

She hesitated in surprise at my inquisition. Without offering response, the maidservant ensured no one stood around to overhear our dialogue.

"Meet me at the rear of the house, near the forest, at dusk. If my master asks of you the reason for your exit, tell them you wish to stretch your legs in the cool autumn air."

It was at this moment Rachel Griggs embarked into the galley and, upon perceiving me, gave a frown to her niece. She offered me a smile and politely informed me that handmaidens are not to be disturbed while preparing the evening meal.

"Yes madam. I offer my apologies."

During the meal at which the elderly couple and I were the only attendees, they inquired of my journey thus far, what the cause was for my excursion, and my final destination. I spoke to them, letting the couple know I originally intended on traveling to Virginia, but gave them the implication of not wishing to abscond so quickly. Periodically throughout supper, I spied Elizabeth and other servants of the house, but none were permitted to join at the table. Finally, at the end of the meal, I excused myself and went back to the bedroom to rest. I bided the time remaining until the sun set, and when I knew the moment arrived, I exited the house, giving the couple the same excuse provided me from Elizabeth prior.

I waited for her at the edge of the forest; when she arrived, I was stunned by the way she looked, and felt completely underdressed. Her gown complimented her features so much, and I became lost in her deep beauty. Her lips appeared dark and nearly red, and her cheeks were almost rosy, although it did not appear as though she wore anything on her face to improve her complexion. The dress looked like one a princess would wear at a ball, light blue and lacy, tight around her waist and streaming down to just above her ankles. Her eyes were the same shade of blue, as though her dress were deliberately dyed to match.

"Shall we, my dear?" Elizabeth offered me her arm. I stammered while attempting to answer her. She smiled at my reaction; I took her arm, and we walked between the trees. She smelled of roses, an aroma I inhaled with enjoyment, and I knew I would always associate with her, and with this evening.

Unable to discern any pathway as we descended into the darkness, I wondered how there could possibly be anything back here. After all, if there were a person or living quarters worthy of any occasion, there should be a marked roadway, and it would not be so completely hidden.

"Where are we going exactly?" I asked.

"We are almost there."

The shadows from the trees swallowed us up, and the dark was thick and heavy. I heard movement in the blackness from unknown creatures of the night. Owls hooted, bats seemed to flutter their leathery wings, and I felt a fear crouch upon me; I slowed my breathing, trying to keep the tremor within my soul from moving to my body. I did not wish for Elizabeth to recognize the fright I had of the unseen forest.

A moment later, as if appearing magically before us, we came upon a clearing in the middle of the forest, where a huge building towered above, brightly lit with music playing, although I was unable to see any clear entrance from the forest leading into this location. It was seemingly isolated from the town, and I wondered if many residents were aware of its existence.

We entered through the front door, where Elizabeth led me down a short hall. This opened into a huge ballroom filled with couples dancing in the spacious area. Other individuals stood around along the edge of the room, chattering and laughing amongst one another. Those not dancing held glasses filled with either white or red wine, sipping as they talked, enjoying themselves in the company. Overhead, a massive chandelier cast an orange light upon the floor, glowing through thousands of sparkling crystals dangling beneath it. A quartet of stringed instruments provided the music, played by four gentlemen, tall and pale. At the rear of the ballroom, several steps led up to an elevation where the host of this engagement sat upon a luxurious seat like a king upon a throne. Standing behind him, arms wrapped around in an embrace, was the slave woman introduced to me previously. To his left and right were two young girls, laughing and giggling. Elizabeth led me across the dance floor, directly to this mysterious gentleman.

"This is master Lucius Fergus. We are in his home."

"Pleasure to meet you sir," I said, bowing my head respectfully.

"Welcome to my celebration."

"Pardon me sir," I asked. "But what is it we are celebrating?"

"Why, my arrival to the village, and the beginning of an era to be spoken of for generations."

"Let us dance," Elizabeth said pulling my arm towards the dance floor. I nodded my head to Master Fergus and followed her, pondering this era of which he spoke.

The music was beautiful, and the violins played rapidly. We moved our feet along the floor and became lost in the moment. As I looked into her beautiful eyes, I thought I was falling in love, though I hardly knew the girl. The song came to its coda, as did our dance. She smiled at me, and before I could react, Elizabeth pulled my face towards her and kissed me. It was not a quick osculation, but a deep, passionate one which took away my breath and made my head spin. After several moments, she broke the kiss and leaned towards my ear.

"You are never going to forget this night."

Pulling me into the dance floor again, we held each other and pirouetted all around the ballroom. The music played slowly, then steadily picked up pace. The violin players became exuberant as they moved the bows back and forth across the strings. I glanced over Elizabeth's shoulder and spied another dancer, who looked directly at me with fiery eyes, bright like coals in the heart of a fire. Shaking my head in confusion, I looked again and the young lady was perfectly normal. *It must have been my imagination*, I thought. We continued to dance, and I looked over and saw another person, this time a male, looking at me as he danced, his eyes an deep crimson glowing with unearthly light. *What was happening?* Another person leered at me, and as she did so, her eyes lit up red and her grin revealed hideously sharpened teeth like some wild animal. I jumped in surprise, looked back at the woman, and she appeared normal again.

My heart pounded with a fear a thousand times greater than that which I felt in the darkened forest. I knew, without truly knowing, that my life, my existence, my very soul was in mortal danger, and yet I could not stop dancing. I watched the musicians as they played the instruments furiously. When their bows rubbed against the strings, bright specks of light flew into the air from the violins like sparks from a flame. Suddenly, the eyes on all four gentlemen illuminated, their color like blood.

"What's hap—?" I said, but Elizabeth placed her finger to my lips.

"Shhhhh. Don't worry, just dance."

I felt under a trance while I observed human faces changing all around to something not of this earth. The musicians' pale skin turned red, and the orange sparks evolved into a flicker of fire. They ignored the impending danger, and continued playing their instruments. Suddenly they became enflamed, and within the conflagration, I saw their appearance change completely. Their faces were demonic and filled with malicious evil. I looked back at the dancers and saw that an opening had been made in the center of the floor, with Elizabeth and me isolated and surrounded by the rest of the guests. All save six young girls had transitioned into devilish entities, staring at me with smiles on their faces, their teeth coming to jagged points. Elizabeth pulled away from me and shoved me with an unexpected strength. I fell down in the middle of the circle.

Lucius Fergus stood from his seat and held out his hands to the crowd. I could hear cheers of excitement. Suddenly he thrust both fists into the air. Two things happened when he performed this action. First, his false appearance fell off like a layer of clothes, revealing an appearance of such a creature who could only be the devil himself. Second, a circle of flames rose up around me, trapping me where I remained on the ground.

The devil stood and bellowed out an evil laughter; Tituba, the slave woman, stood by him as if she were a bride or lover, her hands rubbing over his body affectionately. Seven girls stepped out from the crowd and danced around the flames. Elizabeth was included in this, as were the two young girls, Abigail and Betty, whom I had seen seated beside Lucius. At first, they moved their feet softly and elegantly, appearing to be barely touching the floor, almost floating. The demons sped up the music, and the girls shook in convulsions as they encircled me. I screamed as they closed in, walking through the fire but not catching any flames at all. The awkward jittering and shaking stopped, and Elizabeth stood in front of me. She no longer appeared beautiful, but had an evil thirst for blood in her eyes and a long knife with a razor-sharp blade in her hand. Her lingering scent, that of roses, now contained a sickening sweetness that smelled like spoiled fruit. While the faces of the devil and all his demons surrounding the fire were so extremely frightening, nothing froze my heart like the smile Elizabeth made as she extended her knife towards my throat; the possession which had transformed Elizabeth's beauty was enough to drive me mad. My body felt bound by some invisible force, and I was unable to move.

I lost time for a moment, for the next thing I remember was running from the house, into the trees, afraid to look back. Suddenly the music ceased, and I had the urge to return to the clearing. Slowly, I walked back to the home of Lucius Fergus, Lucifer, Prince of Darkness. To my surprise, the house was gone. The demons were gone. The dancers and the band were gone. And the devil, he was gone, too. All that remained were the seven girls, dancing in a circle, led by Tituba in some form of ritual. I moved in closer to see what they danced around, and to my horror, I saw my own body bleeding from a severed jugular, the red liquid pouring from the wound into a wooden bowl. The girls took turns passing the porringer around, each taking a drink.

I heard a voice behind me, turned to look, and came face to face with the Devil. He bellowed a laugh which echoed like thunder; his demons then appeared and descended upon me, dragging me to the place which knows no joy or pleasure.

A SALEM SECRET
Melissa McArthur

"I had another vision."

"They're not visions, Laura. If you'd take your medication, they'd stop," Dr. Carlock said as he folded his hands on the desk in front of him.

"Dammit! They *are* visions! And I'm not taking that shit!"

Dr. Carlock shifted in his seat. I flinched when he slammed his fist down on his desk—a fancy mahogany deal with a leather inset—and swept his arm across it, knocking the vase of flowers to the floor, the glass shattering. The water splashed my bare feet. I wanted to stomp the beauty out of the flowers.

"Sarah, we need some towels and a broom in here. Some valium from the nurse, too, would be good. She's made a mess again." Dr. Carlock replaced the handset into the base on his desk and looked at me again. "Now, where were we?"

"You were telling me that I'm fucked in the head...again."

"Now, Laura, that's not what I said at all," he chided.

"No, but that's what you meant. That's what you always mean." I crossed my arms and stared at him, eyes boring deep into the lines on his face.

The shard of glass was hidden in my hand. I stood and leaned over the large desk, my gown brushing my unshaven legs and making them itch as I moved toward him. "Laura?" he asked. I leaned closer and reached up to touch the lines on his face, made deeper by age and a constant scowl. The skin split easily, blood thick and hot as it coated the glass and covered my hand. I dug my fingers into the opening and —

A brisk knock interrupted our stare, and the blood on his face disappeared. The skin unmarked, glass still on the floor. Sarah came up behind me. She was a small woman, older, and wore the khaki pants and

16

pale blue shirt required of all Salem Sanitarium employees.

"Oh my, what's happened in here, Laura?" she asked, her voice gentle and soft. An angel dressed in a janitorial uniform.

"The good doctor here insists that my visions are just hallucinations, figments of my imagination. Something I should ignore or take more pills to get rid of." I looked up at Sarah, who stood beside my chair with a roll of paper towels under one arm, her other hand warm on my shoulder. She never treated me poorly.

"Give the girl a break, Dr. Carlock. She's had it rough. Losing her family and all, that has to be hard."

"Do not overstep your bounds, janitor. Clean up the mess and get out." Dr. Carlock's eyes grew dark and his face reddened. I'd seen him angry a few times before. Someone usually got hurt. Sometimes it was me.

"Don't be a dick, doc," I said, hoping to deflect his anger back toward me and away from Sarah.

"Yes, sir," she said as she swept the broken glass into the dustpan and dried up the floor. She emptied the dustpan into the trash, tossed the flowers and paper towels in on top of the broken glass, and turned to go. "The nurses will be in with the medication right away."

I believe you, she mouthed to me before she left. A soft click of the door, and she was gone.

The rest of our session was unproductive, and I was taken back to my room, my cell. I should have known that as soon as I mentioned the visions, it would be all over. I spat out the valium and rinsed the bitter taste out of my mouth with the cup of water beside my bed. I flung myself backwards onto the thin mattress with a grunt of frustration.

"They're supposed to help, you know. You should try it. The colors are pretty if you take enough of them..." my roommate—I couldn't remember her name—slurred from the bed beside mine.

"I don't want to be a zombie. I need to find a way to get out of here and help her before she gets burned at the stake."

"They don't burn witches at the stake anymore, do they?" she murmured before she passed out. I heard her snore and knew it was no use talking to her. She'd be gone in a few days at most. They never stayed with me long.

I stared at the ceiling for a while, held my arms and legs aloft until my muscles burned, and counted all the bricks in the walls. I'd counted them before. Each one. Never using the math I'd learned in school. Just counting. I lost count and started over again. And again.

The woman came to me and knelt by the bed. Her hair was a blaze of red, windblown and tangled. A thin cut marred her otherwise perfect skin, and her green eyes stared into mine.

"They don't believe me," I whispered.

"Make them believe, Laura. It will begin soon, whether they believe you or not."

The woman backed out of the room, sliding through the closed door into the hallway.

I laid my head back on the mattress—I had no pillow, a reward for good behavior—and slept.

* * *

Morning came along with the medications. More medications I pretended to swallow and then gagged back up as soon as they were gone.

My current roommate didn't take morning medications and snored through my dosing. I lay awake listening to the sounds of her snoring for a long time, and when she woke, I spoke to her, continuing our conversation as if she'd never gone to sleep.

"I think she's a witch from the witch trials," I said.

"Who?" she asked.

"The woman. The red-haired woman from my vision."

"Oh, God...that again." She rolled over, turning her back to me, and threw an arm over her face to shield her eyes from the sun.

"It's true! What if I am meant to change history or something?" I replied, but my voice was overshadowed by shouts echoing down the hall.

My roommate leapt up and poked her head out the door.

"Get back in your room and keep the door closed!" Dr. Carlock barked as he ran past our door.

"Laura!" My roommate jumped onto my bed and shook me at the shoulders. "It's a fight! It's a fight! There's gonna be blood!"

The violence excites her; perhaps that's why she's here, I thought. I stared as she shook me harder, bouncing on the bed in delight. Her face faded away and the red-haired woman took her place.

"I'll burn tonight if you don't help me. They've built the pyre in the town square, tied me to the pole. Help me, Laura. I'll burn if I don't freeze first."

"I can't!" I cried.

"What?" my roommate said as she brought her face down closer to mine. Her face was hers again.

"The visions. They're coming so fast." A tear ran down my cheek. "She'll be burned tonight. In the square. I have to get to her. Help me!"

"You're nuts," she said, and started to back away.

I reached up and grabbed her neck with both hands, the only thing I could reach, and shook her. She screamed. The door flew open and the white-clad men pulled her back and out the door. She coughed and gasped and cried. "Tried to kill me!" I heard her say, her voice hoarse.

The men held me down. I gasped at the pain. Nothing is ever gentle here. "Damn full moon," I heard one of them mutter. The needle pierced my skin and the darkness clouded over me. I fought to stay awake, and the world shifted, swirling around me in waves. I squeezed my eyes shut, hoping the world would quit spinning.

* * *

My roommate was gone. I was alone. Silence lingered in the darkness.

My door opened spilling light from the hallway onto the floor. A figure stood in the opening, a shadow of night outlined by the hallway light.

"Who's there?" I whispered.

The figure came in and closed the door. Approached my bed.

"Shhh...Laura, it's Sarah."

"What are you doing here? You don't work at night."

"This is a dangerous place when the moonlight comes. Listen, I think these visions you're having are real. Tell me what the woman looks like."

"She has red hair and green eyes. She's not dressed like we do. She's wearing a long white dress and is always barefoot. She's beautiful."

"As I suspected. Don't help her, Laura. Get her out of your head. She's going to kill you."

"What? Why?" I was confused. I was meant to help the woman. That's why she came to me, wasn't it?

"She's a witch—"

"I know!" I said, voice rising. "She's going to be burned at the stake if I don't help her!"

"No, it's dark magic. I've seen the runes." Sarah looked to the door. "I have to go. I'm not supposed to be here. *Get her out of your head.*" Sarah backed out of the room and closed the door.

I pressed the emergency call button and asked for the doctor.

Soon, the door opened again. Dr. Carlock stood over me.

"Laura, these visions are not real. They're your imagination, a result of the trauma. If you'd take your medications and rest, you'd see."

"Sarah believes me! She told me just now." I felt my face flush with frustration and anger.

"Laura, Sarah resigned. She isn't here, hasn't been here."

"Yes, she was! She told me she believed me about the woman, and that I needed to convince you! She's going to be burned at the stake. Tonight..." I started to cry, and Dr. Carlock just stood over me, watching without emotion. The red-haired woman appeared at my side, silently pleading.

"Don't you see her? She's standing right there!" I screamed, the muscles in my neck straining as I poured my soul into my voice, trying to save her.

"Laura, there's no one here but us. I know it is a shock to you that Sarah is gone. Her resignation surprised all of us. She'd been here longer than any of the others. You have to relax and let the medication work. A hard sleep will do you good. You've scarcely slept in days."

Tears pooled in my ears, making his voice sound far away.

"Hmm, perhaps Salem isn't the place for you, Laura. You may do better somewhere warmer, and with less history. Perhaps Florida." Dr. Carlock pulled out his notepad and jotted something down.

"Salem is my home." My voice broke and the tears fell faster. Snot bubbled at my nose, and I didn't bother to wipe it away.

"I'll arrange for a transfer. Goodnight, Laura. Get some sleep." He slid the pad back into the pocket of his lab coat and moved to the door. He was gone.

I slid my feet into my threadbare slippers and stood. I sat on my roommate's bed and looked out the window. Blackness outlined by white painted brick. Full night had fallen. The shadows in Salem were at their darkest.

The room melted away and I was home. My old quilt soft against my skin. I looked down at my legs, smooth and tan folded under me on the bed. Home.

"Laura?" Mom called.

"Coming, Mom," I said as I got up and moved toward the door.

"Come help me in the attic, will ya?" she said from the end of the hall and disappeared around the corner.

"Yeah, ok." I climbed the wooden steps into the attic and shivered at the freezing air. The attic was usually stifling hot in the summer.

The boxes and sheet-draped furniture were gone. The walls glowed with carvings illuminated from within – runes?

"Mom?" I said to the room.

"You've come," came the voice of the red-haired woman. I looked around, but I was alone. "Here," she said. I turned to the sound of the voice and found a mirror on the wall. It hadn't been there before. The voice came from the mirror.

"Laura!" Sarah hissed and shook me. "Come back!" Her uniform was gone and replaced by jeans and a forest green sweater. I tried make sense of her as my vision cleared.

"Sarah?" I asked.

"You can't stay here. Let's get you back to your room. You're safer there. They never die in their rooms."

"Where are we? How did I get here?" I asked, panic rising in my throat.

"The morgue," Sarah said with a finality I'd never heard in her voice before.

The red-haired woman stepped through barred door. My eyes widened as I saw her, knife glimmering in her hand, come up behind Sarah.

"No!" I screamed. But it was too late.

Sarah fell against me, eyes frozen in a terrified stare. She grabbed me, and we slid to the frigid cement floor together. The knife had gone all the way through her, the tip protruding between her breasts as the crimson stain widened, staining the forest green a red, nearly black.

"Save yourself," Sarah said in bloody bubbles before she crumpled to the floor.

"What have you done?" I screamed to the red-haired woman.

She turned her head to the side and spoke softly. "It was you, not me. The knife is in your hand." I looked down and saw that the hilt of the blade was indeed grasped in my hand.

"No, I saw you…" I whispered.

"Nothing can be done now, Laura. Help me with her. We can use her blood. There's only one way to save me."

Had I killed her?

The red-haired woman and I dragged Sarah's body out of the morgue and down a shaft to a floor that I didn't even know existed. I'd always thought the morgue was the end of the line.

The room was small — candles lining the walls, an old-fashioned operating table in the center.

"Lie down here," the red-haired woman said. "Rest a little while."

Body cold and mind racing, I did as she suggested. I climbed onto the table and laid down. She pulled a rough sheet over me and put a hand behind my head, lifting gently to place a pillow underneath.

"A pillow?" I whispered.

"Yes. You should be comfortable. It's the least I can do for someone trying to save me."

"Are you from the witch trials?" I asked around a yawn.

"Yes…" she said, voice shrinking as the world fell away.

The moon was full, the air cold. An owl hooted in the distance. Warmth tickled my bare feet. Where were my slippers? But the rest of me was ice. A long white gown whipped around my calves in the biting wind. I couldn't move.

I opened my eyes to the candlelit room beside the morgue. The red-haired woman was still there. Runes like the ones in my attic marred the walls. I tried to sit up, but my body was too heavy. I was tired. I closed my eyes again.

The wooden pyre was rough against my bare arms, the skin raw and cold. Men and women approached, coming out of the nearby woods with torches and pitchforks. Women cradled children to their chests, wrapped in heavy cloths. "See the witch?" they'd say, pointing at me. "She's got the devil in her." The children would look, wide-eyed, at me.

"It's time, Laura," the red-haired woman whispered. She'd painted her face with Sarah's blood and held a wicked blade to my forearm. The pain was sharp as she slid it down my flesh. She held my arm down and let my blood flow into a silver bowl. She dipped her fingers into the bowl. "So warm," she whispered as she traced the carvings on the wall with her blood-soaked fingers.

"The blood of three, the life of two. The third will make it complete."

Three? I thought. *Who besides me and Sarah?* The fight in the hallway this morning came to mind. *Was that only this morning? Coincidence or design?* I wondered and tried again to move. My body was free, but I was powerless.

I closed my eyes and felt the fire burning the wood at the base of the pyre. The men shouted and threw their torches into the flames. One spat at my feet. I turned my head and red hair whipped across my face catching the wind that fed the flames. I screamed as the first orange flame licked my bare foot.

"Embrace the flames, Laura," Dr. Carlock said as he appeared before me in the candlelit room.

Then he was gone, and I was in the forest again.

Sparks exploded around me as the men—and now women—of the town, of Salem, threw sticks and branches into the fire dancing with delight as I burned. "Burn the witch! Cast out the devil!" they chanted.

The flames grew, and I screamed as they charred my legs, melting the white dress to my skin, and climbed further, to my belly and chest.

"Help!" I cried out.

"Help, oh, help me. Aren't you pathetic?" The red-haired woman mocked me. "*Feel the flame, Laura.*"

Dr. Carlock dipped his fingers in the bowl of blood, stirred it around. "It's cooling. Bring the flame," he said quietly.

"Yes, my love." The red-haired woman nodded and knelt before him with a burning candle in hand.

"It's working," Dr. Carlock said, looking at the red-haired woman. "Soon we'll be together, Celeste."

I cried. I felt my skin scorch and melt away as the fire burned hotter. "I'm dying, help me," I whispered.

The men and women began to leave as my flesh melted away. I suppose hatred only goes so far. The cold air stung, and I felt my eyes grow heavy. Death was coming. There was peace.

"He won't help you now," the red-haired woman said as she stood and came to my side. She looked different. Alive. Dangerous. She was no longer an innocent spirit asking for my help.

"No..." I said, my voice barely a whisper as I felt the spark of life extinguished by the flames.

* * *

I sat in the corner with my knees pulled to my chin, arms wrapped around my legs, and sobbed. I had only wanted to help.

"Come play with us," a girl said, giggling.

"Who are you?" I asked raising my head from my knees.

"I'm Mary. I was the first. It's different here, but you'll like it."

"Am I dead?" I asked.

"In a way, yes. In a way, no. The red-haired woman—"

"Celeste?" I interrupted.

The girl screamed and flew into me, through me, face contorted by demonic features.

"Never speak her name," the girl growled.

"I'm sorry," I said. "The red-haired woman?"

"Yes. The red-haired woman. She traps us here. The doctor helps. She gives him…power…in exchange for us. We take her place. Did you burn?"

I nodded, tears that weren't tears slid down my cheeks.

She laughed. "It never stops burning. Now, come play with us."

I looked to the back of the room, damp walls disappeared behind the girls as they timidly stepped forward. They were coming for me. Forever.

INSPECTION CONNECTION
Bill Dale Grizzle

Charles Greyfall's clock went off with the same obnoxious clanging at six-thirty a.m., as it had for the past two and a half years. In the still, quietness of his bedroom he swore under his breath as he slapped it into silence. He trembled in fright. That blasted clock had scared years off his life, he was sure of that. It didn't matter that he was already awake, had been for half an hour, it still scared him. No, he thought collecting his wits, it wasn't the clock that scared me so badly, it was that awful dream again. For the fourth night in the past week that dream, that horrible, blood curdling dream had visited his sleeping mind.

"That does it," muttered Greyfall, "I'm going back again to talk to the boss."

Two hours later Charles Greyfall found himself in Mondo Carvelli's office babbling his case to the very much annoyed head of the building commission for the city of Salem, Massachusetts. As timid, mushy, and non-productive as Greyfall was, he was Carvelli's main man. Mondo Carvelli could talk Charles into anything, snowball him, hoodwink him; plainly speaking, Greyfall was Carvelli's puppet on a string.

"I don't want to hear anything else about that elevator, that....that confounded elevator!" Carvelli was as red-faced as he'd ever seen him.

"What do you want me to do about it? You're the inspector, you signed off on this report," he roared, "It's your hide that's in a pinch if anything happens over there, you understand that, don't you," Carvelli fell into his chair and pounded his desk in anger, "We're two weeks behind schedule on that tower, and we are *not* going to have any more setbacks." His last words were slow and deliberate, each one accompanied by his huge fist as it landed solidly on the mahogany desktop. Greyfall cowered even deeper into himself. "Get out of my office, Charles; I don't want to see you for at least a week!"

Greyfall tucked his tail and ran like a scared street hound to a barrage of insults referencing his manhood. What else could he do? He *had* signed off on that inspection report, *after* his boss forced him to change it with threats of firing him from his well paying, cushy job, and a promise of a visit from Jimmy 'The Knuckles' Rossi. *Geez,* he thought, *what am I going to do? Carvelli has the entire city council in his pocket, the mayor is terrified of him, and his best friends are connected with the Mafia.* Charles slumped into the seat of his city furnished black sedan and leaned forward until his head rested on the steering wheel, and muttered to himself.

"If I go to the police it won't be two days before somebody finds me stuffed into a trash bin with a bullet hole in my forehead. Lousy bunch of cops, most of them are on the take, too."

Rocking back and forth he thumped his head on the steering wheel over and over, just hard enough to cause a little pain. A hopeless attempt to knock some sense into his senseless head, as he saw it.

"How did I get myself into all this mess?" he continued, but his misery was suddenly interrupted by a soft tapping on the car window.

"Charlie, are you okay?" Lana Sandoski, the pretty secretary from the office down the hall from his boss stared through the glass. Shaking his head, Greyfall motioned for her to come around to the passenger side.

"Geez, Lana, you scared me. What are you doing out here in the cold?"

"I had to drop off some letters at the post office. What's going on with you, Charlie? I saw you banging your head on the steering wheel like some kind of crazy person. Are you alright?" Lana cocked her head to one side, expecting an answer.

Charles gave her the once over, taking note of the kindness in her expression. He thought he could trust her, they'd shared a booth a few times at the corner diner, and although those encounters could not be considered dates they *had* always enjoyed each other's company. They had always found something to talk about, and right now Charles Greyfall needed someone to talk to.

"I'm done for, Lana. I just know it, I'm done for." Greyfall's mouth was as dry as gunpowder and his hands shook.

"What are you talking about, Charlie?" Lana placed her hand on his out of concern, but feeling its tremble she quickly pulled hers back. "You're shaking all over, Charlie, what's wrong with you?"

"He'll *get* me yet," Charles sneered, "that dirty, rotten crook. He's got me where he wants me, and now if anything happens out there it will all be on me. And now, if I try to do anything about it, I'll just come up missing. That's how he does things, ya know."

Lana's eyes narrowed as she quietly asked, "Who, Charlie, who are you talking about?"

"My boss, that's who. Carvelli, he's as dirty as they come, Lana, a real gangster, that guy is. I just wanted to be a bookkeeper, a simple bookkeeper. Boy, what a sap I've been. I'm a bookkeeper alright; collected his bribes and delivered his payoffs all over this city. That alone is enough to get me six feet under, and that's not including the phony building inspection reports and all the kickbacks and payoffs he takes from practically every construction company in Massachusetts."

Greyfall shook his head, took a deep breath and sighed. If Lana couldn't be trusted, he'd surely sealed his fate now.

Lana Sandoski was obviously rattled at her friend's behavior and his accusations; her eyes were wide open and her mouth agape, "You're saying that Mondo Carvelli is doing illegal things? You'd better be careful, Charlie, talk like that could get you fired, you know."

"*Fired,*" yelled Greyfall, "getting fired is the least of my worries. I'm worried about getting killed. Geez, Lana, you're as naive as I used to be. Carvelli is a crook, and he's not the only one at city hall."

"Look, Charlie, try to calm down. I have to get back to work now," once again she placed her hand on his and gave it a little squeeze, "Meet me at the diner at six, and we can talk about this some more."

Charles nodded as the young woman exited the car, he then drove to a small park at the water's edge and found a vacant bench in a secluded spot. There he sat for hours and thought deeply about the mess he had gotten himself into.

Washington Street was pretty much deserted, a light mid-March snow had begun to fall some three hours earlier and most of the working class had already made their way home rather than deal with the slick streets. Salem had already received word from areas westward that heavier snow was close at hand. This suited Greyfall just fine. Bad weather might give him some time to lay low and figure out what to do. He gazed out the diner window, almost unaware that Lana had seated herself in the booth across from him. He was wet, snow had worked its way down his collar causing his back to ache. Generally speaking, he felt totally miserable.

"Charlie, you look *awful,*" Lana's assessment carried sharp edges and a disapproving look.

The scolding actually felt warm, like she really cared about him.

"I spent the day at the park, at the waterfront....thinking."

"*Good grief,* are you trying to catch your death of a cold? It's twenty-five degrees out there, Charlie, and in case you didn't notice, it's snowing."

He finally forced his eyes away from the window and met her stare. Her eyes were like bright green embers from a fire.

"What am I gonna do with you? I'm afraid you're losing it," she said.

Yes, he thought, *she does care.*

"Look, Lana, I'm not losing it, I'm just in a jam, that's all. And I could sure use a friend right now."

"Well, *I am* your friend, Charlie, but I'm still worried that you're losing it. Where did you get all that criminal stuff you were saying about your boss? I know you don't care for him but calling somebody a crook, that's kind of dangerous."

The word 'dangerous' seemed to open a door for Charles Greyfall, and he told it all in a low voice that only Lana could hear. Forty-five minutes later, his young lady friend sat in stunned silence. She had heard stories of bribes, blackmail, payoffs, and shakedowns at the hands of Mondo Carvelli, one of the most powerful employees on Salem's payroll. She heard the confessions of the dozens and dozens of times her friend Charlie had personally delivered paper bags, briefcases, even suitcases, and old Army duffel bags stuffed with cash to various drop-off spots. She even heard of the time, just over a year before, when Carvelli had ordered him to pick up a construction company supervisor and deliver him to a meeting at a tavern on the south side of town. That man was never seen again.

Finally, Lana spoke up in protest, "But, Charlie, this is 1954, not the roaring twenties or the days of prohibition that I read about. These are modern times, people can't get away with that nowadays."

"They can and they do, Lana," was his solemn reply, "Every construction project in this city for the past two years has been inspected by me, personally. Every inspection report that I turned in to Carvelli has been altered or rewritten to suit him. I was then forced to sign them under the threat of being exposed for writing false reports, of being fired, and of being beaten to a pulp by his strong-arm."

"We're closing in half an hour," the voice came from behind the counter. Lana and Charles both glanced in that direction and nodded.

"How did you ever get involved with Carvelli, anyway?" asked Lana, "I mean inspecting stuff in buildings, you told me you're an accountant."

"I am. Rather, I was. Carvelli pulled me out of the accounting department two and a half years ago and appointed me the 'chief' building inspector for the city. Somehow he found out that my Dad had been a carpenter all his life and figured that qualified me for the job. The only thing I was qualified to be was his sap." He buried his face in his hands and mumbled a few choice words to himself. After that, Greyfall sat quietly, thinking; he was reluctant to tell her about the elevator and his recurring dream, but what the hay, he'd told everything else, may as well tell her about that, too.

"A week and a half ago, I inspected the elevator in the new tower at the train station. Lana, that thing is a death trap. The cables are frayed and the emergency brake has been disconnected because the foreman said it was getting stuck all the time with his workers on it. And trust me, I'm no electrician but the wiring in that elevator shaft is a joke. I'm telling you, Lana, it's a death trap for sure, it's just a matter of time."

Lana Sandoski sat with a blank stare on her face that made her look plain, she almost looked unconscious, even. Never in a million years had she expected to hear things like this from the young man she had secretly admired for more than a year, but her sad state did not silence Charles Greyfall.

"Carvelli forced me to sign a false report. A report that he'd filled out saying that all was in order with that elevator. I've had this horrible dream about that elevator falling with men on it three times in the past week. The exact same dream, Lana, and each time I wake up to the screams of those men. I talked to Carvelli on Friday and again this morning. He threw me out of his office. If I go talk to the foreman, he'll tell Carvelli, because there's money changing hands between those two. If I go to the police, chances are they'll tell Carvelli, too. What can I do?"

The sound of the diner's owner clearing his throat interrupted what had been a full minute of silence. Lana grabbed her purse and coat.

"I can give you a lift home," Charles offered, "it's kinda bad out there now."

"That would be nice, Charlie, it's only a few blocks."

Stopping in front of Lana's apartment building they agreed to meet at the diner at six o'clock, in three days time.

Unlike their neighbors to the west, Salem was spared the misery of the heavy snows, but not the cold. Frigid temperatures blanketed all of New England, and a constant gusting wind chilled everyone to the bone. Everyone except Mondo Carvelli. How could one with ice-water in their veins be effected by a little chilly weather. He had gotten word that construction on the tower had virtually come to a standstill. So there he was, bellowing at the top of his voice at the foreman, rough-handling the much smaller man with his shirt collar in the firm grip of a massive hand.

"You *will* get that plumbing done!" he yelled, "You *will* get the brick finished this week! You *will* finish this project on time! Do I make myself clear? I don't want to hear anything about cold weather, I don't want to hear anything else out of your whiny mouth except, *yes sir*! Do you understand what I'm saying?" Carvelli then shoved the man down into the corner of his ten by ten makeshift office and towered over him until he could muster the strength to reply.

An hour later the foreman instructed one of his men to have a truck deliver a shipment of fuel oil to the job site, having said, "If we're going to work we need a little warmth. Fire up that heating system."

On the other hand, Charles Greyfall had stuck very close to home. He did venture out to make his usual pick up form Carvelli's bookie, and another scheduled blackmail payment his boss was collecting from a federal judge. The money, all in cash of course, was dropped off at the usual clearing house where it was checked for watermarks or other ways of being traced before it was passed on to Carvelli.

The dream, of course had come again, every night since his meeting with Lana. It was hard not to think that maybe she was right about him 'losing it'. But somehow he knew in his soul this dream would come to pass. He also knew that it would all be on him; he had been set up as the fall guy, all the other crooks would get off scot-free and he would rot in prison. *My poor Mother*, he thought. So in an attempt to salvage something for her to hold dear and close to her heart, he wrote her a long letter explaining everything, proclaimed his innocence, and asked her forgiveness for being such a failure as a son. Charles Greyfall was certain his mother would never see him alive again.

Thursday, he reluctantly left his little rented cottage on the outskirts of town for the drive into the city for his meeting with Lana at the diner. It occurred to him too late that he might have left in time to meet her at city hall at five-thirty when she got off work. But no, in his present state of self-concern it never crossed his mind that she would suffer the two block walk in this bitter cold and wind; now he felt guilty and small. *What the hay*, he thought, *after this she'll not have anything to do with me anyway. Besides I'll probably be in a slab of concrete somewhere.*

Nearing the city center, Greyfall couldn't help noticing the traffic flow was much heavier than usual, and the streets that were normally clear of cars and trucks were clogged and moving slowly. Once he reached the diner and found a parking space, he was ten minutes late.

Lana leapt to her feet and met him with an embrace, relief washing over her at his presence. "Oh, Charlie, I was so afraid for you!"

His look of confusion and failure to respond told her at once that he had not heard the news. "You haven't heard, have you, Charlie?" Lana clenched his hands tightly.

"Heard what?" asked Charles.

"The accident at the new tower, Charlie. It's gone, completely gone, so much like the dream you had. I'm scared for you Charlie, I'm scared for me, too."

Greyfall was stunned. He knew it would happen sooner or later, but this was much sooner than even he would have suspected.

"What happened?" he asked, his voice weak and shaking.

"About three hours ago," Lana began, "just like your dream, the elevator fell. Three men died, Charlie, and that's not all. There was an electrical fire that started in the elevator shaft, and there was a fuel oil leak in the basement, and two tanks of fuel oil blew up, and now the whole tower is gone and there is a lot of damage to the train station. It's just a miracle that more people didn't die."

That was the end of Lana and Charles' meeting. He rushed her home, told her it was not safe to be seen with him, thanked her for being a friend, and said his goodbyes forever.

Early the next morning, and much to his dread and horror, Charles Greyfall was summoned to his boss' office. He was fully expecting Carvelli to be in a state of anger like he had never seen before. However, that was not the case; Carvelli was as calm as he could be.

"Greyfall," he said quietly, "thanks to you my plans have changed. I was planning on leaving here with five million dollars, cash. As it is I'm a couple of million short, but it will have to do. Thankfully the 'accident' at the station yesterday didn't damage the area where the luggage lockers are. If it had, I'd kill you myself. Now, this is how it's going to go. I have every inspection report that you've ever filed here; this folder alone contains enough to send you away for the rest of your miserable life. But just to make sure you're done for, and maybe as a bonus, some of my associates will see fit to dump your lifeless body in the river; here is a list of all the payoffs and bribes you've collected for them. I'd like to thank you for being the pansy I needed to pull this off. That's really all I needed," he coldly added, "so now if you'll excuse me, I am going to phone the police and the DA and turn all this over to them. This will be the last time you see me, Charles, this time tomorrow you'll be in the lock-up, and I'll be in Miami," Carvelli sat back in his oversized leather desk chair and laughed, "And this time next week I'll be sailing to Havana," Carvelli then turned his attention to the folders that lay before him, "enjoy your last day of freedom, Greyfall, go hang yourself or some-"

At that very moment Carvelli looked back up at a speechless Charles. Also in that very moment his thoughts were disrupted, fear blanketed his face and he jumped to his feet.

"*Who are you?*" he screamed, "How did you get in here? *Get out!*" he screamed again in a panic as he backed over his chair until he was flat against the wall behind him.

Out of fright, Charles Greyfall also backed up against the opposite wall. He looked from side to side in search of whoever else was in the room. *Who was Carvelli screaming at and cursing at the top of his lungs?* There was no one else in the room, but Carvelli kept screaming at someone or something that Charles could not see. Soon he was thrashing about and kicking as if something had the big man is a fierce hold. He appeared to throw himself back into his chair and was roughly jostled from side to side; his bellowing head jerked violently back and forth, cuts, scrapes, and bruises appeared on his face and head, blood oozed from his lips, which seemed to Charles to just split open, and suddenly his nose went flat like a blowout on a car. Blood poured out. Then his head slowly and deliberately turned upward, his eyes fixed on a spot on the ceiling, his neck tightened, and he stopped breathing. Carvelli's arms seemed to be welded to the arms of his chair, and all his struggling could not free them. He turned blue. Suddenly with a gasp he was breathing again, and with his breathing came a barrage of curses and screams. This oddity repeated its self once more before his face became contorted, his eyes were fiery with fear and anger, and his mouth gaped wide open. Nothing, however, escaped that great hole but muffled sounds, as if there was something invisible over it. His breath was labored, gurgling through the blood that continued to trickle from his flattened nose. Carvelli fought and struggled for a long while to no avail. Then, paper appeared before him and he took up a pen. He wrote swiftly, page after page, all the while protesting with his hushed moans and vain attempts to free himself from the bondage that held him. More and more pages were produced in his handwriting, and when his free hand managed to grab the pen and fling it in Greyfall's direction, it quickly flew back to him. Carvelli paid for the indiscretion when his arm twisted itself behind his back until the shoulder became dislocated. He screamed a silenced scream of pain, his eyes glassed temporarily, and his chest heaved in terror. And he wrote more.

Charles Greyfall watched in horror as the crazed man seemed to be in a battle of life and death with himself. It was hard to watch, even harder to understand; Charles had always thought his boss absolutely fearless, in a cowardly, crooked way, of course. The drama continued to unfold and eventually Greyfall, although still frightened out of his wits, came to realize he was in no real danger. So he continued to observe, still and quiet, and wondered of the things that were not intended for his eyes.

This is what Mondo Carvelli saw:

The three men who'd died in the elevator had stationed themselves between the shaking Charles Greyfall and Carvelli's big desk. His gaze met theirs when he looked up as he was suggesting to his employee that he might hang himself. Fear gripped his chest so hard that he thought his heart would burst, but even the gruesome sight of charred flesh on the faces, arms, and hands of his visitors, or the repulsive smell of burned hair and clothing, could not squelch Carvelli's natural instincts of survival. He screamed his demands that he be left alone, hurled his huge fists in every direction that the men appeared, and he even pulled a revolver from his pocket, which was quickly wrenched from his hand and deposited in the waste basket. Within a couple of minutes he found himself being thrown back into his chair, the three hovering around the wildly kicking and bellowing man, punching him, poking his eyes with their charcoal fingers, and scratching him until blood seeped from his skin.

The three spirit-beings tormented Carvelli ruthlessly; one grabbed the letter opener from the desk and slashed both of Carvelli's cheeks, his forehead, and one arm before calmly tossing it in the trash with the gun. All the while they were yelling in his face, explaining in no uncertain terms, what a worthless slug he'd always been. One forced his hand to his head and caused it to pull out great clumps of hair. Three handfuls in all, one for each of the three children he'd left behind. Another, with a firm grip on his ears, jerked his head back and forth so violently that he vomited down the front of his blood spotted, starched white shirt. Then as Carvelli was spitting the last of the vile taste from his mouth, he watched a huge fist slam into it. A fist even bigger and harder than his own, one toughened by honest hard work, ripped open both upper and lower lips. The next blow smashed his nose into a grotesque, sideways flatness, and more blood flowed freely. Carvelli was dazed by these blows, but still he struggled to free himself. That's when a strong arm wrapped around his neck and tightened into a choke hold. Twice he was a second away from crossing that point of no return, twice he thought he was gone for sure, but no, his work was not done yet. Hovering around the desperate Carvelli, and with a big charred hand securely clamped over his wide open mouth, they forced him to pen his confessions and, at the same time, clear Charles Greyfall of any wrongdoing. His verbal protests were muffled and unrecognizable as words, but his eyes told of his anger, his fear. When he did manage to get one hand free, he grabbed the pen from his writing hand and threw it across the room. A costly mistake, the offending arm was forced behind his back well past its limit of motion, and when the joint dislocated with a snap Carvelli urinated in his pants from the almost unbearable pain.

The three spirits watched as the wet spot grew on Carvelli's fine suit pants, a pair of pants like they had never in their hardworking lives owned. Then they burst into loud harrowing laughter that angered Carvelli into a renewed fit of struggling and thrashing and moaning. Still he could not free himself from his captors, and still he wrote.

"We know all about you, Carvelli," said one of the deceased, in a voice so haunting it made him shudder, "Now that we're dead we can see all that you've done in your miserable life. We know all about the deals you've made, the payoffs, the blackmailing, everything, and everybody you're hooked-up with. We're gonna visit some more of you slime balls real soon. If fact, that low life weasel of a superintendent is gonna hang himself tonight. Naw, he ain't really got the guts, just like he didn't have the guts to stand up to you, but we're gonna help him. And next week, that crook of a mayor is gonna shoot dead all the councilmen that's in your back pocket."

Carvelli's eyes bulged with fear, but still he wrote.

"Ah, don't worry so, man," spoke up a second spirit-being, "he won't rat on you. He's gonna take care of his business before he gets out of the parking lot. Too bad he won't have time to get rid of them list of names. You know them names of all them fellows that work out of that warehouse at the wharf. Yeah, we know all about them guys, and lots more, Carvelli.

We know about your plan to frame that poor fellow there, too," he pointed a fleshless, charred, boney finger at Greyfall who was pushing his back to the wall as hard as he could in an attempt to get as far from what was happening as he could, "The only thing that man is guilty of is falling in with you, for being too weak to stand up to a mangy dog like you are. You just about done him in, Carvelli, but we can see the good in him and you're going to clear his good name if it's the last thing you ever do."

Mondo Carvelli had now completed more than two dozen pages, and he laid down his pen and involuntarily opened the bottom desk drawer. From a secret compartment that absolutely no one else knew about, he extracted a small leather-bound black book. The little black book contained the names of every criminal contact that Mondo Carvelli had ever had, along with the details of every transaction he'd ever made. The discovery of his precious black book generated a new round of muffled cries and strains to free himself, but there was no escape. He took up the pen again and continued to write.

The third of the dead men, the one with his big hand clamped solidly over the squirming Carvelli's mouth, spoke now. Although he was a big, strong man, he was a soft spoken, gentle person and displayed this trait by speaking quietly and close to his ear.

"Mondo, we know about your plan to leave the country with a load of money. Do you really think that would be the right thing to do? We don't, so, just to let you know, there's been a change of plans. Those bags of cash you've got stashed in locker 319, well, you're not gonna need that where you're going. Don't look so surprised, boss man, we know all about that cash. We even know about lots more cash that you stashed around in different places. Don't worry about it though, we're gonna take real good care of it. Now you just carry on with your writing like a good fella, and when you're done we'll get on with the rest of our business."

So Mondo Carvelli wrote on, compiling some fifty pages, before he finally dropped his pen. On these pages he had indeed cleared Greyfall of any wrongdoing, placed the blame for the accident squarely on himself, confessed to countless crimes, including murder and kidnapping, and told everything he knew about every crook in the whole of Salem.

Much to the distress of Greyfall, this had gone on for three hours. He had actually tried to leave but the door wouldn't budge, and he'd been forced to witness the whole thing; whatever this thing was. Relief did come, however, when suddenly Carvelli virtually leapt from his chair and stumbled to his office door, the door that now opened with ease. Still fighting the unseen force that had held him captive for hours, he left his office flinging his arms like a mad man, screaming and swearing at the top of his voice. Witnesses turned in amazement as the mad man kicked the doors of city hall wide open, stumbled and fell down the marble steps, and like a fish out of the water flounced and floundered his yelling and screaming and cursing way toward the street. Carvelli tore at his clothing, pulled his own hair, and swung his fist in a rage while he cursed the three men that tormented him; the three men that no one else could see.

Scores of passers-by paused to watch the crazed man bash his head against a streetlight pole until his scalp was laid open to the skull. Droplets of blood flew in all directions, and the handful that had drawn near to assist him withdrew to avoid the red rain. Then in one last screaming, thrashing, cursing fit of rage, he threw himself into the path of a city bus. In an instant Mondo Carvelli lay dead in the street. Women screamed in horror, men gasped in disbelief, and within seconds they gathered to view the mangled body of Mondo Carvelli. He was recognized, of course, by a few onlookers, but not one person saw the small brass key leave the pocket of the deceased man and fly out of sight.

Charles Greyfall stood in stunned silence on the steps of Salem's City Hall. Little did he know that he had witnessed the first of several unusual deaths of city employees and businessmen suspected of illegal activities.

Two months later, after the District Attorney had cleared him in the disaster at the train station and also determined that he had nothing to do with the death of Mondo Carvelli, Greyfall was awakened one night by the dinging sound of a small brass key being dropped on his bedside table. A handwritten note lay beside the key.

"Make haste for the train station will come down before the years' end. Locker 319. This money was come by illegally, although you cannot return it to those from which it came, much good can be done with it. Trust that you do so."

The following spring, Charles Greyfall and Lana Sandoski were married in Salem, where they lived the rest of their lives and raised three children. Charles managed to remain an employee of the city and eventually became the building commissioner. During his tenure he developed a strict and trusted team of building inspectors.

Charles knew he was always being watched. Every March on the anniversary day of the tower disaster, he was awakened by the dinging of the small brass key as it dropped to his bedside table. He and Lana, through contributions too small to draw attention, assisted a countless number of citizens of Salem.

WITH NEITHER LOVE NOR MERCY
Nancy Brewka-Clark

The day before my thirteenth birthday, I came upon Billy Edgars on the bank of the North River. It was almost twilight and the sky was filled with wheeling gulls. He was whittling a chunk of wood, white ash by the look of it. "Have a seat," he said, pointing to the grass at his side with tip of the knife.

"What are you making?" I asked him, not quite daring to rest my bare brown leg against his when anyone could venture by at any time. We were both stokers at Master Norton's tannery in Blubber Hollow, lads who fed the flames beneath the huge black iron cauldrons where whale fat was rendered down to a thick, brown goo, but there was never a chance to further our acquaintance during the hours of mutual toil.

In answer, he pursed his lips to whistle in the manner of the bird of the Massachusetts forest called whippoorwill. From the few chances we'd gotten to speak, I knew his heart was set upon moving far north up the coast beyond Kittery to clear his own land for a farm. It was said that in this Year of Our Lord 1735 Salem was overtaking the town of Boston in industry. I could well believe it if the tanneries springing up in Blubber Hollow were anything to go by. When I asked nothing more, he said, "Venture a guess, Peter."

The wood shavings lay curled in the grass like a girl's hair, blonde and sweetly scented, and I felt a pang of—something—regret?—an instant of doubt for my heart's yearning?—too sharp to acknowledge. "I wager you're designing a poppet for your sweetheart."

"Aye, I'm supposing you could say that." He looked at me with a sharp, bright glint to his brown eyes, amber like the spring sap of the maple in the last glow of the setting sun. "Fancy a walk?"

I stretched in heady languor, knowing he was drinking in the sight. "After such a hot day's work, we could go down to the spring."

Silently we stood and left the town behind us. In the gathering shadows we made our way down the well-worn path to the small freshet that bubbled up ice cold no matter how intemperate the day, giant ferns slapping at our legs to release the sweetly spiced scent of living greenery. Without a word we ventured further into the forest until all around us the great boughs wove a canopy over our heads and the great trunks rose from the soft bed of earth like angels standing sentinel.

And we made love.

One star glowed so brightly overhead it was like God's eye following us to our homes. At his door, aware of his widowed mother waiting alone on the other side, we said nothing but instead waved our farewells beneath the watchful eyes regarding us secretly from all the other houses in the lane. Barely aware of my surroundings, I went on to my home on Herbert Street where my own mother was in the midst of putting a brood of younger children to bed. Each child represented a fleshly keepsake of a time when my father, a sailor, had come home from the sea. True to form, he'd left behind yet another in Mum's womb. He might perhaps, but not necessarily arrive home in time for its birth with his pay in his pocket, which meant my wages would have to stretch to feed yet another mouth. But that no longer meant dreary labor. Rather, it promised that I'd spend my days being near to Billy. In a bubble of bliss, I went inside to drift up to my own pallet and dream of him.

The next morning Billy failed to appear for the first firing of the day which commenced exactly on the sixth stroke of the clock in the meeting house steeple. Billy was tasked with the particular placing of fresh wood which was then lit with a brand from the deep brick well in the warehouse. The foreman, a low-browed pious fellow by the name of Hodgkin, who kept scrupulous track of his men, needed no timepiece to be aware of Billy's transgression.

When Billy did arrive six minutes after the hour, Master Hodgkin was puffed up with ire and importance. "So, you decided to leave your bed and join us after all, did you, Edgars? For your indulgence I shall dock you six shillings in wages."

"Dock me if you must, sir," Billy replied, "but six shillings? Nay, in fairness it should be sixpence."

"Do you answer me so impertinently because you wish to be docked twelve shillings?" Master Hodgkin sneered, feeling the eyes of all the others upon him.

"Indeed, I do not sir," Billy responded, "because I would be compounding your error."

"What?" Master Hodgkin advanced upon him. "Go home. Your

services are no longer needed here, Edgars."

To my horror, Billy swung a punch.

"Rebellious cur," Hodgkin screamed. "I'll have you whipped."

"I'll see you in Hell first," Billy snarled and sprang at him.

"Help!" Hodgkin cried, his eyes bulging as Billy throttled him. "Men! Bring down this madman!"

In the mayhem that ensued, men poured from the drying rooms while others came galloping from their steaming pots, and yet others stampeded away from the stacks of fly-ridden hides, brandishing their flaying knives like devils. Billy was knocked to the ground and vanished beneath a legion of stamping feet. When he was finally hauled to his feet by two men, his face streamed with blood.

"Take him away," Hodgkin panted. "Straight to jail."

"Sir?" One of the tanners from the inner works was stooping to snatch something up from the ground. "He had this on his person, sir."

In a flash of fearful knowledge, I shut my eyes.

"Ho, then, what's this?" Master Hodgkin's eyes bugged even more than they had when Billy was choking him.

I blinked back tears as the tanner held up Billy's carving of a naked man in a state of rapturous arousal. Perfecting my present—a few more strokes of the knife while the clock sounded his doom—had cost Billy his job and his freedom.

An angry murmur ran through the men.

Barely able to summon breath, Hodgkin rasped, "Lord God, have mercy on us all." His eyes rolled as his voice rose. "We've been harboring a sodomite."

The men's shouts were rising to the howling pitch of a storm at sea. "Filthy bugger! Ganymede! Idolater! Pagan! Blasphemous prickshite!"

As my arms and legs pumped to carry me down the road to Salem Neck, I heard the screams. Although they pierced my heart, I only ran faster, but not fast enough to be out of earshot of that last fearsome shriek. Flinging myself down in the brush at the side of the road, I wept, and puked, and wept until I fell into a sleep-like state that bordered on the loss of the will to live. But it passed. And I went back.

There wasn't much left of him. The dexterous use of flaying knives and judicious application of boiling water had seen to that. His skeleton sat in the bubbling cauldron almost jauntily, one elbow propped against the rim.

"Hey, you. You!" Still in a state of high excitement, Master Hodgkin marched toward me. The front of his jacket bore splashes of blood and both cuffs were soaked, but he didn't seem to notice. "What's your name, boy, and what are you doing here?"

"Peter, sir, Peter Palfrey, and I—I work here. I'm a stoker. For—

there—that kettle, usually."

"Where have you been then?" He thrust his face right up into mine, his jaw working.

"I—I—I was—sick."

Master Hodgkin grabbed my shirt and bunched it in his grip. "Not a sodomite yourself, are you?" When I shook my head, he tightened his grip. "Are you certain, Master Palfrey?"

My eyes rolled helplessly toward the cauldron. The blank sockets of my lover's eyes stared directly at me, right into my heart. "No, sir. I mean, yes, Master Hodgkin. I am certain."

And I told myself I was, even in the face of Billy's grin.

LOVE AND OIL
Jonathan Shipley

"Welcome to Redwood, the Redridge House on Chestnut Street in Salem's premier historic area." Maggie Bederman smiled as she ushered a group of tourists into the long front hallway of the house museum. She tucked a strand of graying hair behind her ear and began in earnest. "The name Redwood has nothing to do with California and everything to do with the original oxblood color of the house. It was built in 1794 by the Redridge family, restored in the 1890's by the Dunlaps, and acquired in 1973 by the Society for the Preservation of New England Antiquities. It is one of several properties the organization operates here in Salem and a prime example of early Federal architecture."

"Is it haunted?" a young woman asked.

If only, Maggie thought to herself. Maybe it was growing up Salem, but she'd always had a deep interest in the supernatural. "No indication of ghosts," she replied. "But we keep hoping."

That raised a little ripple of laughter from the group. It was her stock answer to a common question. But then she caught a glare from Director O'Neill listening at the back of the hall, possibly about the ghosts or possibly for the dig about California, but more probably for referring to the Society for the Preservation of New England Antiquities. They weren't supposed to dredge up that name. SPNEA had been gone for over a decade, renamed into Historic New England. Maggie didn't actually approve of the name change, but then she loved the past and loved Redwood. Docenting at this historic house for over twenty years made her a little possessive of the house, but now that was catching up with her.

She and the new director -- much too young for the job in her opinion -- had been having words of late about deviations from the standard docent

39

script. So far she had been able to stand her ground without being openly oppositional, but it was fast coming to a head. He had the authority, but she was the one who knew the house inside out. Dammit, for years and years she had written her own script, using the tidbits from the archives to spice up the Redridge story. But now some . . . kid . . . from California was telling her she had to adjust her tours, just because he had a degree in preservation management. And he had even threatened her with probation -- *her*, the most seasoned docent on staff.

With a final "we'll talk later" look, O'Neill retreated down the basement steps to the staff area below. Maggie felt some of her tightly bottled tension fade away with her unwanted audience. She took a deep breath of candle wax and polished wood and continued.

"There are eight rooms on the two main floors of the house. The basement and third floor are used for storage and administrative purposes and are not open for touring. But I believe you'll be amply intrigued with the history of the rooms on display for some of those bits of history are . . . well, let's just say they're not in the guidebooks. There has been scandal and mystery in this house from the start."

There. Now she had the whole group hooked on the upcoming bits of gossip she would sprinkle into the standard script. How was this not a better tour than the bone-dry version O'Neill insisted upon?

She was just leading the way into the parlor when the doorbell rang -- an actual door bell, not some electric buzzer -- and she backtracked to admit the latecomers to the tour. But it was FedEx with a crate, not more tourists. A crate was not exactly historic ambience, but she had him leave it in the entrance hall since it had to go somewhere.

The sturdily built wooden crate was perhaps three feet by three feet and very thin. Maggie could tell at a glance it had to be a painting. That surprised her. She knew every wall of the exhibition rooms and no wall had space for additional art. Something would have to come down for something new to go up, and that also surprised her. The collection of paintings in the house was a nice balance of early and late 19th century work, and mostly original to the families who lived here. In her opinion, anything new would have to be exceptional, either historically or artistically, to claim wall space. Then she shrugged. It wasn't her decision. The new regime wasn't even interested in her opinion. She went back to her group in the parlor.

Three more afternoon tours brought the day to a close, but Maggie lingered in the front hall until O'Neill appeared with a screwdriver and crowbar. Looking at the crate all afternoon had made her very curious.

"May I assist with the uncrating?" she asked stiffly.

He looked about to refuse on principle just because it was her, then hesitated. "Actually, yes. Four hands are better than two where artifacts are involved. Thank you." His California accent was peculiar to her ear and his answer was as stiff as her offer, but still it was a yes.

They sat down on the floor on level with the crate and silently began. The work went slowly and midway, Maggie had to get up to turn on the lights so they could see. But piece by piece, the crate fell away, leaving layers of wrapping cloth. The frame came into view first, old burnished gold leaf over gesso, so probably period 19th century. Then the painting itself.

An oil portrait, Maggie noted as part of a torso came into view, a male torso in a dark coat with embroidered waistcoat. More anatomy was revealed, ending with the head. She sat back to view the overall work and gave a nod. "Handsome devil, isn't he?" The wavy hair and thin moustache made him a cross between Lord Byron and Clark Gable.

"I assume you recognize the subject," O'Neill said with a superior smile.

She hadn't, but immediately scrutinized the face for clues. There was something familiar about it beyond the Clark Gable moustache. "Ah," she said after a moment. "I believe this is a much younger Captain Mason Redridge." The portrait of the captain that hung in the upstairs hall was painted several decades later. "I hadn't heard he was so dashing in his youth."

"This painting appeared at auction in New York, and Mrs. Bradley-Smith, our ever-generous benefactress, happened to recognize the captain. It's a generous gift to the house."

"How expensive was it?" Maggie asked, but immediately saw from his expression that he found the question impertinent.

"I don't actually know," he said tightly. "One doesn't ask Mrs. Bradley-Smith such things. She did share, however, that the bidding went higher than expected because he was such an appealing subject. Thank you for your help, Mrs. Bederman. I can hang it by myself."

She heard that as a dismissal and got to her feet. "Who is the captain displacing?" she asked on the way to the door.

"The watercolor landscape at the head of the stairs. It will share the hall with the portraits of older Captain Redridge and his wife Sarah. I'll need to adjust the docent scripts accordingly."

And the evening ended on the uncomfortable note of docent scripts.

* * *

"Welcome to Redwood, the Redridge House on Chestnut Street," Maggie began the next morning with her first group. "It was built in 1794 by the Redridge family, restored in the 1890's by the Dunlaps, and acquired in 1973 by the Society for the Preservation of --"

A distinct *thump* interrupted her spiel. Followed by another. It seemed to be coming from the second floor, which was empty, to the best of her knowledge. She was the only docent in the house with the only tour group. Even the basement office was empty this morning.

"What is that?" one of the kids in the group asked as another *thump* sounded. He had a nasal Texas twang.

"Probably just a loose shutter banging in the wind," she improvised. "But I really should see to it" -- yet she couldn't leave the group unattended -- "so if you'll bear with a slight change in sequence, we'll start the tour upstairs and work our way back down to the rooms here on the first floor."

She didn't even try to speak as many feet tromped up the wooden staircase behind her. It always sounded like a herd of elephants. At the head of the stairs, her gaze went immediately to the empty picture hanger to her right. That was where the watercolor usually hung, but supposedly it had been displaced by young Captain Redridge. So why was there nothing on the wall? She gave a shiver. At least it didn't seem to be the worst scenario of a picture falling off the wall, for there was nothing on the floor.

"This is the second floor hall directly above the entrance hall," she said, slipping into her script, though her mind was still wrestling with questions. "There are four bedchambers, two on either side of the hall whose furnishings date to the Dunlap family ownership. They were also the ones to convert the original closets into small jack-and-jill bathrooms --"

"What does that mean?" the same Texas kid asked.

"It means a bathroom shared between two bedrooms, like Jack and Jill carrying a bucket," Maggie rattled off quickly. Young tourists never knew that term. Maybe they weren't used to sharing.

"And why is the air conditioning running full blast," the boy continued.

"The house doesn't have air conditioning, only central heating," she began, then paused as she realized it *was* very cold up here. Oddly cold. Someone might have left a window open, but it was June, not December. It was actually very pleasant outside.

"So we have a little mystery," she continued, recovering quickly. "If you will follow me to the front bedchamber, you will see on either side of the door two oil portraits of Captain Mason Redridge and his wife Sarah, the first owners of Redwood."

"Why is she so much older?" the boy twanged again.

Wasn't he a little Lonestar livewire? "It was common back then for gentlemen of means to marry much younger wives to ensure years of childbearing --" Then she realized that wasn't the question he had asked. Glancing at the portraits, she saw Sarah Redridge was in her customary place, but on the other side of the door was the new arrival, Young Captain Redridge, not the one from later in life. That hadn't been the plan. And where was Old Captain Redridge? She scanned the hallway and saw a painting sitting in the corner, facing the wall. She stepped over and turned it around. Old Captain Redridge.

Well, this was a mess. "One moment, please," she said and quickly hung the young captain at the head of the stairs so the old captain could have his place back. "Now, if you will follow me into the front bedchamber, you will see a poster bed carved by Salem son Samuel McIntire . . ."

* * *

"I'm sorry but this is the last straw," Director O'Neill said to Maggie as she closed the door on the last tour of the day. "You know that docents are expressly prohibited from handling the valuable artifacts in the house."

Maggie assumed he meant re-hanging the portraits upstairs. But what else was she supposed to do? Leave Captain Redridge on the floor? "They were out of place," she said sullenly. "It reflects poorly on Redwood to have its valuable artifacts scattered around like so much trash."

"What?"

"You're referring to repositioning the portraits, are you not?"

"Of course. Those paintings have been hanging as a pair beside the bedchamber door since before even your time, Mrs. Bederman. I am shocked -- yes, shocked -- that you would break up that historic placement on a passing whim."

Maggie frowned. "But I didn't break them up. I put the pair back together. Someone had miss-hung the new portrait as a pair with Sarah."

"And they still are miss-hung," O'Neill huffed. "A very flimsy excuse, Mrs. Bederman, I must say."

"No, the portraits are correct now *because* I rearranged them," Maggie insisted. "Let me show you." She led the way up the steps and pointed to the wall space at the head of the stairs where there was . . . an empty hanger.

She turned and hurried down the hall to the bedchamber. Just as before -- Sarah on one side, Young Captain Redridge on the other, Old Captain Redridge on the floor. "This is not how I left them," she frowned.

"A flimsy, flimsy excuse," O'Neil sniffed loftily as he went about restoring order to the portraits. "You see I have no choice but to dismiss you from service." He hung the last one at the head of the stairs and held out his hand. "I'll need your keys."

She gave them up grudgingly and slunk down the stairs to collect her coat and purse for the last time. She never dreamed O'Neill would manufacture such a blatant reason to fire her. Maybe she could appeal to the Board of Trustees, but she didn't have many friends in those lofty circles. At the door, she turned and looked straight him in the eye. "You're a fool, Director O'Neill," she began. "I'm the best docent the house has, and it's the off-script parts of my tours that people remember. If you really wanted to get rid of --"

Thump.

The sound echoed eerily down the stairwell.

Thump.

"What in the world?" O'Neill sputtered, heading back for the stairs. "Is someone up there?" he called up the well.

No answer.

He started up the steps; she followed. At the top of the staircase, an empty hanger. Down the hall, the same rearrangement as before. The doors to the bedchambers stood propped open as usual, showing no one else on the second floor.

O'Neill shuddered. "Why is it so cold?" he murmured, though that probably wasn't the top question on his mind.

Fool me once, shame on you, fool me twice . . . Maggie took a deep breath of frigid air, finally fitting the pieces together. She had longed for this for years, and finally it had come. "It's a haunting, Director. This hallway has become a cold spot."

He gave her narrow look. "A haunting? Why would I believe that?"

"Because this is Salem, where odd occurrences have been happening for over three hundred years, even before the Witch Trials. And it seems that the new portrait is causing all this, possibly spirit-possessed."

She paused a moment, knowing how ridiculous that all sounded but surprisingly, the director was not dismissing her words as nonsense. Of course, it was hard to dismiss sub-zero temperatures and roaming paintings. "But I have no idea," she continued, "why a spirit would attach itself to an earlier painting instead of one closer to the time of death?"

"Vanity?" O'Neill suggested. "He wants to be remembered in the prime of youth and not as an old man?"

"Vanity is seldom the cause of an earth-bound spirit. It's more usually incomplete business or a violent death."

"And what violent death would that be?" O'Neill asked with a shake of his head. "Both Sarah and Mason Redridge lived to ripe old age and died peacefully in bed."

"But that was exceptional for a time when life expectancy was only about forty years. Infant mortality, infectious disease, and accidents took a huge toll of early populations, especially infant mortality . . . "

Something niggled at the back of her head as she said that. "Are we sure this is Mason Redridge?"

"Over and above the obvious resemblance, the name is chalked on the back of the canvas. But I see you want a look -- allow me." O'Neill carefully lifted the young captain painting from its hanger and turned it around to display its backside. "It feels like ice," he shivered.

"The focal point of an active haunting would," she muttered absently as she leaned in to study the name. It was an old cursive hand with some smudging over the centuries, but the second word was definitely "Redridge." The first name was harder to decipher, and she read it letter by letter backwards -- n-o-s-a -- with a smudged capital at the beginning. "Something –as on," she murmured. "But that first letter doesn't look like an 'M.' It has a tail to it -- perhaps a 'P' or 'J'."

"Pason, Jason." O'Neill shook his head. "That means nothing."

"But the old family Bible does indicate there was once a Redridge brother," she pointed out. "Because there's no later reference to him, we've always assumed infant mortality. The Bible is on display in the north parlor."

Carefully, O'Neill re-hung the portrait, and the two of them left the frigid zone for the more normal temperatures of the parlor downstairs. The Bible sat under a glass dome on the side table. Gingerly, O'Neill opened the front cover and studied the family tree inked on the endpapers. "Grayson Redridge," he said. "Born 1772. . . the same year as the captain."

They stared at each other. "Twins," they said in unison.

"And not at all an infant death if Grayson lived long enough to be painted as a young man," O'Neill added.

"But not mentioned in any of the family letters of the time," Maggie mused. "That's strange enough for me to suspect a scandal, carefully hushed up. And an unquiet death that left behind an unquiet spirit." She mulled a moment more. "Ah, of course. The portrait tells its own story by its actions."

"And?"

"Grayson and Mason were both in love with Sarah. But Mason prevailed, perhaps in a duel. With all the public outrage over the Aaron Burr-Alexander Hamilton duel in 1804, contemporary with the Redridges, it would have prudent to keep any death by duel quiet. Moreover, if this was an affair of the heart when Mason and Sarah were already married, then the whole of it definitely would have struck out of the family documents."

O'Neill gave her a long look. "You're just making up all of this."

"It's a hypothesis that fits the known facts," she countered. "There's nothing wrong with embellishing. It gives the tours zest."

He didn't respond to that, but seemed to be considering it. "And the big question," he finally said, "what do we do with the haunted portrait of Grayson? Refusing to display a gift from Mrs. Bradley-Smith is not an option."

"Well," Maggie considered the problem from a dozen different angles. "We could split the time with Sarah between the two twins. In the winter, we leave Mason in his place by the door and store Grayson in the wine cellar. But during the summer when it's a little muggy, we display Grayson."

"And let tourists enjoy the cold spot as natural air conditioning?"

"More supernatural, I'd say."

He was quiet a long moment, then slowly handed back her keys. "Perhaps I was overly hasty in my conclusions. Perhaps a little zest goes a long way."

* * *

First tour of the new day. "Welcome to Redwood, the Redridge House. The name Redwood originally meant only the color of original oxblood paint, but nowadays it's a nice connection with California. The house was built in 1794 by the Redridge family, restored in the 1890's by the Dunlaps, and acquired in 1973 by . . . Historic New England. It is one of several properties the organization operates here in Salem and a prime example of early Federal architecture."

So Maggie Bederman could change. If O'Neill could unbend a little, she could as well. There was such a thing as being too tied to the past, too much in love with it. And every time she thought about the spirit of Grayson Redridge stuck in a portrait by the strength of his love, it reinforced her resolve. This was, after all, Salem, where odd occurrences had happened.

She didn't want to end up as one of them.

LITTLE BROTHER
Richard Farren Barber

Michael hesitated on the sidewalk outside the arcade and a wave of sound crashed over him: the electronic ping of games and the rumble of voices shot through with excited cries. A pop song that he vaguely recognized blared out, although the words sounded strange, corrupted. Beneath that came the clatter of money and the mechanical whirr of slot machines. It wasn't fear that stopped him from entering, not quite; it was more complicated than that.

He felt the muscles in his chest tighten. He tried to breathe, to drag into his lungs the scent of cotton-candy and grease.

Sandy laid a hand on his arm. "Are you okay?"

He nodded, he didn't have the air for words.

"We can come back."

Michael didn't take his eyes away from the entrance to the arcade. She didn't get it. She tried, but she just didn't get it, and he couldn't explain it to her. He'd told her about the other times. He'd told her about standing on the far side of the road and watching kids scuttling in and out of Salem Willows like ants working their nest. This was the closest he had come in twenty years. He could reach out and touch the metal poles at the side of the arcade. In a couple of steps he would be inside. No, if he didn't manage it this time he couldn't try again.

"I'll be fine." His words sounded weak and strained. He didn't believe them, so there was no reason to think that Sandy would.

He turned to her and smiled. "It's okay," he said, and he wished that was the truth. He felt something settle within him; not quite peace, but acceptance, a recognition that this time it would be okay because it would have to be okay, and he stepped off the melting sidewalk and onto the wooden floor of the arcade.

Nothing happened. Michael paused for a second inside the doorway, as if waiting for a lightning bolt to come down from the heavens. Or for all the children inside the arcade to turn away from the video games they were standing at, put down the paddles on the air hockey machine and together, as one, look at him and shout that he didn't belong there, that the arcade was theirs now. But the kids were immersed in their games and if any of them noticed him entering the arcade they didn't respond.

"This was where you came as children?" Sandy asked.

He knew she was trying to distract him. Just as she had done on the drive up from Boston. Sitting beside him in the car and chattering about old movies and favorite concerts and whether they would finally get to a game at Fenway after three years of broken promises. He knew what she was doing, and he loved her all the more for trying.

"Every summer. Mom and Dad used to hire a cottage by the river and we'd take the train up from North Station." He paused. Looked around the room. It was impossible to be certain, but he would swear that nothing had changed in the twenty years since he had last stepped inside the arcade. The same games, the same rides, even the same kids crowded around the screens peering through the glass as the next high score was racked up. The pinball machines clanged, and if he closed his eyes he was ten years old again.

A small kid brushed against his side and scurried to the games. Michael turned and outside on the sidewalk the boy's mother peered into the gloom, her hand raised in a half-wave.

Reality crashed over him. Drowned him. He felt a rush of heat flood through his body and in that instant he knew he was either going to faint or vomit. He took a step toward the exit on legs that melted beneath him. It was like walking through saltwater taffy. He took another step. The mother outside on the pavement stared at him, and he imagined falling to the floor and lying there, unable to walk. Having to drag himself outside.

Sandy held him. Without her he would have lurched out onto the sidewalk, maybe even onto the pavement before he stopped.

"For Jimmy," she said. Nothing more. Her voice so quiet it was impossible to hear her above the crashing machines, and yet somehow he did. He looked at her, *Do you know what you're asking?* She couldn't, and yet somehow she understood at least enough to stop his flight out of the arcade.

Michael staggered across the floor and slumped against one of the yellow machines used to make change to feed the video games. Anywhere else his actions would have drawn attention, but everyone was too focused on the games to notice what was happening around them. There were a couple of older women feeding the slot machines with quarters from plastic cups. He heard the regular ker-thunk of the machine each time the lever was pulled. Somebody could have set off a strip of firecrackers next to the women's seats and they wouldn't have noticed.

He breathed deeply, filling his chest, tasting the arcade at the back of his throat. Someone should bottle that scent, they'd make a fortune. What had Jimmy called it: eau D'Willows. He'd said he was going to create a chewing gum flavor out of it. It was going to make him millions. Make *them* millions – Jimmy had said they'd split the profits evenly: seventy-thirty.

"He loved this place," Michael said. "*We* loved this place," he corrected himself. "Mom used to say that if they'd had beds we would have stayed here for the whole week. I guess she was right."

"Did he have a favorite game?"

"Asteroids. First day of the holiday he would make straight for it and see what the high score was, and he'd spend the rest of the week trying to beat it. You know... where you get to put three letters next to your score. His was JIM, or would have been. He never got anywhere near the top ten scores. He was good... but there must have been kids who lived in the town and came in every week because Jimmy—"

Michael stopped.

"Go on."

"Jimmy used to say that when he grew up he was going to buy an Asteroids machine and play it every day, and then he was going to come back here and fill the screen with his high scores." Michael heard his voice crack, and he wiped a tear away from his eye before it had a chance to properly form. "I'd forgotten about that until just now."

He stood a little straighter. Took his weight off the change machine. He looked out to the sidewalk and the sunlight poured in, just as he remembered; like that was another world out there. There was Salem Willows, and there was everywhere else.

He passed the punch bag and smiled at the memory of Jimmy winding up his arm and barely registering on the scale when he finally thumped it. They'd stood there together, two brothers side by side, and watched some muscle-bound Jock smash the punchbag through the machine and out the other side to impress a girl. How old had he been? Ten, maybe eleven, which meant that Jimmy would have been about eight. Eyes wide as saucers at the feat of strength. The pair of them thinking that they would never grow up. Never be able to hit the bag that hard.

Michael stopped in front of the machine. It was too early in the day for it to see any real use. Once it was dark and the older kids started to drift in there was often a line of guys out to impress their dates, but for now the punchbag was abandoned. The brown leather was shiny in the spot where it had taken the knuckles of thousands of youths. He rummaged in his pocket for a quarter and dropped it into the slot. The lights flashed around the edge: Weakling through to Strong Man. He tapped the bag with his closed fist, not hard enough to rock it. He looked to his left, and Sandy was watching. To his right Jimmy was standing, that same wide-eyed look on his face.

"You know I can do it?" he asked.

Jimmy said nothing.

Michael punched his fist through the bag as hard as he could, and the machine clanged and flashed in response. "There," he said, but Jimmy was already gone. He thought he saw his brother disappearing between two lines of kids. Just a fleeting glance as he headed deeper into the arcade. He heard the rubber soles of Jimmy's sneakers on the wooden floor.

Michael pressed past a row of video games with small kids lined up in front of them. He could drag a bloody corpse along the ground behind him, and they wouldn't notice. For now all they wanted was the screen and the noise and the feel of the joystick under their fingers. He remembered the sense of being so immersed in another world that nothing else mattered, and for a moment he yearned to relive the experience.

Michael wanted to explain, but he couldn't because he didn't understand what was happening. He'd come back to Salem to try and recover what he had lost when Jimmy had died. He knew Jimmy wasn't here. Not the twenty-eight year-old man he would have become or the thirteen-year-old boy he had been when the car had knocked the future out of him. Jimmy was a pile of bones in a wooden casket six feet under the ground in Forest Hills. Whatever he was following through Salem Willows was not his brother. Maybe it was the memory of his brother. More likely it was some eight year old kid who looked vaguely like his brother and dressed in the same clothes that all eight year olds wore: faded Converse High-Tops, a dirty t-shirt, and ragged jeans

The sound of the video games dragged Michael back twenty years to a time when the only thing important to him had been his score on Galaxians and Spy Hunter. When swapping tips in the school yard had been the whole point of recess. Jimmy had been even more obsessed.

There was a moment, Michael realized, when he could have turned and walked out of Salem Willows. He had achieved what he had set out to do — he had come into the arcade. But instead of setting the ghost of his dead brother to rest it had the opposite effect. Jimmy had never been far from his thoughts during the intervening two decades, but now he was there, actually there in front of him, turning his back and leaving him felt like letting him die all over again.

He took a longing glance back over his shoulder to the bright world outside the arcade, and then plunged into the gloom.

"I knew you'd be here," he said. Jimmy was too far ahead to hear anything, and yet Michael felt that his brother knew he was following him. He had his back, because that was what brothers did, right? Any scrap

Jimmy got into in the school yard, and Michael would magically appear at the edge of the crowd. He didn't always intervene, because Jimmy could handle himself, but on more than one occasion, when the fight had been uneven, he had waded in to scrape his knuckles against the chin of some brat who was picking on his kid brother.

"Wait for me," Michael said. He hurried down an aisle, bumping the back of a kid on a Space Invaders game who was too enthralled to register the contact. He turned the corner just in time to see Jimmy disappearing behind a pinball machine.

Michael increased his pace through the arcade. Behind him he heard Sandy call, "Hey, wait up!" and his allegiances were torn. Except Sandy would understand, and she would still be there when this was over. He had a strong sense that if he lost Jimmy now, he would never find him again.

"Hey, Jimmy! Slow down!" he called. He passed a pinball machine, a *Funhouse* with a high score of 666,666 posted on the glory board.

And Jimmy was waiting for him.

Michael sucked in a breath of shock. He tasted it at the back of his throat – sweet and hot.

It was Jimmy. No doubt about it. His brown hair messed up, eyes blazing deep blue. There were freckles across his nose and Michael recognized every single spot on his cheeks.

"It's really you."

Michael felt each double-thump his heart made. He tasted each warm breath sucked into his lungs.

Jimmy was playing on one of the machines. His eyes were fixed to the screen, and if he heard his older brother he gave no indication of the fact. For a moment Michael just stood and watched him.

In Salem Willows you didn't interrupt someone when they were playing. It was one of the rules. Instead, Michael walked up to the machine next to Jimmy's. It was Space Invaders. The original; it had been old even when they had been kids. He checked his pocket for a quarter and put it into the slot to interrupt the demo playing out on the screen. For a second the glass went black. Only it didn't because over the years the after-images had been burned into the screen so it was possible to see the ghosts of the houses and the rows of aliens hovering above them.

Michael covered the controls with his hands and when the electronic music started he began firing at the aliens coming down and eating away his world. As he played he looked to his left. Jimmy was still engrossed in his own game. Michael had so much he wanted to say to him. About Mom and Dad. About what had happened to their friends. He wanted to tell him that he was sorry, that he never meant to hurt him. More than anything else he wanted to tell him that he never meant to hurt him.

"Hey, Jimmy," he hissed. The boy beside him did not respond.

"Who are you talking to?" Sandy asked.

"I've found him."

Sandy looked down the aisle. "Why didn't you tell me? Where?"

"Right there." Michael's hands did not pause in their work on the controls, and he nodded across to the other machine where Jimmy was still engrossed in his game.

There was a silence. In the cacophony of the arcade there was a moment of perfect silence and he looked across to Sandy. Her expression was a mixture of confusion and concern.

"That's not Jimmy."

"Course it is." He let go of the controls and watched as a moment later the aliens ate through the remains of the houses and came to land on top of his tank. The legend 'Game Over' rose up through the screen.

He broke the rule. He reached out and grabbed Jimmy by the shoulder, and then immediately pulled back from his little brother. He was cold. Not just cold, but freezing. It was like plunging his hand into a bucket of liquid nitrogen and immediately all the nerves in his fingers burned.

The boy at the next machine didn't respond to the contact.

Sandy took a step closer, until she was standing beside Michael. Another step took her in front of him. Next to the machine Jimmy was playing.

"Don't scare him away," Michael said. He heard the panic in his own voice as he spoke.

He heard Sandy's breath. Deep and measured. It felt like they were wrapped in a cocoon – just himself, Jimmy, and Sandy. The three of them pulled out of existence so that Salem Willows no longer existed.

"I've been looking for you," he told Jimmy. Somehow it was easier to speak when it seemed that the boy wasn't listening to him. "I've come every year. I knew you'd be here. No one believed me, but I knew I'd find you again."

Jimmy whirled around to face him. His eyes were silver discs. His skin was gray-blue. He opened his mouth to snarl and his teeth were long and pointed, like a row of uneven razor blades.

Michael took a step back and raised his hands to protect himself. He staggered against a video machine and the edge of the cabinet smacked against his hip. Jimmy snapped his mouth closed and returned to his game.

"Jimmy?" Michael asked. His stomach flipped in terror. He could feel adrenaline coursing through his veins, pushing up his heart rate. His body screamed at him to run. But it was just Jimmy. Just his little brother. Now that Jimmy was staring at the screen once again he looked like any other kid in the arcade. He twisted his body in sympathy with the game's controls.

Michael leaned forward.

And Jimmy turned, silver eyes blazing hate, sharp teeth bared. He lifted a hand from the panel and instead of fingernails he had talons; cigarette-yellow claws that scratched the air. His lips moved but Michael couldn't hear what he said, and he realized he didn't want to hear.

"Who are you?" he asked. For a moment he saw his kid brother through the distorted features of the thing in front of him, rising up from the depths before fading back again. "What happened to Jimmy?"

His brother's lips moved, chewing words that were never allowed to escape. His teeth cut into his gums, scarlet slashes on pink lips. Blood trickled from his mouth and down his chin to fall in large drops on the wooden floor of the arcade.

"Jimmy's gone." At first Michael thought that it was the creature who spoke. Only after a moment did he understand that it was Sandy.

He shook his head. "No. He can't be. I won't let him."

Jimmy turned back to his game. A drop of blood fell from his lips onto the joystick.

Michael reached out to him, but Sandy held him back. "Whoever that is, it isn't your brother."

"You don't know that."

"But you do."

Michael dropped his head. It was impossible to accept that she was right. He'd made the journey up from Boston every year, stayed in the same B&B on Essex Street. It had to be Jimmy.

He stared at his kid brother. Maybe he should just let him go. Maybe he should finally listen to his friends, his parents, Sandy.

"No!" he shouted. He reached out and pulled Jimmy away from the game.

They came from both ends of the aisle. Kids and teenagers and young adults. A ten year old boy wearing a smiley Nirvana t-shirt, and a pock-marked eighteen year old girl, her make-up not quite thick enough to hide her acne scars, pushing against each other, filling the aisle with their bodies. Silver quarters blinding their eyes. They held their hands in front of them, outstretched fingers gripping the air and tearing it apart.

"They can't hurt us," Sandy said. Michael wasn't sure if it was a statement or a question. He didn't know the answer. It was impossible to believe that his kid brother could – or would – hurt him, but he wasn't so sure about the others. It was hard to see how he could be frightened of a ten year old; the boy was thin as a stick, no muscle on him at all. Michael could pick him up and snap him in two. There was no way the boy could threaten him, and yet Michael couldn't ignore the terror he felt. It was the same with the other children: there was an other-ness about them. They were wrong. They didn't belong here.

The ten-year-old grinned, revealing his mouth full of razor teeth, and, although he said nothing, Michael knew perfectly what he was thinking: *Oh, but we do belong here.*

Where were the adults? The people in charge? Michael wondered. And then he laughed – he was an adult, he just didn't feel like one at that moment.

"Jimmy?" he said. He didn't quite know what he was asking – for an explanation? For protection? His kid brother glared at him with silver eyes. There was no warmth there, no recognition.

"What do you want?" Sandy asked over his shoulder. Michael wondered what Jimmy's response would be, and then he realized she wasn't talking to his brother, she was talking to him.

What do I want? He almost laughed. *To get out of here alive. To see my brother at peace. To say sorry for every bad thing I ever did to him when he was alive.* But he wasn't sure what was possible any more. He couldn't just run away, not now he had seen Jimmy like this. He would be haunted by the knowledge that his little brother was trapped in this place.

Behind the boy with the Nirvana t-shirt came a girl, a year or two older, floral dress and silver quarter eyes. She held a plastic pot of money in front of her, and the coins rattled inside. Behind her was another girl, fifteen or sixteen with a cut-off top exposing a pierced navel. She had a tattoo just above her hip bone; a Chinese symbol.

The aisle in front of him was packed with children now. The fluorescent lights overhead reflected in their eyes. The pumping music grew quieter until it felt like the aisle was a cocoon of silence trapped within the crashing music and flashing lights of Salem Willows arcade.

Michael thought about taking Sandy's hand and pushing through the bodies of the children. Crashing through the crowd and forcing the kids aside. That was what his body wanted to do: escape. Just get the hell out of there. But he'd found Jimmy, after twenty years of searching he'd found his kid brother, and he wasn't going to give him up that easily.

He snatched forward to take Jimmy. The boy hissed and drew back.

"Come with me," Michael said. The other children moved closer. "Are they holding you here?" He glared at them, as if they were responsible for what had happened to Jimmy. "They can't stop us."

He lurched again, trying to snatch Jimmy's arm and pull him away. He had an idea that if he got him out of the arcade then the rest would be easy. Away from the sounds and flashing lights of the video games Jimmy would open up and explain what had happened to him and how he was still the thirteen year old boy who had died all those years ago.

Michael's fingers touched Jimmy's cold skin. It was hard and dry. Still, once Michael had him he didn't let go. He pulled Jimmy toward him. The boy's rubber-soled sneakers squealed against the floor of the arcade.

"Come on," Jimmy said. Over his shoulder he was conscious that the other children were crowding in, bodies packing the aisle to stop him from leaving.

54

"This way," Sandy said. She pushed kids aside, forcing a narrow path through the bodies.

Michael followed, dragging his brother after him. Jimmy reached out and his fingers found the controller of a Pac-Man machine and, as Michael pulled, his brother stretched like a torture victim on a rack. He couldn't think of anything to do except to keep pulling, until Sandy stepped around him, and pried Jimmy's fingers from the machine, one at a time. When his pinkie was released he lurched forward and the pair of them crashed into the pack of quarter-eyed kids.

"If I can get him outside..." he told Sandy.

At the end of the aisle he dared to look over his shoulder, the entrance to the arcade was washed in pale sunlight, and it seemed an impossible distance away. It was like trying to cross a desert carrying a huge boulder. But he couldn't give in, not after all these years of searching. He *wouldn't* give in.

The hands of youngsters grabbed at him as he pushed through the pack. Their nails raked along his arms, carving through his shirt to his skin. The edges of the tattered cloth stained red with his blood.

Jimmy caught hold of a metal pole supplying the machines with electricity and wrapped his arms around it. Sandy paused to extricate Jimmy from the obstruction, and when he was freed Michael picked him up to carry him the remainder of the way to the exit. The hot stench of fried electricity filled Jimmy's breath.

They stumbled on, Michael's head bowed to the floor so that he saw only the few inches of space that Sandy cleared in front of him. He focused on the heels of her shoes and each staggered step was a victory. He wasn't going to make it. There was no way he was going to make it, but he was determined to get as far as possible.

The weight of the children behind him pushed him to his knees and when he fell, Jimmy rolled from his arms. Michael rose to his feet and dragged his brother across the old floor. "You've got to get out," he said.

He stumbled out of the arcade onto the sidewalk. Jimmy stood, still inside the arcade, staring out.

"You've done it," Sandy said.

Michael shook his head. The toes of Jimmy's sneakers barely brushed the line that marked the divide between the arcade and the sidewalk. His brother was still locked within Salem Willows.

With one last pull he could drag him out of The Willows. He could free him. He looked into Jimmy's face. For a moment the silver quarters disappeared, and he was looking into the blue eyes of his younger brother.

Michael opened his hands and let go of his brother's arm. "This has to be your choice," he said.

Jimmy stared at him.

What was that look? Fear? Anticipation?

"What are you doing?" Sandy asked.

"It needs to be his decision."

"But…"

Jimmy stood on the threshold of the arcade. Behind him the press of young bodies left a clear semi-circle of bare floor. Michael wondered what he would do if they reached out and tried to draw Jimmy back into Salem Willows. Would he fight?

Yes. Then he would fight. But for now it was Jimmy's decision. Jimmy's and no one else's.

Michael thought he saw Jimmy looking out, past him and Sandy. Staring out over the sidewalk and the pavement. He wondered how far he could see. Across town? Across the park to the Atlantic?

Jimmy looked behind him, back into the shadows of the arcade. His eyes flickered; from blue to gray and then back again, and in that moment Michael was sure that he had won, that his brother would step onto the sidewalk to join him.

And then Jimmy turned, his eyes flashing silver, and faded into the crowd and the depths of the arcade.

THE PARSON
Brian Malachy Quinn

In 1697, in Massachusetts Bay Colony, the Devil smiled a wicked grin as flying witches filled the night sky; enchanted apples cast spells, and shape shifters morphed from human to animal, did mischief and then became human again. Just five years earlier, fourteen women, five men, two dogs, one chicken and a black cat, condemned of "wickedly, maliciously, and feloniously" engaging in sorcery, met a violent end at the hands of the righteous – or were they? Innocents hanged, refusing to confess to something they had not done, but the guilty had escaped – so many believed, including Jonathon Williamson, who was to-be sixth parson of Salem Village. The farming community had not been kind to its previous five holy men, one in the ground and four driven out. His immediate predecessor, whom he came to replace, mysteriously died in his sleep after only three months in Salem Village, found with his mouth agape in mid-scream, eyes bulging out of their sockets.

Religion was an integral part of the Puritan life, Scripture referenced for everything from making cider to mediating neighborly disputes. A Puritan devoted himself to constant and extensive examination, his minister there to guide him to heaven. A New England pastor was judge, counselor, consoler, and guide as he led the people, born in sin, to the grace of God. So valued, he received a princely sum of eighty pounds a year, putting him at the top of income earners in Salem Village. So the contract stated, however, when the constable came around to collect the tax, he often fled empty handed, target of projectiles launched by angry farmers, chased off the property in fear for his life, dogs nipping at his heels. The village was born out of the frontier of Salem Town, the second busiest port in the Colony, as a loose farming settlement. Contentious to its core, even born so - the town elders, wanting nothing more to do with the farmers' complaints and demands, gave them their own village, a buffer between the frontier full of savage Indians, wolves, and demons and their Salem Town.

However, it seemed the very nature of the Massachusetts Puritan to be a thorn in the side of his spiritual guide. Escape clauses became standard in contracts as in the words of Increase Mather, "he was free to leave his parish if the Lord called him elsewhere, if his pay proved insufficient, or if he suffered persecution by his congregation." Ideally, the relationship between a pastor and his flock was like that between a husband and wife, but in all practicality, often a nagging wife that drove her husband to leave the wedded bliss that never existed. Many ministers left to become merchants, tired of living on the little that they received, tired of sacrificing in this world, only rewarded in the next. Dismissals frequently also occurred if the ministers became too severe or rankled feathers, especially those of the powerbrokers of the community (In Salem Village, the Putnams and all their relatives) or appeared not devoted enough in their holy avocation, a fine line to walk.

Jonathon Williamson, age thirty-five, had come to the pulpit late in life. A merchant in the West Indies, the loss of his first wife in childbirth caused him to search for purpose, first in the bottom of a bottle of rum, later in Scripture. He entered Harvard, received a degree in Divinity, and Salem was his first assignment. Even though assignments were hard to come by, and there were more ministers in the Colony than pulpits, Salem remained unguided, a dark cloud hanging over it. Salem Village was in grave danger, so Increase Mather had informed him when he conferred the office, the Great Deluder hiding in every shadow.

Williamson arrived in Salem Village late in the day. It was one of the coldest winters on record. He went directly to Thomas Putnam's house, the largest house in the village, the family's wealth evident. A young man in fine clothes, though having a disheveled look about him, opened the door, not welcoming him in the house, not identifying himself, saying something incomprehensible under his breath as his face distorted in a rhythmic spasm, clearly afflicted - mutterings being the Devil's music.

"May I speak to Thomas Putnam?" Williamson asked, knowing this person was not Putnam since the leader of the village was much older and more distinguished.

"He is busy," the man said, not making eye contact, his mouth pulling up on the left in a grimace, exposing yellowed teeth, spittle dripping down his chin, "cannot be disturbed, important man, important business."

"But I am the new minister."

The man began to close the door.

Williamson put his hand against the door stopping the motion, "Well, surely you can lead me to the parsonage?"

"No," and the man again tried closing the door.

58

"Well, at least give me directions."

The man gave terse directions, his English ill-formed, this time more forcefully attempting to shut the door, all the while his eyes darting around wildly.

Williamson quickly said, "I will give my first sermon tomorrow at noon, perhaps I can meet Goodman Putnam there?" before the door closed with a thud.

Williamson stood facing the closed door, confused, frustrated. Salem Village consisted of ninety families and fifty isolated farms, many living a full mile from his nearest neighbor, and the parsonage was on the outskirts. He followed the directions and along the way, the few people that braved the frigid cold did not even give him a simple greeting or acknowledge him.

The steep roofed clapboard parsonage left the minister in shock. A two-story house on two acres of land, everything in disrepair, the house with missing shingles, the fence around the fields collapsed to the ground. Ownership of the parsonage and the land by the village was a sore point in the contract negotiations, usually only granted to the parson after a long and uncontentious period of service. He inspected the outer buildings, the supply of firewood was sparse, the root cellar full of moldy vegetables. Surely, the people understood how important he was? Their eternal souls were at stake! Inside a howling wind roared down the cavernous chimney in the center of the house and out of the four fireplaces bringing snow swirling in. The four-whitewashed rooms had little in the way of furniture and what was there was crude and cheaply made. In the bedchamber upstairs he saw the bed – was that where his predecessor had died? Did they expect him to sleep there?

The sun was low on the horizon, though still early in the day, it was late in the year, so he decided to prepare for the night. After putting his horse in the ramshackle stable, he gave it what little oats were in supply and brought in some wood to start a fire in the hearth. He picked through the moldy turnips, carved away what he could not eat and made a weak soup. Tomorrow, Thursday, he would give his first sermon. In the sermon, he would reinforce basic principles of the faith and stress covenant obligations. He had been preparing it since he received his office. The first sermon would set the tone for his relationship with his parish. He needed to be commanding, demonstrating knowledge of the Scriptures. For the rest of the day he would contemplate his discourse, study Scripture, hone his delivery replete with dramatic arm movements and pronounced hand gestures.

A minister's life centered on the sermon, delivered on Thursdays and Sundays. Its crafting began with the studying of, reading of, and meditating on Scripture. A minister's wife was an integral partner in this as she was the testing board for the sermon as it evolved, giving advice on content, length, and presentation. Williamson's second wife, Rebecca, had stayed back in Boston with their six-month old daughter, Abigail, and he missed both of them dearly. He would send for them once everything had been prepared. One of the other roles of the wife of a minister was to read and discuss the Bible with the village's children and even to teach the children to read. To achieve his ultimate goal of stealing souls, Satan needed to keep men from knowledge of Scripture, and if they started young by establishing a love and reverence for the Bible, they had a better chance of attaining salvation.

However, a minister also had to provide for himself and his family and maintain his property. He stopped harvesting corn only to preside over a prayer meeting, consoled grieving parents of children that died of sickness after hunting game, and made cider before performing baptisms. His sparse provisions made it clear that he was unprepared to finish the winter in his current condition. Cotton Mather had said that "The starving of ministers was always a way of Satan taking over the land." He would address his situation with the village elders; it was unacceptable, especially when his family would soon be joining him. He continued to go over his sermon until late into the night, praying in bed until he fell asleep, wary of ghosts that lingered in this place where dark tragedy had recently struck.

The minister awoke from a restless sleep to a sound on the roof right above his bed. Perhaps it was hail striking the surface. He listened believing he imagined it, but the sound continued – a clip clop of hooves going back and forth. The night was moonlit, and he could see his breath when he exhaled; the fire had gone out. The minister tried to quiet his breathing, trying not to make a sound – if whatever it was could not hear him, maybe it would go away. It continued, and he believed he heard children's laughter coming down the chimney. He rose from his bed and approached the fireplace, sticking his head under the mantle, peering up. He heard sweet voices uttering blasphemies, foul words that only the vilest of people would speak. Suddenly a black mass shot down the chimney; jerking back to avoid it, he struck his head on the mantle and dropped to the floor, the darkness overwhelming him. In a disorientated state, on the cold floor he became aware that he was not alone in the room. A smell of lavender grew in strength as the sound of soft feet came closer, a sweet smell but overpowering. Struggling to rise, he heard whispered songs of dark rhythms and then blackness overcame him.

He awoke on the floor, the sun shining, unaware of how much time had passed but the night was long gone. His body was stiff from the cold, his head, where he had struck it, ached. He became aware of a burning sensation on his right arm, placing his hand down the neck opening of his night shirt, he felt a bump slightly below his shoulder which was sensitive to the touch. Awkwardly, he rose and lifted his bed shirt over his head and looked down to see a black, raised, circular mark. *What is this?* Perhaps he had bumped his arm when he had fallen.

There was a fierce draft coming up the stairs, so he put all thoughts of the mark out of his mind. Dressing quickly, he descended to the first floor. The front door was swinging back and forth and snow had gathered in the house entryway. Rushing to close the door, he saw prints in the snow, cloven and deep, leading out of the house.

Williamson drew in a deep breath and let it out slowly. Something had entered his house, something most unnatural, clearly not of God's design. The Lord was testing him because he believed in the strength of his faith. Singled out to do combat with evil, a testament to the purity of his heart, he would confront it and strike it down. Sure in his task, he put on his cloak, hat, and gloves; with his walking staff in hand, went out to do battle.

He followed the prints on the path, which headed directly for the forest, where darkness dwelled. After a half an hour of trudging through the ankle-high snow, without breaking stride, the footprints abruptly changed from cloven ones to human. The hair raised on the back of the minister's neck, and his heart beat faster, as if it would explode out of his chest. To strengthen his resolve he attempted to pray, to invoke the names of the Father, Son, and Holy Ghost, but the words came out in a rush, incoherent, as if in the language of a savage from some dark corner of the globe. He could see from the well-formed toes of the footprints, clearly the one responsible wore no foot coverings; shocking as he, though heavily clothed, felt the cold to his very bones. The creature's stride was not long as there was little space between the tip of the toe of the previous print and the edge of the heel of the one above it, moving unhurried, unafraid, unaffected by the cold. He grasped his walking staff tightly, solid in his gloved hand, striding forward, following the tracks as they wound through the woods. The wind drove through the trees, stealing his breath, which came from his mouth in frozen gasps.

As he came over the rise, expecting to see some horrid creature, he saw - her. Not quite in her second decade, she wore only a short, white underdress, which rode up her thighs and caressed her slender form, her skin a deathly white. She stood facing him, as if she had been awaiting his arrival, her long, straight, raven-black hair danced in the wind. Her irises were a striking emerald green; she smiled, a laugh on her sensuous lips. Parting those lips, baring her teeth, the length of the pointed incisors caused him to doubt his sight.

Turning, she walked slowly away from him. Overcome with a paralysis of indecision, he was unsure of what to do: follow, or return to the safety of his house. As if sensing this, she turned with a strand of hair caught between her crimson lips, slowly brushed it aside with a long finger, smiled, then proceeded up a slight rise, the motion of her hips entrancing him. The changeling disappeared around a massive oak; compelled, he quickly followed. Upon reaching the oak, the tracks disappeared. Hearing motion above him in the tree, he fearfully looked up and staring down at him, perched on a low limb, sat a great white owl, unblinking. Seeing his reflection in its eyes, thinking his soul captured, he turned and ran, half-stumbling, half-lunging back up the path.

He was not aware of his journey, only of reaching the parsonage. He had lost his hat and staff, his face rubbed raw by the wind, the mark on his arm burning. Grabbing the door handle, he pulled, but a small drift of snow had formed, stopping its motion. Frantically, dropping to his knees he clawed the snow away, forcing some up his sleeves. Finally inside, he slammed the door closed, his back against it, and he slid to the ground, his entire body shaking. When his legs could support him, he hurried to the fireplace and started a fire; he rubbed his arms, his fingers ghostly white and numb.

He warmed his body by the fire, praying for strength. How could he convince the people of the village that the devil was back? That witches once again walked amongst them after the recent happenings, with what people chalked up to hysteria. On the title page of the Malleus Maleficarum, the witch hunter's bible, which he kept alongside his Bible, it stated, "Not to believe in witchcraft is the greatest of heresies." He would have to convince the good people of the village that the devil was here and that they must act. He prayed for guidance, that he choose his words wisely when he spoke to his flock.

When it was near noon, he dressed, saddled his horse and headed for the meetinghouse. Along the way, he felt eyes on him, his horse was unnerved, and both anxiously looked into the suffocating pine forest, hearing movement with nothing presenting itself.

The minister, in a dark gown and a flat linen collar, stood in the austere, dim meetinghouse, its broken windows boarded up and birds' nests in the rafters. He was shocked as walnuts flew from the galleries, children ran up and down the stairs, there was spitting, laughing, flirting, and a grizzled old man in a back pew whistled a rude sailor's tune while he whittled. Some people slept while others gossiped, spreading vicious rumors, casting dispersions on their neighbor's character. The pulpit was well worn, a hand-me-down from Salem Town, the tankards on the communion table, pewter, not the polished silver of the finer, more established Boston parishes. This was a place of worship, the center of their existence! At the First Church in Boston, the parishioners came with paper and pen to record the divinely inspired words of the sermon, the centerpiece of the week; Williamson saw no such preparations here.

Before the meetinghouse fell into complete chaos, Williamson took to the pulpit and started to speak; the congregants ignored him. He pounded the pulpit and raised his voice to battle the noise, but only a high-pitched sound escaped his mouth. The meeting hall erupted with laughter.

The minister cleared his throat and spoke in a louder and more commanding tone, "The Devil is among us."

There were groans from the people; a child giggled.

"The girl, the woman… with hair the color of night and cat's eyes – who is she?" He scanned the pews searching for her, "I do not see her."

The man whittling in the back, with a milky white eye peering out from behind a shock of unkempt greasy hair, grumbled, "She is a daughter of Salem."

"She is not here? Why is she not here?"

"Because she is dead and buried in the graveyard!" the man said with a low laugh.

"Protect us," the minister said, eyes closed, head lifted to heaven. Looking back toward the congregation, he nodded his head, "Ghosts leave their graves and walk among us. We are besieged by the Dark One."

"And how did you meet this ghost – Good Minister?" the old man asked with a sly smile on his face.

"She came to me in the night--" there were ooh's and ah's from the congregation.

"You were with a woman, not your wife, at night?"asked the man with one eyebrow raised dramatically.

"She-- I," the minister stammered.

"Rather unseemly," the old man said, this time directing his words to the congregants, and he received head nods and words of reproach about the minister.

"I--I--,"the minister stammered again then regained his composure," We must prepare for battle. I declare a village-wide fast and devotion to the Scriptures." There were exasperated sighs and groans of disapproval from the people.

Throughout the whole sermon, the villagers were curling and uncurling frozen fingers and toes, stomping feet to regain circulation, and rubbing arms. The constant sound of coughs and sniffles competed with the rattling of the shutters as the wind pounded the building. Addressing these conditions and the unrelenting winter, the minister spoke of the lessons of affliction, "Afflictions humble and instruct, they keep us vigilant, and sanctified afflictions are choice mercies." Williamson then picked up the papers with his sermon and began reading, "The Lord tells us in Exodus: "Thou shall not suffer a witch to live", we know that--"

A man in the front pew, dressed in the most exquisite of clothes, with an air of superiority, stood and interrupted, "That is all well and good Minister, but it is most cold today and it will be the death of us if we stay. I suggest we all go home and," with a smile added, "reflect on your words."

There were snickers from the pews. A service could last from three to six hours, and the people felt reprieved from an unpleasant, prolonged ordeal.

"But my sermon--" Williamson said in disbelief, "and who are you to command this?"

"Why, I *am* Thomas Putnam," the man said in a loud, arrogant voice.

The people responded with "yeses" and emphatic head nods.

"I will, we must--" the minister started, but Putnam turned to the pews and with a lifting motion of his arms, directed the people to rise and leave. The noise of their motion drowned out the minister as he tried to address his fleeing flock.

Seeing it was futile, Williamson rushed down toward Putnam saying, "This is most unheard of!"

Putnam turned to him, and with a disingenuous bow said, "As you commanded, we will all go home and read Scripture and search our hearts." With a smirk on his face, he put his back to the minister and walked toward the door.

"I do not have enough wood or food – was that not part of the contract?" Williamson shouted out.

Without facing the minister, Putnam said, "You will be taken care of, I assure you of that. Salem Village has always," and he lifted a hand pointing in the direction of the graveyard, "taken care of its ministers. See William Allen, your neighbor, for food."

Williamson stood in the empty meetinghouse in a state of shock. "What will I do?" he asked. After some time, resolved, he nodded his head, "Yes, I will return to the parsonage and read Scripture and it will give me guidance."

As he began to leave, he noticed an object on the pew where the man had been whittling. Approaching it, he saw a carving. He picked it up and, realizing what it was, dropped it to the ground as if burned by the contact; a crude carving of a woman, unclothed, her breasts and other parts large and exaggerated.

"This place," he exclaimed, "is the very gateway to hell!" Not wanting to touch the pagan idol, already feeling unclean by the brief contact, he kicked it down the aisle and out the door into the snow.

Williamson returned to his house, and again he felt watched by something unseen. As directed, he went to his nearest neighbor, William Allen, who farmed four acres with his wife and two daughters. Upon approaching the door to the house, he heard movement to his left in the woods; he turned and peered into its darkness.

"Minister," said Allen, a large man, appearing without a sound, startling Williamson. Seeing the reaction the farmer said, "What troubles you?"

"I fear there is something out there, perhaps a wolf."

"Surely the Lord will protect you," the large man said with a smile,

"Thomas Putnam said you would come."

"But how could you know? You were not even at services and I came here directly."

"Come," and he began walking to the house, not answering the question.

"I need food and oats for my horse, I just arrived yesterday. Why weren't you at services?"

The man said nothing in reply and continued into the house.

The house was similar to his in structure, four rooms on the first floor with a large chimney in the center, though it was in an excellent state. He was shocked to see the two daughters, not quite past their first decade, playing in the parlor. They showed no deference to him, no sign of respect, speaking loudly as they and their dolls engaged in some disruptive activity in front of the roaring fire. Beside them sat a large black cat that watched the minister intently.

The ideal Puritan girl was a combination of modesty and piety, and engaged in tireless industry; she spoke neither too soon nor too much. When she was not doing work about the house, helping her mother or stepmother, she was reading Scripture. The girls should be spinning or weaving, not being idle. As Cotton Mather said, "When the devil finds an idle person, it is as if he were to call to more of his crew: Come Here! Come Here! A brave prize for us all!" A girl was to learn the art and craft of housewifery, a boy a trade. The duty to discern God's will was the lifework of a Puritan, selected before birth for salvation or damnation, and a child, above all else, should be frightened that he or she was damned, not playing without a care in the world.

Allen came from the kitchen with a package wrapped in cloth and a jug, "Some bread and cider."

The minister pointed to the girls, "Are those poppets Goodman Allen?" he asked.

"They are only dolls."

Poppets were crude figures used for witchcraft, the person it represented would be afflicted with pain by the placing of pins.

"If they are not working, should they not be reading Scripture or a book about the lives of the holy?"

"Come, I will get you oats," the farmer said, ignoring the holy man, and walked out the door.

The minister looked again at the girls, one of whom, the youngest, pinched the head of the doll and gave him a dark look. The cat bared its teeth and began growling. The minister quickly left. A Puritan was to be watchful and wary. The presence of evil affected them all; if the neighbor of an elected saint sins then the saint sins, also.

With supplies in hand, Williamson returned to the parsonage. He gave his horse more oats, then went inside the house and began working on his Sunday sermon. He read Exodus, the burden of Moses as he led the Israelites in the desert to the Promised Land. Of course, Moses would never see the Promised Land himself, even though he suffered through the trials of overcoming the mutinous Israelites and their idol worshipping. Would the minister ever see the Promised Land as he led his flock through this period of darkness and bitter cold? He began to doubt himself, his leadership abilities, and the strength of his heart.

An hour after eating the cake and drinking the cider, Williamson doubled over with stomach pains. He began to vomit violently and sweated profusely. Williamson wished his wife were with him, she would know what to do. Rebecca had such a calming influence over him. Exhausted, convulsing, and wracked with fever, he struggled up the stairs and fell into bed, smothered in the darkness of doubt. He fell asleep and dreamt of Rebecca, a most pleasant dream of her gentle caresses. Dreams became reality. Still not fully awake, with reason not having total command, he found his wife beside him in bed, her soft body in contact with his, the warmth of her breath upon him as her head rested on his chest. He began touching her hair, caressing it, the silkiness pleasing, the fragrance of lavender scented it. Did not his wife use rose water? He looked down at the woman, she looking up at him, with deep green eyes, teeth bared and glistening in the moonlight. Jumping out of the bed, he landed awkwardly on the floor, his right arm burning and useless, the disease now spreading to his torso.

He looked at the person who had shared his bed, her long black hair cascading over her naked body, the changeling witch. She began to laugh, a low rattling noise, like the sound a dying man makes while breathing his last. With his left hand, he grabbed the poker from the fireplace, lunging at her. She flew through the air and descended the stairs, her deathly white flesh naked with raven black hair flowing behind her. The front door opened by no earthly hand, and she was gone into the night.

He followed her out, and in the field before him was a large bonfire with people and strange creatures dancing about. A dark rhythm filled the night, a music of the dead with the people cavorting about in harmony with it. Approaching the group, the poker lethal in his hand, he recognized many of those that he had last seen in the meetinghouse. The creatures around them were dogs, cats, wolves, and some that were not natural. As he came closer to the fire, one abomination, a lion with eagle's wings and a large mastiff head with powerful jaws came toward him.

It was then that the group became aware of the minister's presence. Thomas Putnam stepped out, stopping the creature in mid-step, its powerful jaws open, saliva dripping and burning the ground where it landed.

"Look, the Good Minister has joined us!" Putnam exclaimed.

"What is this?" Williamson exclaimed in horror.

The people moved away from a tall, distinguished, white-haired man. He wore an expensive, dark, serge suit; a high crowned hat on his head. Though his hair was white, he was a young man, quite healthy, without a blemish or any apparent affliction; the contrast was striking. His eyes flickered with the flames of the bonfire, changing colors. The closer Williamson approached, the taller the man became. In his left hand he held a red ledger and beside him was the succubus that had bewitched him.

With a commanding presence, in a deep melodic voice, the gentleman said, "Welcome. Do you not want to live forever? Be rich beyond all imagination?" he smiled and looked at his congregation, "Come write your name in my book," and presented the book to the minister with a leather covering of dyed human skin, the names written in the ledger in blood.

A look of disgust came over the minister's face, "I will not! I know who you are!"

"Who am I?"

"You are the Prince of Hell!"

The devil bowed and sang, "To rule in hell than serve in heaven," and he began to dance with the witch beside him as if at a grand ball.

The minister turned away.

"Wait," the fiend said with feigned distress, "your daughter, she is sick." He shook his head dramatically, "So sad. Yes." He offered the book to him again.

"My daughter?"

"Yes my good man. "

In great turmoil, the minister shook his head, "No. No."

"So small, and such a sweet child. I can save her, *you...* can save her."

"Not my Abigail. Please no!"

"Did you not already lose a child? And a wife? Dying in childbirth and-- Oh, you were not there. Does that not eat at your soul?" The foul thing paused and then said in a deep tone, "Write your name in my book."

With tears streaming down his face the minister said, "No! No!"

The witch began to approach him, her feet not touching the ground, soft whispers coming from her mouth.

"No! Better she dies and is saved than live forever and be damned," the minister cried out.

"Salvation and damnation, is that all that occupies your mind?" the Devil said closing his eyes. Then, he opened them wide; they were a bright glowing red. He ran his long tongue across his pointed teeth. "Death, yes, I know about death. Has anyone died that has embraced me?"

The people shook their heads saying, "No."

"Have any of your children died?"

Again, they said, "No."

"Has anyone that has written their name in my book, gotten sick? Been attacked by Indians? Starved?"

Again, they said, "No."

"I will protect you and your family," the devil said softly, "Oppose me and you will suffer. Those that hung five years ago – do you think them guilty?"

Thomas Putnam spoke up with a wide grin, "They were not witches, I assure you. They opposed us and we used their own righteousness against them – women, children, old men," he did a little jig, some gallows humor, imitating a person hanging with legs jerking about, "We are witches and we are still here, we will always be in Salem."

"All of you escaped justice," the minister said to those around him, "I will strike you down!"

"Think of your family," the devil offered the book again to him.

"I cannot!"

"Very well, your daughter will die and she," and he gestured to the witch beside him, "this child of the night will come for you," he smiled a toothy grin, "The pain in your arm from her kiss will spread. The food that you have eaten is poisoned. Your body will rot. If you make it to Salem Town, I might let you live, at least past tonight." The people laughed.

The minister turned and fled to the stable, not even taking the time to saddle the horse. With only one good arm, with great difficulty, he mounted and rode away at breakneck speed in the direction of Salem Town, his left hand clenching the mane of the horse. Some of the creatures from the bonfire gave chase, the wolves being the fastest, lunging at the hindquarters of the horse. One sunk its teeth into the equine flesh, and the horse in a frantic motion reared up; the minister slid off onto the ground. The horse fled into the night in terror.

The minister struggled to his feet; the wolves followed but did not attack. He turned, looking back; there was no bonfire, no one there, just the moon lit night. Had he imagined it all? The wolves stood between Williamson and the safety of the parsonage. When he made a move back toward it, the wolves lunged at him. Salem Town was five miles away. The night was most cold and the minister was not dressed to be out in it. He made another move towards the house and, once more, the wolves lunged. Could he make it to the town? He must, his daughter's life was in danger; he had to get to her, to save her.

He trudged through the snow, more falling heavily from the sky, making his progress slow. The pain in his arm and chest was excruciating. He doubled over several times and vomited from the poison in his body. His legs became stiff with the cold, his feet numb, and his pace slowed to a crawl. On both sides of the road, he could see eyes glowing in the forest, moving as they kept pace with him. He questioned himself, "Did I imagine it all?"

After some struggling, putting one agonizing foot in front of the other, he saw dim lights in the distance– Salem Town! It was then that he heard giant wings flapping from behind. Looking into the sky, he saw a large mass descending quickly, striking him, knocking him hard to the ground - the abomination from hell. He tried fending the beast off with one arm but it was too strong as its teeth sunk into him, over and over again. Where its spittle fell his flesh burned. His legs failed him and he could no longer get up. Salem Town was there – just a few strides away, but he would not make it. He attempted to say the Lord's Prayer but the words would not come to his lips. Battered and torn, he bled out in the snow. He thought of his daughter and his beloved wife. There was laughter from the forest, the scent of lavender; he felt a soft caress and finally the dark of nothingness.

NO HOPEFUL VERSE
Patrick Cooper

"Looks like Marvin's going away for a long time, man."

"Looks that way."

"Why you think…why would a guy go and do something like that, ya think? Something so…so fucking morbid?"

"S'pose he just lost his damn mind for a minute there in the woods."

"He did it in the woods then?"

"That he did. Want a refill?"

"You having another?"

"Sure. Gonna be a long night."

"Then I'll have another. If you're having one, I'll have another."

I signaled the waitress for refills. Fisher slurped down the rest of his gin and tonic. I sucked on an ice cube that tasted like ginger ale. That's all I was having. Ginger ale. Couldn't tie one on. Not tonight. The waitress brought over our drinks. Our conversation picked up where we left off.

"The woods behind South Campus, was it?" Fisher said. He took a sip of his gin and tonic and winced. "I said, goddamn! That's a strong pour."

We were sitting at one of the back tables in Major Magleashe's. It was quiet for a Thursday night. Regulars lined the bar. A handful of college kids occupied the tables up front, being more rowdy than they had to. Putting on a show. Best burger and beer for the buck in town. Bet on that. A classic local watering hole. And yeah, they've got a helluva pour.

"There's a trail there behind South Campus," I said. "Winds up through a thick patch of forest, up a hill. Students go up there to drink beers around a fire or whatever. Up there, where no one can see them. Not so much in the winter time. But yeah, that's where the rumpus was. That's where Marvin did Dickie and Mathieson."

Fisher shook his head and lapped his gin through a straw, like a child sucking down strawberry Quik. It made him look dim. He said, "I still don't get it, man. I thought they were tight."

"Love makes friends do stupid shit. Love and money."

"It was over a girl then?"

I nodded and sipped my ginger ale. "A girl and money and things you find in the woods. Things you're maybe not supposed to find."

Fisher scowled. "The hell you mean?"

"You're a city mouse, I forgot. There are parts in every wood that are a little darker than the rest. Where the sun don't shine as bright. Where there's a wind that sends a cold from the other side right into your guts. It's best to avoid those dark parts of the woods."

"You lost me, man," Fisher said. He took the rest of his drink down in one gulp. He drank fast. That was okay with me. It'll be easier if he's drunk later on.

"You got time?" I said. "You wanna hear what happened to Marvin and Dickie and Mathieson up there in the woods?"

"You paying for the next round?"

I signaled for the waitress and began.

* * *

Marvin couldn't find any work. He got his B.A. in history from Salem State but lack of ambition made that degree nothing but B.S. In the three years since graduation, Marvin had worked at a deli and as a barista (which Marvin insisted was Italian for *jackass*). He lost both jobs and wound up working for a landscaping company that serviced a lot of commercial jobs in Salem, Beverly, and Danvers. Pushing a leaf blower wasn't his "calling" or anything, but Marvin liked the physical work and getting to be outside all day was okay with him. It beat slinging coffee and slices of cheese with a phony smile plastered on his face.

Mathieson owned the landscaping company. He started it almost a decade before with just a lawnmower and his pick-up. Through some family connections, his small company grew into a monopoly on commercial properties, and Mathieson was making cash hand over fist. He bought a house on Chestnut Street. A real money street. The type that gives out full-sized candy bars on Halloween.

It's at that house that Mathieson and Marvin bonded over post-work beers and pizza. Mathieson was 15 years older than Marvin, but the two got along. Mathieson didn't seem to have many friends. It was just him and his wife Joyce sharing that big house. Joyce. Deserves to be said in two syllables: Ja-oiyce.

Like Marvin, Joyce was younger than Mathieson by over a decade. They met at a karaoke bar where she was waitressing. Directionless and leggy, that was Joyce. Eyes big and brown like saucers. Freckles that would make a Catholic burn his bible.

Mathieson got on stage and sang "Across the Great Divide," looking at Joyce the whole time. She looked back at him. This stocky, commanding

71

man going grey around the ears, she looked back at him and saw a purpose. A path. She saw cash.

He waited for her out in the parking lot. Asked her if she wanted to grab coffee at Dunks. From there, wedding bells. They tied the knot two weeks later at the city clerk's office over on Washington. With a love like theirs, there wasn't any time to plan a wedding and fill out invitations.

You know what they say about the candle that burns twice as bright? It ain't worth a shit when the big blackout comes. And it came for Mathieson and Joyce in about a year and a half.

That's how long it took Joyce to realize how miserable she was. Mathieson had forced her to quit her gig at the karaoke bar. "No wife of mine is going to be serving drinks to wasted assholes, getting her tail grabbed all night for slave wages," he said.

He insisted she stay home every day and handle secretarial duties for his landscaping business. Answer calls, cut paychecks, manage expense spreadsheets. All that droll, droll. Like the passing of the Halloween season in Salem, the thrill was gone.

Then along came Marvin. It began like something out of a movie. Their eyes meet across the lawn on Chestnut Street. They bumped into each other in Mathieson's kitchen. Elbows graze hips. Palms touch stockings. Next thing you know Marvin and Joyce are screwing right there on the counter while Mathieson's passed out in his pint glass out back.

They started meeting out in the garden behind the house. Mathieson's routine was strictly routine: get home from work, shower off the day's grass cuttings and grime, drink until he passed out. It was a steadfast routine - more reliable than the MBTA in winter. Once Mathieson was blacked out on the couch, Joyce would sneak out and meet Marvin in the garden, under the umbrella of an elm tree. The yard was bordered with a tall wooden fence stitched with thick veins of ivy. The lovers were shielded there from the street and surrounding homes. Screwing like in the movies.

The way Marvin is telling it to reporters, it wasn't long before him and Joyce decided they needed to kill Mathieson. Now I know, that's a big leap. From romance to murder. Why didn't she just ask for a divorce? Well Joyce had casually brought it up once to old Mathieson and it nearly got her tossed down the stairs. See, Mathieson was cut from an old school Catholic cloth. Divorce is a sin and all of that. So that was out of the question. Besides, if they divorced, Joyce wouldn't get any of his money. And believe you me pal, she wanted that money. Mathieson had to die. Cha-ching.

That's how Dickie got involved. Marvin, he didn't have it in him to kill Mathieson. He was just, y'know, Marvin. Dependable Marvin.

But his old friend Dickie was another story. They grew up together here in the Witch. Like kids do, they'd get into some shit once in a while. Shoplifted candy or sodas or whatever from the convenience store. Dickie always had to take it to the next level though. He'd go back and throw a brick through the store window. Just for kicks. This pattern continued on through his teens and adulthood. That's how come he found himself down there in Suffolk doing an assault bid. Smashed a bottle over some poor slob's head outside Tavern in the Square and ground his face into the sidewalk with his boot. Kicked his teeth all down Washington Street. Slob had to go to Mass General for reconstructive surgery. Dickie had to go to Suffolk for seven years.

It wasn't just that Dickie was crooked. He was a mean bastard. But he got along with Marvin, them being old friends from the neighborhood and all. So Marvin calls up Dickie and tells him about Mathieson and the cash he's got tucked away. He left Joyce out of the conversation. All Marvin told him was that Mathieson was his boss, and he piled cash in his house. That's all Dickie needed to hear.

Marvin and Joyce figured they should make it look like a robbery. They also figured Joyce shouldn't be there when it happens, that way it won't be hard for her to play stupid when the cops question her on details.

So that one night in autumn, Marvin and Dickie went to Mathieson's house while Joyce took in a movie downtown. She took a cab and made sure to make conversation with the folks working behind the concessions counter. That way there'd be no question where she was that night. A lot of people saw her go to that movie.

What no one saw was her steal away through the theater's emergency exit about halfway through the film.

It was a dark night with a small wind. The type that might make someone uneasy if they were walking alone. Marvin brought over a handle of Mathieson's favorite cheap whiskey. That was his key to getting them in the house. They parked Marvin's car in Mathieson's driveway, near the gate to the backyard.

"Mathieson, this is my old pal Dickie," Marvin said. "We were in the neighborhood and I figured, what the hell? Why not pop in? Have a few?" He waved the handle of whiskey in front of his boss like a talisman.

Mathieson eyeballed the booze hungrily and waved them inside. By the way he leaned on the knob as he closed the door, it was clear he was a few drinks deep. They settled down in the backyard. Mathieson had a picnic table out there next to the garden. It was his favorite autumn drinking spot. That garden. Marvin looked over at the garden, at the umbrella elm tree, as he sat down. The sight made his loins warm.

They bullshitted for 30 minutes or so. Dickie told some prison stories, but Mathieson steered most of the conversation to himself and his accomplishments. Marvin looked at his watch. Any minute now. Tick tock. Tick. Tock. There it was. Mathieson blacked out. Head down on the picnic table. Forehead on the cool wood.

Dickie rose from the table and took the plastic Dunks takeout bag from his back pocket. In an almost mechanical fashion, he walked around the table, positioned himself behind Mathieson, and stuck the bag tightly over his head. He leaned backwards and let Mathieson's drunken slumber do the rest.

Well, almost. Mathieson came to. Big guy shot up from the table like a firecracker in the Point. Arms thrashing at the bag. Elbows swinging back and forth trying to crack Dickie in the face.

Dickie said, "Grab him, Marv! Yo, grab him!"

Marvin got up from the table and stepped back, uncertain.

"I said fucking grab him!"

Marvin ran to them and tried to get a hold on Mathieson's arms. Mathieson punched him. Smeared Marvin's nose across his face.

Marvin cursed and put a hand to where his nose had been. Dark blood oozed between his fingers.

Dickie pulled back harder on the bag. He knew it wasn't enough. He held the bag in one fist and started delivering kidney punches with the other. Mathieson threw up in the bag. The vomit pooled up. That's what got him. The vomit. He choked on it. Hell of a thing.

"Thank for all your help, Marv," Dickie said, slipping the bag off Mathieson's head with two fingers, like he was picking up dog shit. Vomit dripped out of the bag. Dickie went over to the trash bin and buried it under some garbage bags. He said, "Man's got vomit all over his face. Get the hose, Marv."

"I think he broke my nose."

"Get the fucking hose, Marv."

Holding his nose, Marvin complied. He sprayed Mathieson's face off. Then they carried Mathieson's body over to the gate leading to the driveway. Marvin ran out to the car and popped the trunk. Then they put the body inside, next to the shovel.

"I gotta fix myself up, man," Marvin said. The front of his denim Sherpa jacket was stained red. His nose had stopped bleeding, but the break was making his eyes water and blur and black up. It was his only jacket.

"Fix your ass up while I'm counting that cash," Dickie said.

Marvin cleaned himself up as best he could in Mathieson's downstairs bathroom. He shoved balls of toilet paper up his nostrils in case they started bleeding again. Dickie jetted up the stairs and into Mathieson's office. Right where Marvin said it would be, there was a large painting of a shipwreck in an ornate gold frame. A print, not an original. But it looked the shit. Dickie took the print off the wall and revealed the safe behind it. He took the slip of paper out of his pocket. Written in Joyce's precise handwriting was the combination.

After that oh-so satisfying click, the safe swung open. Four stacks of cash greeted him. All hundreds. He removed another Dunks bag from his back pocket and filled it with the green. He whistled "Across the Great Divide" while he worked.

* * *

Fisher belched. "You say Marvin and this Dickie cat killed Mathieson and robbed his ass?" His eyelids were looking a bit heavy.

I swirled the ice around my glass of ginger ale. "That's what they did. There was a murder on Chestnut Street and nobody heard or saw a thing. This is all from Marvin's mouth now, up in Suffolk. This is what he's telling reporters and the cops."

"Ain't he got a lawyer? Why the hell would he be spilling his guts about all this horrible shit before trial? Making himself look as guilty as a wolf in a hen whore house?"

"Because, Fisher my friend. That killing of Mathieson? That was nothing. That was a Saturday morning cartoon compared to what came next..."

* * *

They drove to Salem State's South Campus. The infamous "horseshoe."Parked Marvin's car as close to the path's entrance as they could. This was at about midnight. Marvin and Dickie sat in the car for a while, watching the lights go out in the dorm windows.

That last light hung on for some time but eventually went out. They got out of the car and hefted Mathieson's body out of the trunk. They had only killed him about an hour ago. Rigor hadn't set in. The body was pliable.

Marvin fumbled with the shovel, tucked it under his arm. They managed to carry Mathieson from the car to the path leading up into the woods.

"You sure about this spot?" Dickie said.

"Positive," Marvin said. "Used to go up there all the time in college. Get high and neck and shit."

He had already explained it all to Dickie. In the woods, Marvin said, there's one path going up and one going down. It forked. All the college kids go up, snaking up the side of the hill. You can overlook the Witch up there, in all her glory.

Nobody followed the path leading around and down the hill. Some say it was because it was darker than the other path. It didn't let in any light. The darker part of the woods.

Others who had gone down that way, they weren't the same. It just didn't feel right, they'd say. This path, the one that led down, is where they decided to bury Mathieson.

They carried the body down the path, like they were moving old furniture out to the curb. Marvin took the torso, walking backwards. Dickie took the legs and balanced the shovel under his arm. It was slow going. They both stopped a few times to catch their breath and adjust their pants. Despite their aching muscles, the men kept on. Marvin driven by Joyce. Dickie driven by all that green. Nothing is green like cash. It's a relaxed, casual green nothing else has. Glory be.

Eventually they came to the fork. Right side led up, to college, Dionysian debauchery. Left side led down, to the cold, cold parts. Marvin and Dickie nodded to each other. They hoisted the body and the shovel and continued to the left.

They gradually rounded the hill, their lefts to Swampscott, their rights to Salem, and began to hear noises. Things like the rustle of an old branch behind them. Like browned leaves shriveled and creased under feet that had already passed. Like warped tree boughs scraping together. Trying to touch their faces, like the blind. Like someone's footsteps trying to pass them without a sound.

The sky disappeared behind the grotesquerie of elm branches holding on to one another. Leaves fell dying on to Mathieson's body as it swung between the two men. The little cries of the wind trembled through the tree's fingers as Marvin and Dickie moved on.

He dug for an hour, until the blisters on his fingers howled so much he could barely hold the shovel. After all that work there was hardly a hole, let alone a grave. The ground was frozen and Marvin's work barely made a dent. Dickie shrugged and they threw Mathieson in and kicked dirt over him. They stomped his ankles down to cover his feet. Still, Mathieson's head remained, peeking above the dirt and the leaves.

The men looked down and sighed. Dickie said, "Gimme the shovel, Marv."

Marvin obeyed. Dickie stepped back and spread his legs like a golfer.

"Oh fuck no," Marvin said right before Dickie swung the side of the shovel into Mathieson's neck. Blood sprayed out, but not that much. The heart had stopped beating.

"You wanna take a shot, slick?" Dickie said, holding the shovel out to Marvin, who shook his head no. "Didn't think so." Dickie swung again. And again. And again. The sound was like wet cabbage being harvested. On the last swing Mathieson's head come loose of the tendons and rolled off the path, over rocks and bark.

Marvin turned to Dickie and said, "And what now, man? We gonna carry that back to town? Walk down Derby to Chestnut with his fucking head?"

"Asshole," Dickie said. "Remember that pond we passed five minutes back? The one's almost iced over? We toss it in there. Stop being such a baby. Yellow baby."

Marvin shrugged. He just wanted this night over and done with. To get to Joyce. Ja-oiyce.

He walked with Dickie off the path to get the head. Mathieson's head. After walking about a minute they realized it couldn't have rolled so far. Not in this choppy terrain. Where was it? They must've passed it.

They came to a rock that violently pierced the hill. The gate of the dark place. That's when they started to hear the voices. In the dark.

Marvin heard Joyce calling to him. Lamenting his name and whispering flirtatious come-hithers at the same time. Dickie heard the familiar tone of his old man. The tone he'd take before slipping off his belt and beating him over the back with its business end. These voices swelled in a way that urged Marvin and Dickie forward off the path. Cries of rage, sympathy, and sorrow. Cries of welcome. Sad and horny at the same time. Follow the head. Follow the head. Follow.

"Joyce!" Marvin said. "Joyce it's me!"

"Dad!" Dickie said. "Yo, stay the fuck away from her, dad!"

They stepped forth through a thick brush of tangled branches into a clearing. What they saw, Marvin says it was bottomless. That's what he called it: "bottomless." And what they heard? He described it as a string of verses that man and animal were incapable of making. Like the whole city was tone deaf and singing backwards. Marvin said the voice sounded guilty. How he put it. Guilty.

They continued forward, tripping over roots that crested the earth in waves. The rock they saw piercing the hill became an altar. A stone steeple blended with untouched wilderness. Untouched by witch shops and tourist stores selling tees to tired teens bussed in from the South Shore. Untouched by dizzying drunk dudes and the dolls they carry like mascots on Halloween. A site unknown to the city council meetings and their ward managers deciding the path of progress. Unprofitable maritime history versus witch exploitation bent over Rebecca Nurse's table while Slick Dick Willie Stoughton comes through the speakers like a hound.

Marvin looked into this dark place and saw a veiled woman. He saw Joyce. She walked towards him. One of her hands drew him closer. The other warned him back. He drew closer.

Dickie looked into this dark place and saw his old man. He wouldn't be caught dead wearing a veil. One hand drew him closer. The other swung a belt over his head. He drew closer. One hand drew him closer. Closer.

Through this dark place a figure called, "Bring forth the converts!"

Marvin and Dickie tried to step away from the voice. They really did. They tried.

Later, Marvin swore he ran away at this point. But he says someone, maybe many people, were grabbing his torso, pushing him forward, deeper into the woods. Towards the catechism. Towards the communion in the dark. There in the woods. Into that dark place.

* * *

"And the last thing Marvin remembers seeing is his Joyce," I said. "Then he woke up the next morning in the woods with the heads of Mathieson and Dickie under his arms."

Fisher slurped the remnants of his drink. Each time he blinked. His eyelids got all heavy. It was a struggle to get the shutters up again. He said, "And that's how they caught him? Caught Marvin?"

"No. Marvin turned himself in that morning. Turned himself in, that morning."

Fisher nodded slowly. I was ready to catch his chin if he blacked out. His head dipped and he said, "Here's the thing I don't get, man."

"Hit me," I said. I fingered an ice cube to suck the ginger.

"How's come..." Marvin wobbled as he spoke. "I mean how come you know all these details? About the spot in the woods and all 'a that? I read the papers. Marvin didn't say half the shit you did, man."

I signaled the waitress. Let her know we were ready for the check.

"You wanna know how?" I said, leaning across the table toward Fisher. The waitress brought the check. His eyes rocked but stayed steady on me. I took the green out and laid it on the table. "You wanna head home? We can cut through the woods."

A SHOCK OF FEATHERS
Alec Anthony Firicano

Lately, it's not the cold that leaves me shivering on nights like this. I try as hard as I can to robe myself in the warm memories of the not-too-distant past, but when one of these chilly March storms rolls in across Salem Harbor and the rain comes down in unrelenting sheets, I find myself huddling in my corner and staring down at the dark pools of rain water which gather in the empty streets, and I am filled with the deepest trepidation. From high on my perch on this encrusted ledge in the alley next to the old Russian American club on Pickering Wharf, I observe the ripples in that dark water as they glisten in the glow of the street lamps. As the clouds darken from deep gray to black overhead, the cold seems to emerge from those dark pools like a pair of invisible hands. They slink up the brick walls of the building and enclose me in their icy grip. Their fingers chill me deep into those dark, hollow spaces between my bones and a stinging voice echoes there in that empty darkness - a voice that knows my name.

Like these streets, the club too has been empty for months now, shuttered for repairs. The old, brown-painted, wooden attic window beside me is no longer brightly lit, warm and inviting. It looks nearly as cold in there as it is out here, devoid of the light and happiness and the wonderful music that once filled it and spilled out from the gap left by the missing brick at the window's edge. No longer do the teenagers gather in the attic of the club, the owner's two sons, Matt and Steven, and their friends in the youth group. They once regularly met there to play their role-playing games at a table in the center of the room or watch movies they would project onto a make-shift screen - a large white sheet they hung in the corner. Every other weekend in the summer, they would invite big groups of kids and stage concerts in the hall downstairs. I'd stand by my hole and listen as the entire building vibrated with a wondrous noise - but no longer. The table is gone. The sheet, used as a projector screen, has been taken down and lies haphazardly in the corner, thrown over the remains of a broken chair like a shroud. The room is otherwise empty, save for a plastic bucket which collects the rain water as it sneaks into the empty darkness from gaps in a tarp hung loosely over the holes in the roof. The bucket is nearly full now and the steady clop of the dripping echoes like a metronome playing on at the music's end.

I wish I could say my stomach was as full as that bucket, but I haven't had a proper meal in weeks. Not only did musical sustenance flow through that hole by the window, but the kids from the youth group would feed me the best treats. They'd leave little bags of potato chips or cookies for me, but no more. Not in forever, it seems. Yes, the joy seems to have flown from this place, as I perhaps should have done myself months ago.

One of my cousins stopped by the other day. He remarked at my thin form and told me I should have moved on back south to Revere Beach, but I can't bring myself to leave. I still hold out hope of a return of the good times. I can't wake from my dream of freedom and adventure, and the memories of the better times still linger. They linger like the sweet, herb-scented smoke which used to waft through the hole on summer evenings. In those more pleasant times, I would nod my head against the window sill, feeling the cool, salty sea breeze flow up from the nearby wharf, and listen to the music as it echoed into the dark streets late into the evening. I rested there with a full belly of salty sweet treats and let my mind drift to places of fantasy.

These days I still mostly stand around, waiting and staring, but the food and entertainment aren't as good. I'll find myself pecking at the odd snail or millipede that crosses my path. Sometimes by daylight, I listlessly fly down to the pier and look out to the churning waters. I try to let the good memories fill my head as much as I can in order to keep the darker things at bay... those events dark and strange whose shadow persists in welling up from the depths. I might almost be able to fancy that my mind was playing tricks on me, and that the events of that night were all a strange dream. But when the night comes... and the winds blow the dark clouds across the moon... I can almost hear that voice again on the wind... and see something out on those waters... so I retreat to my perch.

This listlessness has begun to consume me lately, and I don't know what to do. Perhaps what I truly need is to face these fears, and to revisit those thoughts which persistently have crept in these last few stormy months. It would maybe be a sort of purging for me if you allowed me to voice them to you. I've never really had a chance to tell a story before, you see. I do love stories, and well, I suppose in some ways that may have been my undoing all along. That urging to discuss events with other caring and sentient beings may have led to this odd happenstance which now haunts me.

Would you then? Would you be kind enough to be an audience for my tale? If so, I would be greatly honored. But... excuse me, in all this blabbing through melancholic thoughts, I seem to have misplaced my manners. I failed to even properly introduce myself. My name is Harry. Actually, my friends in the youth group, they used to call me "Harry the Seagull".

Yes, I'm a bird. Is that surprising? I suppose it should be, but I don't fashion myself to be an ordinary sort of bird... and perhaps that is another one of my issues. Back in more pleasant times, not so long ago, the kids from the youth group regarded me as a sort of a pet, or as I'd more generally prefer to be known, a mascot. But before I mention them, I should probably first explain how it was I came to be among them and how I happened upon this place. That is the proper way to set up such a tale isn't it? All my tribulations haven't been for naught. I'm learning, you see.

Anyway, I flew up to this area from Revere Beach about a year and a half ago. It wasn't that I necessarily hated life on the beach, although it could quite literally be what you humans refer to as a "rat race" at times. It was more my difficulty in getting along with the company. In particular I could no longer stand the incessant goading of my cousins, who made up the majority of the flock. I was fed up with the life of an ordinary gull, and they didn't understand anything outside the ordinary.

Every morning our flock would scrounge around the dumpsters behind the roast beef restaurants on the boardwalk, then we'd head out to the beach and pile into the surf to fight over clams and crabs with a hundred other birds from varying flocks. I would stand on the outside of this violent mass of birds, observing them as they pecked at each other for scraps... pushing, scraping, clawing... beaks clacking. I just couldn't take a part in this barbarism anymore. Don't get me wrong, I am not completely anti-social. In fact, as far as birds go, as you've probably surmised, I can actually be quite talkative when you get me going... it's just that this particular crowd was a bit... I don't know... we'll call them 'unsophisticated', I guess. In the aftermath of these melees all they ever wanted to talk about was how the fish smelled that day or how high they had flown that week or how fast they could dive.

I was never the most competitive bird, nor the most athletic. I was never given to the new trend of 'speed flying'. However, mind you that while I don't like to self-aggrandize, the truth is, when it came to depth-diving I could out-dive the best of the beach. It was just an innate natural talent of mine, I guess. I wasn't much of a flier, so it took me a good while to reach a suitable height, but when I fell into a dive, I could penetrate the depths of the water far deeper than any of my cousins - maybe deeper than any bird any of us had heard tell of on Revere Beach before. On the rare occasions when I my cousins convinced me to utilize my talent, they would

81

stand by the shore waiting for me to emerge with the fattest, juiciest fish they had ever seen, but they didn't know I wasn't diving for fish. I was only interested by the wonders that transfixed me down in those dark depths.

After I burst through the surface of the waves and the friction of the water slowed my descent into the blackness, I would float there and look up toward the penetrating sun whose light was distorted by the rippling liquid. I was fascinated by the strange creatures I observed, writhing, slinking, and flying in their own way beneath the waters. Not far from shore, not far from sight, there was a whole strange world full of not just brightly colored fish, but sharp-toothed eels, flowing umbrella-like creatures, and steely crabs much larger than the ones we scrounged for on the beach. Sometimes I would linger there so long, turning over and over, feeling the currents washing over me, and losing myself in deep thoughts, that I would almost forget I had to breathe. I'd suddenly be shocked back to reality by a survival instinct and a fear that I would be consumed by this new world and never see the surface again.

When I finally would emerge, gasping and exasperated, I would be subjected to not only the disappointed snarls of my cousins, but also their outright mocking. They called me a "waste of wings" and though I hated to disappoint them, I just didn't have the drive to make scrounging or diving my full-time occupation. I found that I preferred to hang around the boardwalk, lounging around and reading the odd discarded newspaper, and maybe hoping that some human would toss me a couple of their fried shrimp tails - yes, I still loved eating, as all gulls do.

One day, however, something I found in the dumpster changed my life. I was trying my damndest to get at a discarded carton of Mallomars in the dumpster beside the convenience store, when I discovered an old anthology of fantasy stories. This was wholly unlike the newspaper articles I had happened upon at the beach. I had never read any kind of fiction before, and I would never have imagined the magical places it could transport my mind to. It was like taking a hundred meter dive into the deepest ocean, but I didn't have to emerge for breath.

I stood there on the dumpster, enthralled for the entire afternoon, flipping through page after page with my beak as my eyes ingested tales of dragons and witches and wizards and high adventure, strange planets and time travelers who saw an age ruled by dinosaurs and talking robots. When I returned to the beach later that day to meet my cousins, my stomach was empty but my mind was overflowing. I couldn't wait to tell them what I had found. I soon realized, however, that there was absolutely no one willing to discuss it with me. Not only did no one share my new found lust for the magic of adventure and exploration, but furthermore, my enthusiasm toward the subject was met with laughter and mocking like I'd never known before. The rest of the flock couldn't believe I had spent the entire day staring at pieces of paper when there was good food to be had on the surf. They called me mad and pecked at my feet.

Then there was the final indignity. My cousin Carl snatched up the anthology and pecked it apart before my eyes. All I could do was stand there with my beak agape. When he was finished and my fantasies were reduced to a pile of what looked like nonsensical fortune-cookie papers, he remarked, probably without irony, "Hmph, needs ketchup," and he flew off. I saw the wind pick up the pieces and blow them away into the waters, where they were drowned forever along with any hope I had of fitting in.

I decided then and there that I must leave the beach. I resolved to seek out the wondrous weird worlds I had read about in the anthology, or at least find a place where I could read more about them. I knew then had to make my way apart. But how? I had no direction. Luckily, fate soon intervened.

About a week later, in the same dumpster in which I had discovered the anthology, I found a curled up flyer. It advertised something called the "City-Wide Halloween Bash" to be held in a place called Salem. The flyer had pictures of men in space suits, skeletons, witches and robots. I couldn't believe my eyes. Here, I thought, must be a ticket to the gateway of the fantastical places I had read about - it was all real! I determined at that moment that it was my destiny to travel to this wonderful place and make a home there, where magic and fantasy, and hopefully some good food, would fill my being all the rest of the days of my life.

I asked Barry, one of the older, more well-traveled birds, if he knew the way to this place, Salem. His normally lazy eyes perked up and he became agitated. He sternly advised me against traveling up there. He said, "I took flight up there years ago. There's nothing there but hordes of pesky humans who line the over-crowded streets in strange attire. They walk around with the oddest looks on their faces - looks like you've never seen before, and they'll heed you no mind. They'll push you away if they see you and step on you if they don't.... and the worst part is that the trash cans are all well-covered!" He told me I shouldn't be traveling any further north this time of year, and that I needed to stop dreaming and start storing provisions for the winter. But I begged him to show me the way, and finally he relented, shrugging off my youthful naiveté. He said, "You only need to follow the coast north past the jutting island and fly around the rocky peninsula, and where the waters calm to the harbor, and you'll find that place." I thanked him and headed off to gather my meager belongings for the trip.

That night I left behind my family and everything I'd ever known, and struck out for the north coast. Something guided me through the darkness, and the calm winds seemed to push me onward to my destination without pause. I flew past the jutting island and reached what I somehow knew to be Salem Harbor in no time. The wharf was quiet. I encountered no hordes of strange revelers and, contrary to Barry's warnings, to my delighted surprise, I found fresh trash in bins I could access behind a couple of restaurants. After I had my fill, I was set to explore, when suddenly there was a roll of thunder and the clouds opened up in a torrential downpour. A stiff wind blew in, and I knew I had to find some shelter. It was then that I saw the inviting attic light of the Russian American club. I flew up to the alley window and found a ledge suitable for shelter from the storm.

The next morning I awoke to the sounds of men talking excitedly. I found that, beneath an awning below, there was a group of old men that would sit outside in the morning drinking espresso and discussing politics around a small table. When they noticed me waddling around on the old cobblestone street, they threw me some pieces of scones, and we became friends. Even when they realized that I had taken up residence on the platform outside their attic, they didn't seem to mind. I was finally fitting in. The owner, Evgeny, remarked to the other men sitting there that I was an unusual-looking gull because of a shock of gray feathers that jutted out around my neck and lower head. He said it made me look... how was it he put it? Yes, 'professorial', he said. This reminds me... as I see myself in the reflection of the window just now, I realize that these same feathers have now been bleached to a bone white. But, I digress, bear with me, this is where my tale begins to reach its consequence.

Although I spent a good deal of time exploring the city in those first days, flying up to see the strange, drooping trees of Salem Willows and peering at the horrific faces behind the shop front windows of the monster museums, I spent a fair amount of time just hanging around on my ledge. The owner's sons, Matt and Steven were in the attic with their friends quite often, and we soon got to know each other. They were these sort of goth, rebellious types who wore various shades of black clothes and had various shades of multi-colored hair - the styles of which sometimes reminded me of some gulls I've met.

The youths would gather there and play games and watch movies on summer nights. When it was particularly hot, they would leave the window open and in my more adventurous moods I would sometimes venture in to join them. They were surprisingly accommodating with the aforementioned food, and they seemed amused by my interest in the various books they left out on the table near the window. My favorite was a binder called "The Monstrous Compendium" with drawings and descriptions of all sorts of weird-looking creatures, the likes of which I had never seen. There were also various fantasy novels there, and some odd magazines of human pornography which contained political articles that I didn't understand in the least. The one book which I was forbidden to read was an old tome bound in an odd thick sort of sort of wrinkly leather. I caught only a glimpse of its contents before Steven shooed me away from it. Judging by the little I saw and also from my experience in watching some films about witches and séances through the window, I could surmise that it was some sort of volume of magic spells. I knew that Steven fashioned himself to be a sort of wizard, but I never thought much of it until the night they had 'the meeting'.

At first, I thought the group was gathering for their regular Saturday night role-playing game. I liked these meetings because, even though they wouldn't allow me inside, they always left me a bowl of cheese curls on the window sill. I knew something was different this particular night because Matt opened the window and Steven began enticing me in with a piece of a doughnut. They never invited me in on role-playing nights because Steven said I would make a mess of the board. I had one time, and only once, mind you, chewed up one of their red dice when they weren't looking, having mistaken it for a cherry candy. That got me permanently banned from coming inside on role-playing night. The other odd thing on this occasion was that, as Steven led me forward, dangling the piece of doughnut enticingly in his two fingers, I could sense his brother Matt creeping up behind me. I knew the boys well enough at that point that I felt they couldn't possibly have any ill intent toward me, even if they were up to some sort of chicanery, so I followed my stomach toward the delectable crumbs of doughnut which brought me to the center of the room. The card table they usually played on had been oddly pushed off to the corner, and in its place was an interesting chalk drawing of a sort of upside-down star, ringed by a circle with seven black candles melted to the floorboards at intervals around it. When I reached the edge of this circle, Steven said, "Now!" and I felt a sharp prick on the back of my neck. I cawed in surprise - it really hurt quite a bit - but I quickly realized I had lost only a single feather.

Matt was behind me snickering. He had snuck up with a pair of metal forceps and pulled a small single feather from the gray shock around my neck. I said, "Hey, what gives?" but they just ignored me and continued on with their strange business. Steven threw the half of doughnut in the corner for me, and I waddled over to it. He shouted to one of the others, "Hey, make sure he doesn't cross the circle." I was careful not to.

As I stood in the corner munching on the doughnut, I watched as Steven donned a strange hooded black robe with red embroidery that looked like the backs of some spiders I have seen. He proceeded to shut off all the lights and began lighting the candles that ringed the circle. I heard a roll of thunder outside the window and began to hear the patter of raindrops on the roof above. Steven then took my feather and some other items and placed them in a small golden bowl in the center of the circle. He then poured some dark, syrupy liquid into the bowl and took up the book that I was forbidden to read. He began to speak strange words from the book, in a language I had never heard before.

The rest of the kids donned their own strange robes and took places around the circle. They began raising their hands in the air one after another, humming something under their breath as Steven spoke the same chant over and over again. This went on for a few minutes. I stopped chewing and stood back in the corner of the room in the darkness, frightened but also enthralled.

Finally, Steven paused his chanting and produced a long red candle from inside of his robe. He lit it and reached gingerly across the circle to place the candle's burning wick down in the bowl. There was a burst of fire as the candle's end met the liquid in the bowl and a blue fire ball shot straight up to the ceiling and dispersed in a thick gray smoke which flooded the room. This was not like the smooth herb-scented smoke that wafted through the window hole on Saturday nights in the summer. Rather, it was gritty and dry like burnt leaves, and left everyone gasping for breath and coughing. My eyes began stinging and watering, and I decided to scamper over to the window for some air and maybe to dip my beak in my water bowl.

As I made my way from the corner toward the window, however, one of the robed, coughing figures unexpectedly stood up and began stepping backwards toward me. I tried my best to avoid being crushed by her foot, but I was somewhat disoriented from the smoke inhalation, and when I fluttered up into the air to escape, I ended up crashing into another robbed figure who was just then standing up as well, and I managed to trip him. If anyone could have watched that dark and smoky room they would have witnessed what must have been a pretty comedic sight. The youth whom I tripped, threw his arm out to brace himself and in the process whacked me square in the head, sending me skidding across the circle and knocking over one of the candles. When the confusion finally cleared, Steven looked down and shouted "Nooo! How did you let him do that? It's all ruined! Now we'll never be able to conjure Grogsothott and hear his divine wisdom! Good one, Harry!" Someone flicked the lights on. I lay there in a heap, confused and humiliated while they looked down on me. My feathers were streaked with purple chalk and candle wax.

"What are we going to do now?" Matt asked Steven.

"Well... Nothing," he answered, surveying the mess, "There won't be another moon cycle like this for fifty years. Let's go back to the house and play Fallout."

The dejected teens threw their robes off in the corner, revealing their usual black gothic garb, and filed out the door. I just lay there with a sorry expression on my face for a while, watching them go. I wasn't quite sure what I'd done exactly, but I knew I'd ruined the evening for my friends. I figured it would be best if I just exited as quickly as I could so as to not incur any further wrath from my hosts, so I jumped up on the table beside the window and scampered out onto the landing. I watched as Steve placed the book in his bag, blew out the remaining candles and walked over to the window. He looked down at me. I thought he might offer some words of reassurance as I looked up at him with my sorry eyes. "Goodnight birdbrain!" he said, and slammed the window closed. I had never known Steve to be that vindictive. He must have been pretty upset that I'd ruined his ceremony. I chalked it up to a case of teen angst and told myself he would surely forgive me... maybe.

As I sulked on the ledge, my own mood began to mirror the weather that night. The storm really kicked up, the rain was falling in sheets, and there were frequent flashes of lightning as I stood miserably on my perch. I had eaten the doughnut, so I wasn't very hungry, but I was lonely and felt terrible that I'd disappointed my friends. I was overcome by dark thoughts, doubts, wondering if my friends would ever return or if, by my buffoonery, I had lost them forever and become an outcast in the only place I had ever felt acceptance.

As the night wore on, and the rain waters poured down, drenching me, I was consumed by my thoughts. I tucked my head in my wings and began to drift off to a restless sleep. Just before midnight, I awoke to the sound of the custodian locking the door below and just as I began to nod off again, I was suddenly jarred back to consciousness by a tremendously loud crack of lightning which seemed to occur on the street directly in front of the club. This was followed by the sound of sloshing water in the street below. The winds of the storm had calmed but as I stuck out my head, I saw a rush of water deluge the gutter as if a huge bucket had been dumped down on the street from high above. I heard a thick slapping sound which reminded me of the first beating of the wings of a newborn bird as it stretches and emerges from the egg - only this bird must have been a hundred times the size of any I had ever known. I tried to peer around the corner of the building, but could see nothing.

I looked up overhead to see the clouds of the night sky melding and forming a huge swirling unnatural vortex. It was particularly strange because the winds about me were still calm. The clouds seemed to be gathering of their own accord. There was also an unusual green light pulsing in the center of this overhead maelstrom, and it ascended into a sort of tunnel which disappeared far up into the sky. After a second another huge bolt of lightning shot out of the center of the swirling clouds and struck the street again, somewhere out of my view. After that, it all instantaneously disappeared. The clouds returned to normal, the green light was gone, and the rain continued to fall on the windless streets. Suddenly the street lights went out and everything was dark and quiet.

My eyes squinted in the almost all-consuming blackness, but I could sense no movement. All around was quiet save for the light pattering of the lingering rain, and I wondered if I was just experiencing some sort of dizzy spell as a result of inhaling all that strange thick smoke earlier in the night, but I couldn't tell for sure, and then I heard it. A hollow voice echoed through my head."Harry," it said.

I looked all around but from what I could see, the street was barren, I sensed no movement. The shops across the way were closed for the night. The window behind me was dark, there was no one inside, and I was sure the voice had come from street level, anyway. It spoke again, drawing out the syllables of my name in its guttural tone. "Harrrryyyy," it said, this time louder, and I heard an awful scratching and clicking sound like some massive claws were pawing at the cobblestones of the street below. Still I saw nothing.

I looked all around the ledge, but my vision was obscured. I decided to fly onto the rooftop to get a better view, so I hopped off the ledge, circled around and landed on the sloped wooden roof of the building adjacent to the club. For a moment the wind picked up, and I almost lost control and barreled down into the alley, but I was able to steady myself and grab a foothold. I said a prayer of thanks as my talons clacked down on the roof's wooden tiles and came to rest. I searched the darkness as the rain soaked me, but there was nothing on the roof of the club nor any sign of anything below on the street. I stood on the sloped roof looking down as the water splashed on the flat roof top of the club next door, completely perplexed. "I must be losing my mind," I said to myself, ready to hop off the roof back toward the relative dryness of my perch, when suddenly I heard the voice loud behind me. "Harrrryyy," it said again.

I slowly turned my head around and to my shock I came nearly beak to beak with the thing that had called on me. It's hot steamy breath sprayed through its empty, boney nostrils with a noxious-smelling steam that had the pungent stink of decay. I thought it smelled as if someone had collected all the rotting fish and crabs on Revere Beach and steamed them up in a big cauldron and the thing before me had just ingested all of it. I instinctively began to backpedal toward the roof's edge and when my eyes cleared enough to see what was before me, I wished I had hands that would allow me to cover them up in disbelief.

Bearing down on me from less than a yard away was a massive bird-like creature, or something that once was a bird in some age or place that is well beyond the reasoning or parameters of anything I have known in this life. It looked like it was made of the sort of rotting chicken bones I'd find in the dumpster, pieces of sinewy flesh dangling from its inexplicably corpse-like body. I had seen dead birds on the beach before, but nothing quite like this. There was a friend of mine once, named Alex, who had a fight with his girlfriend, which led him to fly away from the flock for a few days. Apparently he had been gnawing on a discarded sandwich on the sidewalk and the wind had carried a piece of it out onto Revere Beach Boulevard. He hadn't eaten in a while, and his hunger got the better of him, so he flew out onto the street to try to snatch up the piece of wayward crust and, well... when we found him a couple of days later, he looked like the closest thing I've seen to the monstrosity that was staring down on me. This thing, however, was huge, probably ten times my size.

The thing had sickening dead hollow eye sockets in its bare skull which glowed with a kind of intermittent electric crackle like bug zappers I had witnessed hanging by the bar patio on the boardwalk. Only the remnant of some sort of feathers at the base of its neck indicated it once wore flesh on its face. In fact, the only actually composed skin left on its body was borne by its horrid wings, and even that was riddled with holes and rot. If my mind was not wracked with terror, I may have considered the consolation that in any sane world, these accursed wings would have nary the flesh necessary to capture wind enough to allow the creature to take to the air, let alone make any kind of lengthy pursuit, but somewhere in my instinctual mind I knew some spectral power was willing this thing, and it needed no wind beneath it to pursue me.

The creature seemed to have been designed for devastating horror. It had a whip-like tail of white bone which swung back and forth behind it as it glared down on me from the slopped rooftop. It rent the roof shingles with thick, wolf-like claws which were connected bone to bone by the barest yellowing tendons. When its jaw dropped, it revealed rows of glistening, razor-sharp teeth caked in a stringy saliva, and a white, fleshy, calloused serpent's tongue slapped along them hungrily.

Something welled inside me. The same feeling of adventure that maybe had spurned me to leave the flock told me I should not wait around to be a late dinner. I turned and leapt from the edge of the sloped roof, into the night sky, hoping that if this thing could indeed fly, that at least it would fly as slowly and awkwardly as the zombies in the horror films I had seen.

As my wings began pushing at the heavy air, I suddenly wished I had taken more interest in athletic pursuits like 'speed flying', and spent a little less time lounging and ingesting so many doughnuts and cheese curls. I hadn't really flown much in the previous weeks and with the rain still falling, my wings felt like they were weighed with lead as I tried to cross the flat roof of the club and swing around toward the horror museum across the street. This somehow worked to my advantage as the creature must have over-estimated how far I'd fly. I actually wasn't even able to fully catch the air with my wings, and I tumbled, fluttering onto the flat top of the building as the thing leapt over me and crashed into the attic roof of the club, puncturing it with its claws.

I was able to right myself and head over the edge of the roof toward the street below. I could hear the thing stuck in the roof above me, struggling to free its talons and ripping at the rubber tiling to continue its pursuit. "Harry!" it growled in its low empty voice again. As it tore itself free, it bumblingly overshot me again and crashed through the plate-glass window of the horror museum at street level. I limped down the cobblestone street, dazed. I felt warm blood spring from my forehead beneath my feathers, but I knew I had no time to dawdle. I couldn't see the creature, but I heard its tail whipping and crashing in the museum foyer, "Harry... I'm hungry," it said in its low, hollow growl.

My scrambled mind desperate tried to form something of a plan. I knew I couldn't outfly the thing, but I thought I might be able to lose it and hide in the drooping tree branches of Salem Willows, which lay only a mile away... if only I could only make it there. Wharf Street where the club was, was short and narrow, not a good place to be caught with a hungry creature who was ten times my size, but it opened up to Derby Street which was a major thoroughfare and had some passing traffic, even at this late hour. As dangerous as it would be to play in traffic, I reasoned that if I could only land on a car that was traveling northbound, there was a good chance it would carry me most of the way to the Willows, and I might even be able to out-pace the thing for it was still stuck in the museum window display and probably a little disorientated itself, or so I hoped.

This proved to be some unfortunate momentary wishful thinking however, as I turned to see the creature pulling itself out of the wreckage of the window display. It paused and turned to glare at me through the raindrops with its crackling electric eyes. "Harry... hungry," it growled again.

I somehow gathered the strength to take flight again, and I just barely lifted off as the thing came crashing down onto the street behind me. I heard its claws scraping at the pavement like a hungry dog while it gathered itself, as I desperately flapped away with my heavy wings getting some slow lift in the thick, wet air.

I tried not to look behind me as I flew into the traffic of Derby Street. A red sedan was headed toward me at a moderate pace and traveling northbound, so I flew up a little higher and, saying a prayer to the departed Alex that I might not join him this night, swung around as the vehicle passed. By some miracle I was able to grab a hold of the antenna on its roof with one of my talons.

I tried my best to fold my wings in, but the rush of air nearly blew me off the back of the car. Thoughts of the creature in pursuit kept my claws clenched in a steely grip though, and I held on. A woman on the street somewhere behind me screamed, and I knew she must have seen the awful thing rising from Wharf Street with its horrid decayed wings whipping up into the air toward me. Luckily for me, the car I clung to seemed to be headed straight up Derby Street where I wanted to go, and in less than a mile I would be at the willows and I could take refuge in the trees, I told myself, as the rainy winds flew past and my tired claws held tight.

A slight kink in my plan formed when the driver of the little red car I clung to must have caught sight of the pursuing monstrosity in her rear view mirror. She hit the gas, and I was nearly thrown off. She proceeded to take a screetchingly sharp turn onto Memorial Drive, and I couldn't hold on any longer. I released my grasp, and the wind tossed me off toward the unforgiving pavement, but by some luckily chance my wildly beating wings caught a sudden gust which served to pick me up just in time.

I took flight down Fort Avenue as quickly as I could, then ascended over the grove of trees which lined the side of the road. Behind me I could hear the thing crashing through the foliage. This slowed it down a bit, and I was able use my remaining strength to push myself to a height from which I could make one of my signature diving descents and pick up a lot of speed. I focused on a large willow tree at the water's edge where I thought I might be able to hide and then broke into a full dive, swooping down into the branches just as the thing crashed out of the upper foliage looking for me.

As I landed on a thin branch, exhausted, and I could hear rustling as the thing closed behind me. I tried to move to the edge of the branch and shroud myself in the long leaves of the tree, but ultimately this did not prove to be the smartest plan. I heard the thing exclaim, "Hungry! Harry where are you?" as it descended at top speed. It must have sensed me by smell or some otherworldly method because it careened directly into the tree branch I rested on, snapping it clean with its formidable jaws. The momentum of the thing carried me, the creature itself, and a good chunk of the willow tree forward and sent us all barreling off the pier and into the harbor.

The dark waters engulfed me, and I was too tired to press on. As I slunk into the cold depths, I remember thinking that this was a strange way to end my journey and perhaps my existence as well. The gulls of my flock back in Revere never would have believed me about this night's events if I would have had the chance to tell them. But as I drifted lower and lower into the cold blackness, I felt a warmth descending from above. I realized it was the force of water pressing down from the beast descending on me with its open jaws and the warmth of its steamy spectral dragon breath bubbling toward me in the dark. I couldn't bear to even close my eyes. I faced my fate, and in that last moment I saw the creature reach out toward me with taloned claw to snatch my entire body in its grasp.

Perplexed, my body fell limp in the creature's gentle embrace, and I looked on as its terrible jaws instead locked around the body of a huge bluefish that was swimming by. Blood filled the water as its sharp teeth clenched down, completely obstructing my view, and everything faded to a dark haze. The next thing I remember was coughing up water on the beach. I looked up and under the yellow streetlight a few paces away from me, I saw the beast munching away at the body of the bluefish. It looked up and spoke to me in its hollow growl, which seemed slightly less intimidating now that it's deadly attention was not fully directed at me. "Food, good. Me hungry. You hungry, Harry? You want fish? I know not why you fly away. You my master. I yours. Harry, you call me."

"I didn't call you," I croaked, coughing water from my lungs, "why would I call a thing like...I mean, I didn't... why do you think I called you? Who are you?" I asked, dazed.

"I Gragsnardel," it replied, "You Harry. You call me out of time. You bear the mark... you call me," it said.

I looked down at my wings. They were still smeared with the chalk from the strange ceremony I had witnessed. "Oh, you mean this... well, you have it all wrong. Sorry about that, ole pal," I said nervously, "I didn't mean to bother you from your endless sleep or anything. I just got a little caught up in this. I was just trying to get a little piece of doughnut, you see... and..."

Gragsnardel tilted its head in confusion. "You want food?" It offered up the head of the fish, whose eye dropped horribly from its socket and sent my stomach spinning queasily.

"Oh, that's just fine, no... no, thank you," I said.

"What you want me do? You call me. I at Harry's command."

"Well, can you just, um, head back to wherever it was you came from? You know, your home?"

Now Gragsnardel was really perplexed for a second. It stood up, dropping the fish head on the sand, and stared at me with its empty crackling eye sockets. It pawed at the surf. "Harry want me leave?" It paused, considering, "No. Harry make joke! He not sacrifice sacred goat and risk wrath of Voldranae for nothing! Harry funny," it laughed in its guttural voice.

"No, really, Grag...snardel, is it? I don't know where you came from..."

"The kingdom of Vadremont in the Ninth Circle..."

"Yes, the Kingdom of Vadremont... of course, but a terrible mistake has been made. I don't need any servants or even any new friends, I have plenty of those, I think. So if you just want to make your way back to the dimensional portal or wherever it is you came from. I think that would be best for all parties."

"Harry really want me leave?" Gragsnardel considered this for a moment, "OK, I go. You want this food?" He held up the fish head again.

"No, no thank you. You take that with you. As...as a souvenir!"

"I thank Harry. I never forget you."

"Nor I, you, Gragsnardel. You be nice when you get back to your kingdom. That's... that's an order."

"OK Harry, I go. You just call if you ever need me."

"OK, I'll see ya. It's been fun. Good times."

And with that, the rotting creature hooked the fish head in its claw, began flapping its massive, holey wings, and ascended into the night sky. The clouds began to swirl in their strange way again, the lightning cracked, and Gragsnardel disappeared into the same sort of portal of green light I had witnessed earlier. The rain had stopped, but a cold breeze blew in from the southeast over the pier. I just stood there under the lamplight on the beach for a moment, shivering. I think I must have fainted and keeled over, because my next memory is the morning sun waking me and the pain of a deep bruise on the side of my face.

Yes, my world expanded quite a bit that night a few months ago. My little adventure that night opened a whole new sense of reality to me, as I came face to face with the strange things that lie just beyond this world's reckoning - things impossibly far off, and yet, somehow just above us, or beside us, or beneath the surface of those serene seas we stare out upon at our leisure. Standing here on my ledge now, I find it difficult to leave these thoughts behind and to return to the sense of normalcy I knew.

I have had strange dreams huddled in these wings the last few nights, drifting through a sort of listless, waking sleep. Just now I was awoken by a rumble of thunder. The winds are rattling through the alley way again, and the cold rain continues to patter on the ledge. The door below creaks.

I wonder if that gate above the harbor ever fully closed, or if I might see my friend from another dimension again someday - or perhaps some other visitor - maybe one not as friendly. I recall the creature's parting words, which I disregarded in my frightened haste to be rid of him, "You just call..."

Sometimes as I drift through these lonely days I think of perhaps taking up that offer. I see myself diving out there into the black waters of the harbor and floating down to meet the unknown head-on, letting it engulf me. I have a desire to see what lies deeper, ever deeper.

Maybe tomorrow will be the day. I'll fly down in the early morning before the sun has risen. I'll take to the pier and do some diving. I've said this to myself many times in these past few weeks, but when the dawn comes, the cold claw of my own conscious sanity drags me back to the surface, just like my strange friend from beyond dragged me from the waters on that night.

So I huddle again. I try to cover my eyes. Still, that new consciousness entices me to open those eyes to the darkness. I stare into that void and in the flash of lightning, I catch a glimpse of my reflection in the window. I see that ring of feathers around my neck and their bleached color reminds me that I have irrevocably changed from the gull that traveled up from

Revere just a year and some months ago. I am a bird of the Salem coast now. This is where I belong.

The rain stopped just now. The streets have gone dead quiet, and all I can hear are my own words echoing in the dark.

THEY GO TO THE DEAD
Kathleen Halecki

The day had dawned to a cloudy grey with low set heavy clouds which threatened to unleash a winter storm. Before the first shadows of light came through the windowpane, Jane had heard her father moving around below, and she had jumped up before he noticed that she was still abed. Her father was a God-fearing man who brooked no disobedience within his household, and many times during the course of her eighteen years Jane had felt the back of his hand or the end of a rod, as had all her siblings. She, more so than the others, rebelled, often refusing to do the seemingly never-ending work that faced her every day. Shaking her younger sisters, Hannah and Sarah, awake she dressed and came down to the hall to wait patiently for the family to be ready to walk to the meetinghouse. Now standing before the fire, she felt the child quicken, and she steadied herself against the large mantle. It was as she had feared, and now there was no doubt that the babe was alive within her. She moved her hands across the front of her dress and felt it move again. Soon, she would need to bind her belly and breast to hide the bastard that she now knew for certain she carried within her.

Jane was sure that she was not suspected, but this was a secret she would not be able to reveal to anyone. Her mind reeled as she wondered what she was to do now that there was no question that the child would arrive. She felt trapped by her situation and terrified she would be found out. Lost in thought, the crackling hiss of the burning logs startled her. For a brief moment she thought she saw a shadow pass behind her, and she felt her blood turn cold. Thinking that someone had noticed her movements, she froze in place, but the only sound was the wood as it burned. As she stood there motionless, Jane heard a slight knocking seemingly coming from the beams over the chimney. The sound was steady and though it seemed to come from the area near the chimney, she

95

could not find the source. She brushed it off as a branch hitting the roof in the wind and returned to her task of waiting trying to push her problem temporarily out of her mind as her sisters came down the narrow stairs to stand beside her.

Later that morning, she sat in the upstairs balcony listening to Reverend Parris deliver his sermon on the confession of sins, rebuking those who persisted in their ways. Reverend Parris could be frightening when he was worked up, and he seemed in a fevered pitch that morning as his words rolled like thunder through the church,

"But if thou goest on in thy sins God will go on in his controversy till he hath broken thy hard heart, by true repentance, or by the showers of fire and brimstone. I will plead with thee, because thou sayest, I have not sinned. It is not God's usual way to return to a professing people in mercy, after he has turned from the in ways of judgment, till they acknowledge their offence and seek his face."

As she listened, Jane could feel the wood cut into her thighs, and she groaned inwardly for her back ached. As the sermon continued, everyone jostled for a comfortable space, and Hannah fell asleep with her head resting against Jane's shoulder, while Sarah leaned against her from the other side. Jane's attempts at waking her sister were fruitless, and to cause any disturbance was sure to meet with swift punishment at home, so Jane stayed as silent as she could. She had pulled her stays so tight it was difficult to breathe and with every shortened breath she took she was reminded of the minister's warnings. Jane could see her father in the pews below, while her mother sat beside her sisters at the other end of the church. She could feel the cold winds of January whistle through the wood planks, and she thought of warmer days.

Jane returned to that day in early August. That morning her brother John had left aboard one of the many vessels owned by Philip English. Although her father was against it, John had argued that he needed to make his own way in the world, and her father had finally relented. Jane envied her brother's freedom, for his voyage would take him to England and then the Caribbean before finally returning to Salem's harbor. The harbor was full of men going to and fro in small boats bringing in the cargo from off the ships into the warehouses. Sailors were gathered around the taverns, which made Jane's father begin a lecture to John on the dangers of drink. The sight of the ships coming in from far-off places had stirred a restlessness inside her to the point she felt she would explode. It also renewed her fears, for she often worried that she would not marry well. Although she had been told not to covet, as it went against the Lord's Commandments, she could not help but desire to live in a great house such as that owned by the English family. Heavily gabled and overlooking the harbor, she heard it was full of fine furnishings brought in from various ports. It did not seem fair, thought Jane, that a woman as plain as Mary Hollingsworth should marry such a man, while she remained without a suitor.

By the time they arrived back home the heat from the sun was relentless, and Jane was given the unfortunate task of tending the vegetable garden. As she toiled outside, she felt as if her shift was a weight pressing down around her body and the tendrils of hair that fell were wet on her skin. By late afternoon it had become unbearable, and her only thoughts lay with the waters of Frost Fish River. The thought of how cool it would be against her skin obsessed her thoughts and abandoning her duty, she finally took off running across the fields stopping only to sneak the earliest apples from the orchard. She knew a secluded spot where the river was shallow enough for bathing, and where she could be alone, for the nearest house belonged to Israel Porter, and he would be busy at the sawmill with his brothers. By the time she reached the water she was drenched in sweat and rushed to pull her clothing from her body. Pulling her hair down she let her long dark curls float in the water. She reveled in her nakedness against the ripples of water that washed over her, wishing that she could be released from the confines of her life and have new adventures like her brother. *Was everything a sin?* she wondered She knew she should not even question such a thing, as she was reminded twice weekly by Reverend Parris that Satan railed against humanity constantly. Yet she could not help herself, for her friend Elizabeth had regaled her with stories of life at court. For many years Elizabeth's uncle lived in London serving in Parliament, and eventually he had come to live in Salem to be among the godly.

Elizabeth had eavesdropped as he told her father what life was like in the court of King Charles. In shocked tones, he had revealed that ladies wore gowns slashed to their breast and paraded around at masquerades. The courtiers flocked to the theatre to attend filthy plays, followed by gambling and drinking until the wee hours of the morning. His Majesty had even taken several mistresses who had given birth to his bastards with no shame. She wondered what it would be like to dress in silks bejeweled from head to toe instead of the same dowdy dress. The only book allowed in her father's household was the Bible, by which they had all learned to read, so Jane could not imagine what it was like to be at the theatre, which was strictly forbidden in the colony. The ministers often admonished those who tarried in the taverns where they sometimes gambled and sang songs. Jane thought it would be nice to dance, but that was frowned upon as well. One time her father caught her with her sisters twirling around in circles as they held hands, and after a smart slap they had been made to return to their chores.

Lost in her thoughts of life at court, she saw a figure advance across the river on horseback, and for a moment she feared it was one of the Porters, and she hastily pulled her shift around her. As the horseman drew closer she realized that she did not recognize the rider. The horse he rode was sable-colored and stood to a monstrous height, while he himself had long hair of gold he wore loose beneath a feathered hat. His waistcoat and breeches were of a fine black brocade, while intricate lace was like a cobweb that has been spun around his collar and sleeves.

"He must be a ship's captain." She whispered to herself. "Maybe he has just arrived from England and perhaps he is lost."

As he came closer, the stranger stared her down, and she lost herself when she returned his gaze. Before she had time to think, he had slipped from his horse to stand before her, and she forgot her nakedness as his hands moved across her shoulders. She abandoned herself to the pleasure she found as his lips met hers, and she was neither frightened nor shocked that she surrendered so easily to his embrace. She had kissed a boy before, behind the parsonage one Sunday, but Joshua's kiss had been awkward and fumbling. As the stranger took her on the ground, the sky opened up to reveal visions she had only dreamed about. He spoke of love and foreign places and murmured in her ear of her great beauty. It was as if she was wandering across the world as time melted away, and the last thing she remembered were the stars the shone brilliantly in the night.

When she next opened her eyes, both rider and the horse were gone, and Jane could not find a sign that either one had been there. There were no marks on the ground to reveal where they had gone, and as she walked home she wondered at what she had experienced. Perhaps it had all been a dream caused by the intense heat and her own longings. She became confused over the time of day for it was as if it was still late afternoon, but she swore that the sky had turned dark when she closed her eyes in his arms. She hoped she had not been missing for too long, or she would be forced to face the wrath of her father. As she neared the house it became immediately clear that something was terribly wrong, for her brother Samuel was running towards her, motioning for her to go in the opposite direction.

"Move quickly, Jane, before he sees you."

It was too late, however, for her father was now running across the field, carrying something in his hand, shouting as he did so that she was nothing more than a wanton and a whore. As she took the beating with the flail it was revealed to her that she had been missing since she ran off the previous afternoon. Somehow she had lost an entire day, and her mother had been beside herself fearing the worst, but her father denounced her as a wretched sinner and an insolent, disobedient child. If not for her brother and a passing neighbor, Jane was sure that he would have killed her in his rage. He was fined for his behavior and denounced for the cruel and excessive beating he had given her, and Jane had smiled secretly to herself believing that it served him right to be shamed before their neighbors for the abuse he had heaped on her.

Now, as she peered over the balcony again, she wondered if her father was right to call her a whore. At first Jane had believed that maybe it was all a dream, but she began to suspect something was amiss within a fortnight when the smell of food had caused her to become ill. She had vehemently denied her pregnancy, but now that she felt the child within her, she was forced to face her dilemma. She began to grow agitated as she sat there, cursing the situation she was in and her circumstances in life. When Reverend Parris was finally finished, she got up as quickly as she could, pushing her sisters off of her, causing Hannah's head to hit the back of the pew. Hannah stared at her with hurt eyes, and Jane burned with shame. She was sure that Reverend Parris was speaking directly to her, yet it seemed his sermons were wasted for she continued to do hurtful things.

As her mother and father would be preparing to take the Lord's Supper in the afternoon, Jane walked home quickly with her siblings, bracing themselves against the cold. Hannah trailed after her all the way home, still smarting from her behavior, only serving to heighten Jane's distress, and she had to stop herself from dragging her sister home. When they arrived, she stoked the fire to warm them up and sat down in her father's chair, which was the largest one in the house. She wished the stranger would return to save her from this predicament, but there was no sign of him anywhere to be found. She had even asked a few people if someone had arrived in Salem matching his description and a few times had gone down to the harbor to see if there was any sign of him. She felt lost and hurt, abandoned to an uncertain fate. If only she could find him, perhaps things could be different. He could take her away from this place to live in style in a large town, where nobody would know they had committed fornication outside of marriage. As these thoughts raced through her head the child moved inside her again. She gripped the carved arms of the chair to keep from crying when she was distracted by knocking on the roof. The sound was still hard to distinguish and she wondered if it was perhaps birds on the rooftop, or a squirrel, although it was unbearably cold for the creatures to be out. As the knocking continued, she silenced her sisters who were chattering on about some local gossip they had heard.

"Do you hear that?"

"Hear what?" Hannah and Sarah both stopped in the middle of the room to listen.

"That sound. Can you not hear it?"

Hannah cocked her head and then shook it. "No, Jane, there is nothing there."

"Are you sure that you hear nothing?"

Hannah took a turn around the room, and Sarah peered out the window, even opening the door, before pronouncing that there was nothing to be heard. Fear crept into Jane, as she realized that she was the only one who could hear it and no matter what room she entered the sound did not cease.

* * *

By May, Jane was near to madness. The knocking was continuous and as the child grew so began the whispers. They had been ever so slight at first, but soon they began to grow louder to the point that it was hard to block them out and focus on her tasks. She could not make out what was being said, but they kept her up at night, and she felt tormented in every waking hour. Sometimes she saw shadows out of the corner of her eye, and she would turn quickly only to find that there was nothing there. Jane's fear that she would need to bind her belly had not materialized since she did not swell as she thought and had little appetite for food. She could not sleep and soon began to grow pale as dark circles appeared under her eyes. Her mother's concern only made Jane feel guilty, for she could not tell her what was wrong. Jane was sure that she would die soon, and she welcomed death, feeling relieved that her suffering would come to an end.

Her pains began in the middle of the night and by dawn Jane knew for certain that the worst was soon to happen. As it was the Lord's Day, she knew that soon her family would leave, and she could beg off from going to be left alone with her sin. Quickly after their departure, Jane somehow managed to pull out sackcloth from the lean-to that she spread before the fireplace. Her hands were shaking so badly she could barely move them, and her insides felt as if a hot poker was ripping through the lower parts of her body. The pain was excruciating, and when she felt the need to push, she bit down hard upon the wooden ladle her own mother had used during her last pregnancy.

On her knees before the fire, she strained to bring the child into the world, as the whispers became a dull roar, and before she knew it the babe was in her hands. Before she could give it any attention, the urge to push was upon her again and soon a second child lay on the sackcloth. She pressed on her stomach pulling on the umbilical cords slightly as she was taught by the midwife so that the afterbirth would follow. Still on her knees, she now looked at the two tiny boys who lay there but refused to cry. Her heart felt like it would explode in her chest as she tried to breathe, shocked by what had just taken place. She covered them with the sackcloth not wanting to look at what she done. She had killed them because she had not wanted to admit to her sins, and therefore she had not looked to the needs of her children. Jane began to cry out, desperate for a plan.

"What should I do? What should I do?" She wailed rocking back and forth. The whispers had the answer and this time they were clear enough for Jane to understand,

"To the well...To the well...To the well..."

She could see the trail of blood that was coming from her and knew that she needed to act quickly before she was discovered. Still shaking, she managed to clean herself off and dress, the babies still silent under the sackcloth on the floor, as the voices continued to tell her to take them to the well. She would not uncover them to look at them again. She would bury them in the old well that had been abandoned in the North Fields. Nobody would find them there; her secret would be hers. With weak and trembling hands she wrapped the babes up and began the long trek to the North Fields, her knees giving way several times as she tripped in the spring mud. As she clutched the small bundle to her breast, Jane was gripped with fear and remorse. She was both afraid of being found out, and sorry for what she had done. She needed strength, but knew that she could not ask the Lord to help her do what needed to be done. She was sure to be damned for this, and rightly so.

Once at the well, she peered over the side to see that the water at the bottom was green and murky from disuse, and she looked at the bundle in her arms. The thought of dropping them into the well horrified her, for they did not deserve to rot in the waters because of her sins. The whispering was quiet now as Jane placed the bundle down and looked for anything she could use to dig a grave. Finding a sharp rock, it felt like forever before the hole was big enough to lay their tiny bodies in and then cover back up with dirt. All Jane could do was mouth, "I am sorry," before she began the long walk back home.

* * *

It took only three days before the bodies were discovered by Goodman Small's dog, who dug up the bundle as they made their way to fish where the Endicott met the Frost Fish River. He had fallen down on his knees to pray upon seeing what his dog brought up, and ran to the constable's home immediately to deliver the dreadful news. By nightfall, all of Salem was talking of the discovery, until word got around to Goodman Symonds. He had not gone to the meetinghouse that morning because he had injured his leg when putting up a new fence and had been out tending to the animals when he saw Jane cross his field carrying an undistinguishable bundle in her arms. Upon hearing this, the magistrate sent for Jane on the following morning.

When the constable and midwives arrived they found Jane in her bed feverish and glassy-eyed, still in shock from the birth. When they explained to her parents why they were there, her mother began to cry, while her father was in such shock that he sat down in his chair to put his head in his hands. She submitted to the humiliating examination by the midwives who had also looked over the bodies of her dead children. When it was confirmed that Jane has recently given birth, the constable escorted her with her parents to face the magistrate. Jane's mother continued to weep as she was questioned, declaring no knowledge of Jane's pregnancy. Jane had been ill, she told Judge Hathorne, in fact she had become so frail that she had feared for her life and never would have imaged that she was with child. Before she knew it, Jane had confessed to the burial of the babies, was indicted, and quickly sent to jail.

Both of her parents were released and had returned home without a word to Jane. It was only her brother Samuel who followed her from her questioning before the magistrate to the jail. He could only ask her, "Why?" and for that Jane had no answer. As she sat in the cold jail cell, she wrapped her cloak around her shivering body knowing that the end would come soon enough. She had not denied that she buried them in secret, and when asked why she had not seen to their wants at birth she could only shake her head. Although when commanded, she could not reveal the name of the father, causing Judge Hathorne to become angry at her stubbornness.

Three days later Jane was remanded to Boston's prison to be kept there until due order of the law. It had been determined that she had knowingly committed a grave offense, and the judge read her indictment to be sure that she understood the charge against her; that she did "secretly bury contrary to the peace of Our Sovereign Lord and Lady the King and Queen, their Crown and dignity, the Laws of God, and the Laws and statutes in that case made and provided." Jane had nodded in assent but said nothing. She did not try to defend herself or throw herself on the mercy of the court, she simply submitted to the sentence of hanging.

On the fourth day of her imprisonment, Reverend Cotton Mather arrived, and Jane was surprised to see such a man of importance offer her counsel. Although they prayed together, Jane knew that her soul could not be saved and told him as much. She had entertained evil thoughts, she declared. She had been rebellious and disobedient. She had not listened to the ministers or her father, but rather her only thoughts were of her own pleasures. She had coveted what was not hers and disrespected the life she had been given. Reverend Mather gave her a stern warning and asked why she refused to reveal the name of the father but instead insisted in taking it all upon herself.

On the fifth day, Jane was led to Boston Neck where she viewed the gallows for the first time. As she stood there, her heart began to beat wildly, her breath became shallow, her palms were sweating and she tried to face the crowd before her. *How*, she wondered, *had it come to this?* She knew the townspeople had come out to see the evil girl hanged, and Jane did not want to look to see the faces of her family, although she could hear sobbing coming from those who had gathered to witness her execution. Standing beside her, Reverend Mather began to expound on Job, trying to make an example of Jane for the many young people who stood there watching,

"If you would know, when the displeasure of God shall break upon the heads of ungodly sinners, you are here informed, *they die in youth*. It seems, that an e*arly death*, a *death* in the prime, and spring of their days, is that whereunto they make themselves obnoxious..."

Jane could barely hear his words, and it no longer mattered if she listened. She looked off into the distance as the sun began to rise, realizing that it would be the last one she would ever see. Then her eyes caught sight of something that brought terror to her soul, and she began to shake violently. Upon the opposite hilltop across the Charles River she could see from the gallows that the stranger stood with the horse beside him. He was looking at Jane, and he placed his arms across two small boys who stood on either side of him. The horror of what she had done dawned on her. The stranger was the one she had always been warned about, the one who appeared to trick and tempt those who were fallible, the one who preyed upon women's vanities and gave them false assurances. He was the one who came in many guises, and she had given in so willingly. She could now hear the voices whispering, only this time she could hear them calling to her, "Mother, Mother," and Jane began to weep uncontrollably. She had given in to temptation and now both she and her children were damned for eternity. Reverend Mather clasped his hands together, relieved that his sermon had moved her so that she was fully repentant, and then the ladder was released beneath her. Jane saw a flash of light, followed by darkness, and then there was nothing.

WICKEDNESS LIVES
M. R. DeLuca

"The good lady looks lost," the voice said from out of the shadows.

Ruth Wickford clutched her shawl and shivered as the cool November breeze swirled around her. The sun was setting and the harbor was nearly empty, all of the merchants either breaking bread at home or away at sea, halfway to their next port.

"I am not lost, sir. I am looking for my son; he broke from my hand." She scanned the wharf for a pint-sized boy with a chestnut mop of curls.

"Brown-haired little fellow with a fancy blue coat?" asked the man, who stepped out of the alley from which he was hidden from street view.

"Yes," she said urgently. She sized up the scraggly-looking man, possibly an off-duty sailor, and concluded that if he was native to Salem, it was more likely the outskirts than the town center.

"He's right over there," he bellowed, his deep voice pleasantly even-toned as he pointed to a streetlamp illuminating two young boys in its glow. One was a neighborhood boy cupping in his un-calloused hands the latest toy from Europe; the other was her son, marveling at his friend's object of pride and no doubt boasting of his own fashionable treasures at home.

"Archibald! Archibald!" She turned to the older man, gave him a little nod, and said, "Thank you, kind sir."

The pitiful creature, who looked as if he had missed more than one meal, had held out an open hand, expecting a token of gratitude.

She scoffed and walked away in a huff. His audacity would make their Puritan ancestors cringe from wherever their final resting places were.

He called out, loud enough only for her to hear, "As a friendly warning, be aware that Jonah, and Jonah alone, will meet his maker when the sun meets the horizon tomorrow eve."

She stopped abruptly, causing her raised silk skirts to pool suddenly and clumsily around her ankles. Her husband, the esteemed Jonah Wickford had, like many contemporary men, made his respectable small fortune in the shipping business. She had never seen this man before, and knew her husband would never deal with the likes of him; yet, he knew her husband's name, and had known that she was his wife.

Ruth quickly collected herself. The bustling Salem hub was as much a gossip mill as a distinguished port. It was not unfathomable that he would hear of and see the Wickfords in his travels and not vice versa. He was only an angry beggar with a struggling business, likely a result of his poor attitude.

She took Archibald by his hand and rushed him home. It was only the two of them, as the head of the household was in the midst of returning from his voyage to Charleston, where he traded a cargo filled with finished textiles. He was to arrive tomorrow night. The boy was happily musing aloud about what presents his merchant father might bring back from his travels, oblivious to his mother's uneasy state. They broke their bread and retired that night without further incident.

The next day Ruth had made it a point to travel to the heart of the town in daylight hours, when the shopkeepers were aggressive with their wares and the customers were plentiful. In the past she had enjoyed the quieter off-hours—it made for much more pleasant shopping— but she welcomed the hustle as a knight welcomes a shield.

Relieved that she went to the market without having seen the strange, aging rapscallion, she returned home with her son clutched tightly at her side. At times, her grip was so firm he squirmed for release, but she just grasped him tighter.

That evening she watched from her gabled windows as the sun set. The clouds were puffy and not ominous in the least. In fact, the sky was a lovely amalgam of blues and purples and reds and oranges. In the distance, just peeking over the horizon, was a speck. She smiled. It was her speck.

The ship came closer and closer. She recognized the figurehead with its long-flowing hair billowing on either side. Her husband had commissioned it with a face and hairstyle based on her own. When she asked why not a generic mermaid instead, he replied he could rely on her to always point him the way home.

It took a moment for her thoughts to stop dwelling on cherished memories and instead return to reality. After that moment, she began to scream. The ship was alight right before her very eyes. Orange flames shot from all directions as both mast and hull turned to ashen black, ironically yards above hundreds of tons of water. Men could be seen jumping overboard into the chilly water, and it was evident that one poor fellow was too quickly swallowed by the fire. She and the other townspeople living on the coast rushed out of their houses as the whole ship collapsed into a pile of wood floating atop the water.

Their emergency system was put into place. Dozens of rowboats went out to the wreckage, the men searching for their friends and family and fellow townsmen while the women waited anxiously on land. Clouds that came from seemingly nowhere suddenly appeared, threatening rain. The search had to be expedited; should a storm begin, all on and in the turbulent water would be lost to sea.

Minutes later they returned with their boats overfilled with refugees. One by one the families disappeared to take care of their loved ones, the shivering men, who were brought into their respective houses to drink tea in dry clothes by nice, warm fires. Before long only the constable and Ruth, both toting coats over their night clothes, remained. No one else wanted to be around to hear how she would take the news.

"Mistress Wickford," Constable Bowham said with sympathetic eyes, "you know your husband was captain."

She nodded. She had witnessed it herself from her house: he was the only one who had not survived. Everyone else was present and accounted for, maybe a bad head cold worse for wear. Her husband had gone down with his ship; rather, up in its flames. She had been mentally prepared for his drowning death, not his burning one.

"The property was so destroyed that we could not ascertain an exact cause for the fire. It was worst in the cargo, however. The blacksmith's best guess is that since the air is thick tonight, as it usually is right before a storm, the metal material in the ship's cargo swelled, collided, and sparked. Naturally, the wood did the rest."

He offered to walk her home. She declined, needing time to herself. He said good night and returned home.

On her short walk back to her house she saw a figure emerge from nearby. It was the man from the alley.

She turned on her heel and walked right, away from the man but also away from her residence. She did not want him following her home, especially since her son was defenselessly asleep.

He walked behind her. "I was right, wasn't I?" His voice was ever so smug. "The only one gone. How brilliant an ending—literally."

She mopped her brow with the flannel sleeve of her nightgown— though the mercury was low in the thermometer glass, the recent moisture in the air made her drip like on a hot summer day.

"Too warm for you?" he asked as he looked to the sky. "I can fix that."

The clouds shortly rolled out to sea, bringing their stickiness with them. A cool, drier breeze threatened to undo Ruth's pinned-up hair.

"What do you want from me?" she hissed, silently praying he would return to wherever he came from.

"I already asked," he said matter-of-factly, "and you refused. So, now I know what I want, and I shall receive it."

He paused.

"But first your son will die of fever as fiery as your temper."

She whipped around to say something scathing, but by then he had disappeared. Ruth hurried home to her son, glad to see him sleeping undisturbed in his bed. She had not decided how to tell him about his father; she was certainly not going to wake him to break the truth. She wasn't sure she would be strong enough the next morning to tell him, after all that happened that night. Thankfully, fatigue overcame her and she fell asleep immediately.

The next morning she was awakened by distressed sounds Archibald was making. She rushed to his room to see him red in the face and choking, as though something was caught in his throat. She opened the windows to invite in the sea breeze, prepared hot water, towels, and blankets, and offered plenty of motherly comfort. As the hours went by, he grew progressively more weak, pale, and frail. She called for the doctor, who said warm compresses, fresh air, and time would be the only remedies.

She sat on a chair in his room all day until she nodded off somewhere in the middle of the night. When she awoke her son was lifeless in his bed.

Ruth did not leave the house for days. The occasional visitor brought her condolences and meat pies, which sat untouched on the table. She barely slept or ate; grief was an understatement.

She finally forced herself out of the house: not because she was ready to face the world, but because she could no longer remain alone without madness creeping in. She ventured out to the market. People dealt with her quietly and swiftly, leaving her be for the most part, and she was appreciative. Afterward, she stood near, not on, the harbor's main pier, where she had once expected her husband to dock and their son to race excitedly into his embrace. She bit her tongue. She did not want to break down in public, so she looked out into the water, thinking of nothing in particular.

The old man, who was nowhere near her thoughts, soon appeared.

"I'm sorry for your son," he mused. His eyes betrayed his lie.

She dared not say a word. She wanted to push him into the violent ocean waves before her, but restrained herself; not because she thought it would be wrong, but because too many people would witness it.

"My name is Franklin Corey. I am a descendant of Giles Corey, if I haven't mentioned it before." His voice was casual, as if he were discussing the weather. "During those trials—you know, the ones a little over a century ago—he was pressed to death by stones for being a witch—or rather, refusing to plead one way or the other. He refused to lie on principle, but telling the truth was not an option either. He begged the executioner to lay stone upon stone on his body, until the breath deflated from his lungs.

"He was angry at himself for being born a witch, so he allowed his death. Invited it, really. Every first son thereafter was possessed with his powers. My father and his father and his father, and so forth. But they did not use their powers, instead they ignored them, denied them outright. Such a shame; the stigma of being a Corey kept my family ever on the brink of poverty. My whole family lives on the outskirts of towns, never the center. Though people claim otherwise, they avoid business dealings with the descendants of an accused witch. We are mostly subsistence farmers, trying to extract life from rocks, while the shipmen and merchants enjoy riches beyond our wildest dreams.

"Refusing to accept mediocrity as my forefathers have done, I have cultivated my gifts, as you may call them. In doing so, I have become very, very powerful. I yield more control of the heavens and the Earth than any mortal could imagine.

"I warned you of what would come when you refused me the first day we met. But you didn't believe me," he smirked. "I think you do now, Widow Wickford."

Her voice was tight but firm as she replied, "Though you may be a son of Giles Corey, he was not a witch and neither are you. My husband died because of an air swelling, your rheumatism likely predicted it; and my son died of a fever not uncommon in boys his age, especially this time of year. They did not die at your hand, and I do not know why you believe you have command over others' demises through some divine authority you obviously lack. All I know is you are but a wretched man who delights in the misery of others."

"You still do not believe me?" he asked with amused incredulity. "I have met stout skeptics who clung firmly to their hesitations, but none as stalwart as you, milady."

When she did not answer, he went on, "Very well then. I must convince you." He snapped his right thumb against his right middle finger. Ruth watched in horror as a dainty flame danced mockingly upon his dirty nails. He blew out the digital fire as quickly as he began it, his flesh nor beds the slightest bit crisped.

"He lit a fire with his fingers!" she cried aloud. A wave of unwelcome concession drowned her disbelief. A swarm of curious citizens halted their various respective activities and swirled around her to see the hullabaloo. Among them was the constable.

"Mistress Wickford, what seems to be the problem?" asked the genuinely concerned Constable Bowham. He had always found her an agreeable woman, with a pleasant demeanor and a pleasant face, and when the proper time for mourning had passed he was prepared to court the widow. If she was prone to hysterics, however, he was glad to know sooner rather than later.

She shakily pointed her finger at the old man, who sported large and innocent eyes.

"He killed my husband and my son!" she screeched. Her eyes were red-rimmed and stained with angry tears. "He set Jonah's ship afire and put a literal pox on my boy! He's a witch—a male one, if you will. A warlock! If there was ever a man in this town that needed to be hanged by his wretched neck, it is this lowly toad!"

Bowham and the rest of the crowd uniformly pursed their lips. They had long been trying to shake the reputation their history of witch mania had thrust upon them. They were rebuilding their city, and their economy was finally healthy enough that many could live better than the New England subsistence farmers that their ancestors were. Should word of another supernatural hunt spread beyond the town borders, other ports would surely close their doors to them, afraid of the witch fever spreading and devouring their own towns from the inside out.

"Mistress Wickford," he said as calmly as he could while grabbing her elbow, "you are overcome with grief. Let me bring you home, and I will personally fetch a doctor to tend to your needs."

"Let go of me!" she struggled out of his grasp; in doing so, she inadvertently plunged her fist squarely into the middle of Bowham's face. His nose instantly gushed scarlet red blood. Then his cheeks turned the same hue.

"Deputies," he barked as he nodded thanks to a kind, young spinster who had lent her handkerchief. "Take her to the asylum at once!"

As he turned to another deputy, Bowham scoffed, "I know she lost her husband and son recently, but really, this behavior is uncalled for in any situation." The deputy voiced his agreement.

During all of this, Corey was quieter than a church mouse. Ruth was dragged to the jail and asylum hybrid, which was a dark and dank underground collection of cells designed to keep criminals and insane women from seeing the light of day, both literally and figuratively. Very few paid him much mind, save the stray Salem resident who came up to the stranger, welcoming him to their humble home and apologizing on behalf of their town. When the crowd dissipated, he went to the town jail.

He met Bowham at the base of the stairs leading to the catacomb-like prison, concealed from the view of anyone fortunate to live above ground. The air was thick with the stench of human waste and bodily odors. Periodic kerosene lamps perched upon the masonic wall inlets shone like beacons in the darkness. The scene was a stark contrast to the briny sea air and persimmon autumn sun enjoyed ten feet above their heads.

Bowham said with an outstretched hand, "As Chief Constable Isaac Bowham, I would like to officially welcome you to Salem, and your new position as bailiff. I trust your trip over here this morning was pleasant?" He looked around and shivered. "It was sure to be more pleasant than this dungeon. I hope you don't dread this sort of work: it's terribly depressing down here."

Corey took it, and though his own hand was bony, the grip was firm. "In my old town, I never stayed in cramped little quarters like these all day, mind you: I went out and about among the people, where the really sinful serpents crawl, often cleverly hidden among the people as upstanding citizens. Another set of eyes and ears can always be used and, as you have seen today, sir, I am glad to lend them." He patted his bony stomach and added, "You would think all of this exercise would make me as ravenous as a bear emerging from his winter's nap, but it has the opposite effect."

He nodded his appreciation and understanding, but he did need clarity on one subject. "My good man, why did you leave your post? You came so highly recommended, the governor was hesitant to let you even leave the state. Providence was doing so well under your purview."

"That was exactly the reason, Constable. It does my heart good to say that I am completely certain the proper souls reside there. The riffraff have been incarcerated, sent away, or left on their own accord. The town is safe and in the perfect position to thrive. I plan on retaining such a goal for Salem; mark my words, before long we will dwarf Boston as the premiere city in all of Massachusetts!"

"Well, thank you for going above and beyond your call of duty. We are not paid well enough for the tasks demanded of us in our nascent city," Bowham said with a chuckle and a friendly handshake.

The old man smiled modestly, "I find it more a life's calling than anything else. All I seek is to purge my charge of evil. Nothing more."

The grateful constable bid him adieu and walked back to patrol the town, having felt accomplished in protecting his beloved town from potential traitorous underminers. Corey was alone at last, except for the chained prisoner, Wickford, watching scornfully from her immuring cell. He sat in his new chair and kicked his feet up on his desk. He snapped his fingers and lit his pipe for a job well done.

THE CHANGING TABLE
Salinda Tyson

Tiffany rushed into the café restroom, pushed the lock button with her elbow, pulled down the changing table with her chin, set Marti down on it, and fastened the safety strap. She fumbled her pants down, plopped onto the toilet seat and peed a bucket full. What relief. Eyes never leaving Marti, who was cooing, hands and feet in the air, tiny fingers grabbing her pink booties, exploring the shape of her feet and toes; tugging, tugging.

"Marti, honey, don't pull your booties off. Not again."

Of course, there went bootie number one, arcing off Marti's tiny right foot. Marti cooed, wiggling her bare toes in ecstasy, her eyes barely following the trajectory of the pink knitted footwear. With both her hands she worked at her left foot.

"No, Marti, no."

Tiffany finished and turned to flush the toilet. The lever stuck so she turned her back on Marti -- just a second -- and lifted her knee to her chest to use her foot to flush. Toilet aerobics, yeah. Dang. She had forgotten again that this was the bad stall with the flushing lever that stuck. Of course, it had been the only one open. Marti was gurgling and cooing, a sure sign that she had wrestled off the other bootie.

Tiffany whipped around to peek at her baby girl. As she turned, a streak flashed by in her peripheral vision. The left bootie? She shook her head. Floaters? Too much late-night online reading? She blinked, then soaped and rinsed her hands, careful to keep an eye on Marti in the mirror.

The mirror had fogged over. Everything was blurry. Tiff frowned at her reflection. Darn. She hadn't run that much hot water. Could heat from the giant coffee makers next to the adjoining wall cause that?

"Oh, Marti," Tiffany almost cried and almost laughed. What's a mom to do? Marti had wiggled out of the left arm of her shirt and was grabbing at her undershirt. Tiff rescued the booties from the tiled floor, pulled them back on her daughter's feet.

Someone pounded on the door, "Hey, you gonna take all day?"

"Just a minute," Tiff yelled at the door, "I've got a baby."

Muttering from outside the door, "Sure, sure. A likely story."

Tiff ditched the soiled diaper, got Marti's shirt back in order, swept up her baby, closed the changing table, collected all her things, purse over her shoulder, diaper bag over her purse, and balancing baby and bag on her right hip, opened the door by bumping it with her left hip.

"Oh, you really do have a baby," said a goth girl outside. Her silver nose ring gleamed.

Tiff remained calm and walked by. Once past she did a private eye-roll and used her left hip to bump open the front door, which was decorated with black cat cutouts, witch on broomstick silhouettes, and cardboard skeletons in top hats and tails. The smell of spicy pumpkin lattes, specialty of the season, followed her out the door.

Such a beautiful day, all Technicolor blue skies, Indian summer in Salem, Massachusetts, with the air turning crisp, and the smell of leaves and their crunch underfoot. She had managed to avoid the tourists who flocked to the witch museum, but wouldn't you know it -- Marti fussed the whole way home.

Needs a nap, Tiff thought.

* * *

A stray cat sat on the doorstep as if it belonged there. Tiff shooed it away. It stared at her, blinked, and stalked slowly off. Marti cried. Tiff had grown used to fussy spells and getting by on hardly any regular sleep. First, she took Marti's fussing in stride, figuring it would end, but it grew worse. Marti drummed her feet on the surface of the cot so fiercely that her booties slipped off. Then she kicked them through the slats of the crib into the far corner of the nursery. She ripped off her clothes in record time.

"You little quick change artist, you," Tiff said, kissing her forehead and nose.

Marti slapped her, the tiny hand open. It stung. Tiff felt a scratch across her right cheek. She grabbed Marti's hand. Ran her finger across the palm, soothing her, and pressing the small fingers open. The nails had grown amazingly fast. Hadn't she just trimmed them? She ran for the baby nail clippers. How could she have missed that?

Marti kicked and howled when her pearly nails were cut. The howls turned into cries.

Tiff abandoned the nail clipping, scooped baby girl up, and bounced Marti on her knee. The cries turned to shrieks.

Crying is the way a baby communicates. *What are you trying to tell me, baby girl?* Tiff wondered. Another few hours, and she made an urgent appointment.

As Tiff laid her on the examining table, Marti peed right on the front of the doctor's jacket. A dark stream that smelled odd.

Tiff was embarrassed. "Is she sick?"

Dr. Earnshaw took a sample of urine, thinking she knew that smell but could not put a name to it.

"What are you feeding her?"

"Just regular things, strained baby food, milk. Nothing different. Do you think it's allergies?"

"We can run some tests."

* * *

That night Tiff noticed that Marti's nails had grown again, thicker and darker. They curved. Marti was not cooing, but gurgling constantly, her eyes closed, but moving rapidly beneath the eyelids. REM phase, Tiff assumed. Dreams. What was Baby Girl dreaming? Tiff leaned over the crib, watching her sleeping daughter. She bent closer.

Marti's eyes opened suddenly.

Tiff jumped. No sleepiness, no confusion. It was as if the baby was staring into Tiff's eyes as an equal, measuring her, almost mocking her. *As if she knew I was watching her, and she wanted to catch me at it,* Tiff thought.

Her skin crawled. She checked the baby monitor and left the room.

Baby girl was definitely different. Constantly fussy. Throwing tantrums. Biting. Licking. Smacking her lips -- its lips -- in an un-baby like way.

* * *

That night Tiff stood listening to the baby monitor. A sound like ripping and wet munching. She waited inside the nursery door, hidden in shadow, willing her heartbeat to silence, watching the crib. A cat, the feral cat Tiff had sometimes fed but had chased away after Marti's birth, and which had appeared on the doorstep, climbed into the crib, a mouse in its mouth. It dropped the tribute onto the baby's chest. The cat straddled Baby Girl, feasting on the back end of the mouse, while Baby Girl ripped into the front end, head and all, growling.

Help, Tiff thought. She swallowed, trying not to vomit. *Is it the postpartum blues, my anti-anxiety meds? Am I going bonkers?* She slipped from the room, hoping, praying, that she was not losing it. *Was Baby Girl possessed?*

Lines of ants invaded the kitchen, marched across the floor and up the wall, forming sharp right angles to the honey jar on the shelf, and at last crawling under the lid. Tiff put the honey in the fridge. The ants kept coming, carrying bits of leaf across the floor. Tiff opened the sink doors and found a nest of leaves and noodles full of lizards with yellow eyes, a big one, the mother, and three babies emerging from green eggs the size of fingernails. The big lizard stared at her and hissed. Outside the kitchen door at night a chorus of bass croaks sounded until midnight. Frogs? Toads? Strange insects with opalescent wings appeared on the windows, as if they were looking into the house. They clustered especially at the nursery window.

The doctor's office left a message that the tests showed nothing — all perfectly normal. Tiffany called her mother to watch Marti -- Grandma and Grandpa just adored the little girl. Tiff hated herself for leaving Marti, but wondered -- if Mom and Dad saw nothing wrong, then was she nuts?

At last, she called Anna. "We've got to meet. I *need* to talk with you." Anna, unlike a shrink, would listen calmly and not dismiss her as a nut case.

Anna, an old friend who could see ghosts, who read tarot cards, who conducted séances. Anna whom she had mocked for her…beliefs, which had ended the friendship. Anna was likely the only one who would not laugh at her, wave a dismissive hand, and mutter about postpartum depression.

Anna did listen carefully. Offered tea and scones in her kitchen. She looked straight at Tiffany. They had known each other for ten years, the last two of that in estrangement, but Anna never said, "I told you so."

Anna set down her teacup, pressed her hands to the table. "There are old stories… I'd have to see her. She seemed fine last time I sat with her. Perfectly normal."

Tiffany shook her head. "Not now. Things…changed. I feel like I'm going crazy, but I've seen things that no baby, no human baby, would do."

Anna raised an eyebrow.

"Ripping a raw mouse apart. Smacking her lips. Maybe my mom and dad will report some weirdness, but somehow I doubt it."

Anna frowned and swallowed. "Like the car not doing the weird thing when you take it to the mechanic?"

"Exactly." Tiff nodded.

"I have to see for myself."

So Anna did. She watched solemnly through the whole gruesome scene late that night. She beckoned Tiff in to the kitchen, shut the door, and stood with her back against it. "Friend: I'd say she's a changeling."

"Like the fairies' nasty trick of switching babies?"

Anna cradled a teacup in her hands. "When did this start? When exactly did normal stop and weird begin?"

Tiffany shook her head in despair. "I don't know."

Anna put a warm hand over hers. "Just think about it. When and where things stopped being OK." She made her friend a wreath of rosemary, had her sniff it, and bundled several small sprigs in an amulet bag with an agate and a pyrite crystal. "For memory and protection," Anna said, "Wear it."

They retraced Tiff's steps, everything she could remember, every place she'd gone the last few days. Crossed and re-crossed neighborhoods, strode by the Puritan statue in front of the witch museum, crossed the Commons, the Howard Street cemetery, visited the Peabody-Essex Museum, checked every bathroom and café and baby clothes store, every park and library and jogging path. Nothing rang a bell.

"A glamour may contain a spell for memory loss," Anna said. "We are close to Halloween. This is Salem. The fey have a strange sense of humor, so this place might provoke them." She touched Tiff's hand. "There was something odd about Marti's dad."

Tiff's mouth tightened. That was as close as Anna would come to an *I told you so*. He had disappeared: Mister Seductive one day, Mister Into Thin Air the next. Tiff was unsure if his name was Ulrik Green. He had muttered something that sounded like that once. As for his birthplace, his parents' names, who knew? The hospital staff had looked at her as if she were to be pitied, or to be questioned about harboring a criminal.

Hours later, they stopped in the Witches Brew Café on Derby Street for a pick-me-up. Tiff stared about her and suddenly paled. "Damn. This is the same café."

"Make certain," Anna said. "Name certainly fits."

They visited the toilet and read the warning on the changing table.

"Do not leave infant unattended," Anna read, running her fingers over the lettering. "They all say that, of course." She looked grim. "Did you turn your back for a second, take your eyes off her?"

Tiff felt sick with guilt,"A nanosecond."

Anna paced. "Might be enough time for magical beings to make mischief. Notice anything weird at the time?"

"I thought I had a floater in my eye. I watched her the whole time in the mirror, but it steamed up. Something flitted in my peripheral vision."

Anna sighed. "What if...it's a portal to the other side? This time of year, near Halloween, All Hallows Eve, Samhain, the boundaries between this world and other worlds, between living and dead, mortal and fey, grow thin. Fragile enough to let things pass through.

"And if we're lucky, things can travel back."

"I'll try anything." Tiff was near tears. "So somewhere past that line, beyond that wall, in some other place, some other creature, has my Marti?"

"I think so."

"How do we get her back?"

"We trade for her. We catch one of them and make a deal to get her back," Anna said.

"Like a POW swap," Tiff murmured. Tears rolled down her cheeks.

Anna embraced her.

* * *

Marti was a model baby for Tiff's parents. Tiff and Anna rigged a ceiling video cam focused on the crib to verify the nighttime visitations. The resulting film horrified them, showing the cat bringing the mouse, and the hideous shared feast. The video reassured Tiff that what she had seen was not due to the postpartum anxiety medications. "A comfort knowing I'm not nuts," She groaned. "Not a story we can tell any doctor."

"We've got to trap that cat, hold it for ransom," Anna said. "It's fey in the worst sense of the word."

The plan backfired. The cat and Marti clawed them. Marti grabbed the cat's fur and it leaped from the window, baby aboard, and disappeared into the neighborhood.

By morning, Marti was in her crib, sleeping fitfully, her eyes shifting beneath her eyelids. There was a smear of blood on her mouth with a tuft of gray fur stuck in it.

* * *

They closed the windows, but the magic opened them wide. The changeling was inviting the cat in.

"Should we use garlic?"

Anna snorted. "That's for vampires."

Just after full moon would be the best time, Anna said, because a banishing spell works best when the moon is waning. Next night they lay in wait for the goblin cat. It came through the window, Marti riding it, her fists clutching the black fur of its neck. It leaped into the crib and Marti rolled off. She crawled about the crib, growling. Anna leaped, stretching a huge linen sack over the top and bars of the crib, trapping the cat, which hissed and screamed and jumped to escape the bag. Tiff spread a circle of salt around the crib, the pale lines joining the iron objects — old keys and antique clothing irons and pyrites —which Anna had placed on the floor earlier. Together the women wrestled the creature down against the sheets, ignoring the claws and teeth that ripped and snapped through the cloth.

"I bind you, goblin," Anna said. They struggled to hold the sack closed. It was like holding Proteus. The goblin writhed and screamed. Flames and steam shot through the weave of the sack, but its claws and teeth drew blood and human blood contains iron. As Tiff's blood dripped down her arm, the horrible cat settled at last, yowling. Marti gave a cry that sounded almost human again.

They loaded the cat inside a carrier and four more bags for good measure and tied it tightly. Anna stowed the writhing package in her large tote bag, along with a pint of cream, salt, and her ritual objects. They headed to the café, where they had to wait in line for the bathroom, of course. Marti clawed and scratched Tiff, who had put mittens on her hands. At last they were next in line. They got some strange looks because of the yowling that came from Anna's tote.

At last they were inside. "It's a unisex bathroom," Tiff said.

Anna nodded. "I'll be as fast as I can." She disabled the smoke alarm, purified the space with sage and candle flame. "They'll think we're smoking in the toilet, but it can't be helped. Make sure the door's locked."

"Pray they don't have a master key."

"Stay by the door, Tiff, in case they try to force it."

The ritual was halfway complete when someone thumped the door.

"Hey," a male voice yelled, "What are you doing in there? You're taking forever!"

Anna locked eyes with Tiff and went on murmuring, chanting a binding and banishment spell.

Anna kept a tight grip on the twisting, howling goblin cat. It got its head free of the bag, but Anna held it tight. The fur of its throat steamed as Anna pressed her iron-bladed knife close. The goblin hissed, snarled, and clawed. The creature began to shrink. The bathroom filled with a rain of red and gold and brown and skeleton leaves, rustling and swirling as if to form a shape. Forest litter covered the tiles and the smell of wet, rotting leaves and mushrooms filled the air. Acorns rolled across the floor. Spiders scurried everywhere, but the black cat hissed, showing fangs like locust thorns. It bit Anna's hand so that she almost dropped the knife. The beast leaped onto the changing table and disappeared into the shimmering wall.

"Door's open," Anna whispered, cradling her hand.

People were pounding the door. Someone landed an open-handed strike that made the wood shudder, but the angry male voice retreated. Next came a business-like clatter of solidly heeled shoes, "This is the manager. Is everything all right in there?"

"My baby's sick," Tiff said, "Please understand."

The heels clicked away down the hallway.

The baby changing table dropped open. Tiffany gasped. The changeling in her arms hissed furiously, scurried onto the table, and vanished into the wall. A shower of forest floor litter, brilliant red sumac and gold maple and oak leaves, dried berries, pebbles, and a tangle of thin branches spewed from the wall and fell onto the floor. There was a snarl and a whistle. A rumble followed, and a cry -- a human baby's cry. Tiff was blinking away tears. Marti slid through with another rain of acorn caps and pine needles, dried mushrooms, and some spiders that swiftly climbed the walls. Tiff caught Baby Girl as she came through the portal. Marti was okay. Crying, but okay. Her diaper was soaked. Her clothes were filthy and her left bootie was gone, but she was back. Tiff cradled her. Blew away the cobwebs twined in her hair and snagged on her jacket. Picked the burrs from her hat. Kissed her all over, tugging off socks and mittens, examining her fingers and toes.

She changed the diaper, scooped up Baby Girl, stood back to close the changing table. A streak flashed out, a scrawny wild-eyed tuxedo cat whose ribs showed. It yowled and raced around the bathroom, batting the air as if pursued by and fighting imps.

Anna pulled a pint carton and saucer from her tote and poured the cat a saucer of cream, which it approached warily. It let her fasten a collar around its neck, a collar with nine iron studs to protect it from future mischief.

"Everything's OK," Anna yelled at the door. "The baby was fussy and sick, okay, people?" She was stowing what remained of the forest litter in the garbage can and a garbage bag she'd brought along. She put the cat in her tote bag and the quartet made a somewhat dignified exit from the café.

"Where did all those leaves come from?" the guy next in line asked.

"Fall colors. They're everywhere this time of year," Tiffany said. She cradled Marti close.

NEEDLE AND BONE
David J. Gibbs

The gentleman was curiously stooped, as if harboring something in the confines of his top coat. He seemed to move quite unnaturally, as if the very joints that propelled him along were filled with an impossible amount of sand. Tufts of unruly gray whiskers feathered out from his cheeks, the rosy hue of his nose giving the appearance of a rather lopsided rabbit. Roderick knew who he was, everyone in Salem did. Reginald Weatherby was a regular fixture among the cobblestone streets and crumbling brick structures in the older section of the city.

Despite knowing the man, and the rumors, Roderick watched with fascination, as Weatherby knelt to pick something up. As the man stood, he turned, a pointed finger pushing the brim of his crooked top hat up a bit, and smiled. It was hideous, a smile that would certainly give children nightmares. The gas lamp held aloft above him cast a gold halo over the man's features, his gnarled, uneven teeth appearing unnaturally large, his eyes vacuous, a void of darkness.

He felt a sharp smack to the back of his head, followed by someone grabbing him tightly across his chest from behind. It was his friend, Darby, who said, in a laughed filled whisper, "Dear Roderick, you'd best watch yourself with old Weatherby."

"Quite right," Roderick said, though his eyes couldn't look away. Weatherby's eyes danced with the light of madness in them as the man looked upward into the gas lamp, staring intently. His bulbous torso, lumpy and uneven, appeared bent on crushing the spindly legs that held him upright.

"Not much left upstairs with that one, quite mad I say. The fool's lost a bit to the bottle, a bit to age, and a bit more to the rot between his legs, after catching something from one of Ms. Hannigan's girls and their nasty bits."

"That's quite enough about his nasty bits," Roderick said, as he turned away, shivering.

"It wasn't his nasty bits I was talking about," Darby managed before bumping his eyebrows up and down a couple of times.

"Well done then young Darby of Salemshire, well done," Roderick said.

"Salemshire?"

"Well it sounded a bit more suited for someone given your station of import to be living there instead of the tired old city of Salem, Massachusetts."

Roderick still stared after Weatherby. Everything about the man seemed somehow skewed or slanted, as if he was seeing the man through warped glass. He was definitely a curiosity.

"Don't let him catch you staring," Darby said, tapping Roderick's shoulder, "he most certainly doesn't like that much."

"Where does he go? And what does the old sod do?" Roderick asked, ignoring his friend's question.

"Are you proffering a job of some sort? Need someone to poke around the old man? Are you looking to provide employ for such endeavors?"

"What are you going on about?"

"It would merely seem you're taking a rather keen interest in a most uninteresting and undeserving individual. One crazed lunatic that the asylum has overlooked. He's mad as a hatter and downright cruel when he does choose to speak to those around him."

"Perhaps, but I daresay," Roderick said, "I am hardly one to offer such advice or employ. I'm a mere pauper among men."

The two of them chuckled, which in turn made Weatherby pause momentarily. He began to turn back toward them, a ragged cough, fraught with phlegm and disease, following the motion. They turned away quickly to avoid his stare.

He followed Roderick back inside the pub, finding their two friends near the back. Making their way through the throng collecting around the length of the heavily polished bar, they grabbed a pair of full mugs, before finally settling into the worn chairs at the table in the back.

"'Bout time you bastards got back here," McDuggan spat, flecking them with beer and saliva, his red hair dark with sweat. He was definitely a bit under the table already.

"Shove it in your bum, you silly bastard," Darby said, taking a few long swallows from his mug and shoving McDuggan sharply in the arm.

"Our young, dear friend here was staring at our friend Weatherby just now. You'd think he was about to propose marriage the way he was gawking at the fellow," Darby said, his hand on Roderick's shoulder squeezing sharply.

"That so? Well, now Roderick. You like the rotten tenders of an old apple, huh?" McGinty asked, winking at him, beer froth in his mustache.

Roderick put his mug down and playing along with his friend, he said,

"Well the older the pauper's vintage the sweeter..."

Roaring with laughter, his friends slapping each other on the back, he took another drink, feeling the beer work its way down his throat. He didn't put the mug down until it was empty.

"That's put a twist on things doesn't it?" Darby asked, his face ruddy from the beer.

He knew they were being loud, Roderick noticing that others around them didn't approve, their sharp glances and head shaking making it clear. Normally, he would've told his mates to pipe down, but figured even he deserved a night to blow off a little steam. It was high time.

"Pub's closin' boys. Last call!" shouted Dorsey, the barkeep, ringing the bell loudly.

Roderick couldn't believe it was last call already. He knew they had been drinking a lot, but it seemed like the time had just gotten away from him.

"I'll settle up," McDuggan said, winding his way unsteadily to the bar.

"Poor bastard won't even remember that he paid for this tomorrow when he wakes up," Darby said, taking the last swallow of his drink.

"Aye, that he won't," McGinty offered finishing his mug and wiping his arm across his mustache, finally froth free.

"Well, I'm not about to be the fool to remind him of it," Roderick said, leaning over to punch Darby in the arm, "And don't you be the one to do it."

"May worms feed on my loins and termites feast on my eyes."

The last of Roderick's beer erupted in a spray across the table. Darby laughed, throwing a peanut at him, McGinty following suit, tossing several of his own his way.

"And to think, you received bad marks in English Composition. You weave such a beautiful tapestry with your flowery language. A regular wordsmith you are. A swordsman armed with sharpened quill and a bit of ink."

"You're drunk," offered Darby.

"As are you, young Darby, as are you."

"That may be young squire, but I'm still able to get myself home and find myself some company for the night without the need of coin."

"Oh come now Darby, that's not hard to do in this neighborhood."

"Doesn't your sister live a few blocks from here?" Darby asked.

"Now that sir, is an asshole thing to say," Roderick said, though he realized that his own speech was starting to slur a bit around the edges.

"Well sir, you are an asshole so it quite clearly fits."

"That doesn't make a bit of sense since you're the one saying it," Roderick said, finally standing up from the table.

"I see. So, you're saying that I'm the asshole?"

"I don't know what I'm saying. I'm drunk. I guess I'm saying we're both assholes."

"Aye, lads the three of us be assholes!" shouted McGinty, causing Dorsey to look toward their table.

Darby laughed and said, "Well, at least you got that right."

They left the pub a few minutes later, the chill in the air biting across Roderick's exposed face, the cobblestones merciless to his balance. *Why the bloody hell haven't they gone to brick like the eastern side of town?*

Rounding a corner to cut down the narrow alley, he heard something from the shadows creeping about. It gave him pause, some inkling that something wasn't as it should be. His hand found the wall of the alley, his head feeling a bit too heavy for his shoulders, when he heard it again. Listening closely, he tried to peer into the darkness spilling outward from the alley.

Suddenly, someone fell into the sliver of light that spilled from one of the upstairs windows, the flutter of clothes and slender figure lent him to guess it was a woman. He was about to start toward her, when he saw something else dart across the light. The animal-like movements confused him; quick and certain, not rushed but slightly frenzied. He realized it wasn't an animal, but rather a man. Admittedly, Roderick was drunk, but he was certain it was Weatherby hunched over her.

As he looked at Roderick, his hand withdrew something from inside his jacket. It was a kerchief, white and feathery in the dark. His stomach rolled inward for a moment, as he watched the crazed man dab the cloth onto the prone form, raising it a moment later, no longer a white and feathery thing, but instead stained and tainted. Far more spry than could be possible, Weatherby deftly drew it into his mouth, his eyes sparkling for a moment, as he sucked on the cloth.

Roderick turned away, his stomach revolting against him, and he wretched several times. By the time he stood up, the stench of his bile making him wipe his mouth with the back of his hand, Weatherby was gone. The woman remained still, her body unmoving in the darkened alley.

It didn't take him long to reach her side, his eyes darting around before focusing on her. The crazed man nowhere to be found, he bent down, staying out of the light so that the woman was illuminated as much as possible. He recognized right away that there was something sinister about her, something decidedly wrong with what he was seeing. The slope of her face was broken somehow, as if a canvas had been pulled over a mirror that had burst beneath, the jagged pieces threatening the very fabric of her likeness. He was terrified to touch her, for fear those shards might slice through and cut him.

Blood seeped from several wounds across her jaw. Roderick assumed that was where Weatherby had dabbed his cloth for whatever insidious reason. As he watched, beneath the glare of the oil lamp burning away above, the chill of the wind biting his face and fingers, he witnessed something extraordinary, something sinister. The woman's face began to contort, strange spasms tugging her head left and right, the bits of shattered glass pushing even stronger against the canvas of her face before settling, their motion finally stopped, leaving her face smooth.

Rubbing his eyes, he wondered if the beer had affected his vision. *Could he be that drunk? Could he have imagined the entire affair?* He didn't think so, but how else could he explain it?

"You there! You there. I say stop!" called someone from the other end of the alley.

Looking up, he realized it was the constable. A shrill whistle sounded as the man rumbled down the alley toward him. Roderick knew he had to get out of there. Gathering his feet under him, he started to stand when something grabbed his wrist. He cried out when he realized it was the woman at his feet. The woman's mouth gaped impossibly wide, as if her jaw had come unhinged, and an animalistic rumbling spilled over him. She used his arm to pull herself upright before suddenly shrieking, the sound making him wince. Not a moment passed before she let him go and raced off into the night, away from the constable who was closing the distance.

Rubbing his wrist, still feeling the biting chill of her grip, Roderick looked down. Blinking several times, trying to get his mind around what had just happened, he noticed the discolored marks on his skin. They matched the extended fingers of the woman when she grabbed him. He shivered, and though if asked he would've said it was due to the cold, he knew better.

"What's going about here?" asked the constable, a stern expression on his face.

"I, I thought the woman hurt and bent down to check on her, she came to quite quickly and then ran off," he heard himself say, his words slushy feeling in his mouth.

"You weren't taking advantage of her?" the constable questioned, though his tone less severe now.

"No, sir. I was on my way to my flat when I saw her," Roderick said, leaving out the part about her face, and Weatherby leaning over her.

"I see. And, your name?"

"Roderick Morrisey, sir," he said, the words still feeling odd in his mouth.

He looked at the markings around his wrist again and shivered, prompting the constable to say, "Very good. I know your father, good man. I won't trouble your further. You should get yourself home and out of the chill. Right cold it is tonight."

Roderick nodded and said, "Thank you constable. I'll bid you a good night."

After nodding to the man, Roderick walked away, his mind reeling with cloudy thoughts, trying to make sense of what just happened. He wasn't entirely sure how he made it home, but he had. Sleep was quick and merciless when it took him a short time later.

* * *

"So, you had a scare then at old Weatherby's expense?" chided Darby, his laughter filling the sitting room of his parents' home.

"It wasn't at his expense. I don't think you're hearing me," Roderick tried again, "he was standing over this woman, I presume mutilating her, and then proceeded to dab his kerchief in her blood."

"So, a regular vampire is he?"

"I'm not saying that."

"Had a mouthful of fangs did he?"

"I'm not saying that either," Roderick conceded, his fingers rubbing his temples.

"Well then please, good Sir Roderick, please tell me what it is you are in fact trying to say and if you say witchcraft, I'll have to call you daft, old boy. I won't believe in such nonsense as that."

He hadn't even considered the woman to be a witch, for most of the witches he knew were confined to the woods, selling potions and cure-alls for any number of maladies from their stoops or traveling carts. They used to come to town far more frequently, selling their wares in baskets, moving door to door, or at the market, but since Doctor Stenson opened his practice, they had been largely shunned.

Roderick had no idea how the woman shifted her face the way she had. That was far more powerful magic than he had ever known of a witch possessing. Her face had been crushed, he had been certain, recalling the sharp bits poking against the underside of her face. *How had she managed to repair such terrible injuries without a surgeon?*

"Darby, I was hoping for a bit of support. I'm at a loss. You can be sure I do not think it witchcraft, and I certainly don't believe them to be vampires either."

"Then how do you explain what you saw?"

Roderick shook his head and shrugged.

"Are you blaming the booze, my good man?" Darby asked, laughing as he asked, patting Roderick's shoulder.

"I suppose I am," Roderick confessed.

The afternoon passed pleasantly enough, polishing off a bottle of wine and enjoying his friend's company. Leaving, Roderick walked back to his home, taking the long way through the village square. Pausing to buy an apple, he rubbed it against his sleeve. Turning from the apple stand, he stopped short, coming face to face with Weatherby.

"Good day l'il wanker," the man spat, his teeth brown stubs, his eyes wide with madness, the breath reminiscent of sealed, musty vaults.

"Hello, Weatherby."

He bit into the apple as he strode past the odd man, having no intention of speaking with him. Roderick always relished that first bite. It was always the best.

"I think we have some unfinished business to discuss," Weatherby called after him, his voice a rough bit of weathered wood.

Taking another bite, Roderick turned and said, "I don't believe we do. Good day Weatherby."

His heart began racing in his chest he realized Weatherby was following him. The man was tossing an apple up and catching it over and over again, his tongue snaking out across his rotted teeth. Eyes wide, Weatherby smiled before first pointing at the apple in his hand and then toward Roderick. It made him look down to the apple in his own hand.

The blackened bit of fruit had been torn open by his teeth, the innards filled with writhing maggots, plump and swollen, appearing ripe to burst. He suddenly spat out bits of apple, his fingers plucking maggots from his mouth and throwing them to the ground with the rotten remains of the apple.

Roderick stared back at Weatherby who merely smiled, taking a bow before walking toward him. Roderick kept thinking there were maggots still in his mouth, his tongue darting along his teeth, in a panic.

"Now, now, my good Roderick, please stop that. They'll call you mad and toss you in the lot with me. There are no more in your mouth."

"What?"

"You've rid yourself of every last one."

"What in bloody hell just happened?" he asked, looking over his shoulder as Weatherby walked beside him.

"You've been touched, friend. Yes, indeed you have the foulness about you now. One can see it easily if one knows where to look."

"What do you mean?" he asked frowning.

Roderick noticed that Weatherby wasn't moving as he had the night before. There was no appearance of sand in his joints today. His hands moved quickly, unexpectedly pulling back Roderick's sleeve and pointing to the dark finger marks at his wrist.

"As I said, you've been touched."

He looked at the marks before asking, "What difference does that make?"

"Still feel the cold there don't you?"

He did, but didn't want to agree with Weatherby.

Roderick just looked at him blinking several times before asking, "I still fail to understand."

"And, you will continue to do so until you finally accept that which you cannot."

Laughing at that, Roderick stopped and turned to face him saying, "That riddle makes no sense Mr. Weatherby. If I am in fact unable to accept that which I cannot, how could I possibly accept it?"

"We should speak again soon," Weatherby said, and turned from him, walking off.

He was about to call after him, when Darby rounded the corner and called to him, "Roderick, there you are!"

"Darby? What are you doing here?"

"I had just heard the news and knew I had to come find you and give it to you firsthand, otherwise you might not believe it."

Something told him he wouldn't like what his friend was about to tell him.

"They found her," his friend finally managed, his face a stern mask of concern.

"Found who?"

"The girl you saw last night. Rose. At least, I think it's her. What you described definitely fit with what the constable found near Witch's Woods."

"You can't be serious. Darby, I swear to you if this is another one of your jokes-" he started to say, but stopped, realizing his friend could not act this well.

"It most certainly is not a joke. After you left, the constable came to the house looking for you. I came as soon as I could to relay the news."

Roderick's blood ran cold with an icy wave washing through him. The sunlight seemed far away to him.

"While I appreciate the warning, Darby, I can't very well run now can I? I did nothing wrong and certainly the constable saw her run away alive and well last night."

Darby stood there, hands on his hips looking left and right, obviously upset by his decision. His friend didn't know to do.

"You're a damn fool," his friend muttered as the constable came toward them.

"Young Roderick," the constable said, "how is it I'm meeting you so frequently of late?"

"Must be the luck of the Irish."

"You're English, you daft bastard," Darby said, still not looking at his friend, anger tingeing the words.

Roderick was nervous, clearing his throat as he noticed Weatherby lurking about one of the fruit stands further down the square. The man tapped the brim of his crooked top hat and nodded in Roderick's direction, face full of the maniacal smile. He was hideous to behold.

"Roderick? Are you aware that a woman was found dead on the outskirts of town?"

"In fact, my friend Darby mentioned the news just now."

"He did, did he?" asked the constable eyeing them both now, a stern look darkening his features.

"I did sir," Darby said, slipping out of his thicker accent to the more proper one.

"Was that so you could get your stories straight? Did you two talk it over? Perhaps you planned this together?"

The constable's voice rose in volume and in timbre as the thick armed man stepped toward Roderick. Roderick couldn't help but shiver and take a step backward.

"What did you use? How did you do it?"

The question was startling, and it dislodged thoughts about the previous night. *Had they found her looking the same way? Was she filled with broken, brittle pieces of glass beneath her skin?*

"Sir, I did nothing. I saw her last evening when you approached me in the alley. You saw, as well as I, that she ran off, very much alive."

"Indeed, I saw her running away, but I have no knowledge of where you may have gone after that moment."

Roderick noticed Weatherby again moving along the other side of the square, another apple in his hand. It made his stomach clench for a span of a few heartbeats, thinking of the vile apple he had sampled earlier.

"I'll need you both to follow me," constable said and turned, not waiting to see if they fell in behind him.

Roderick shrugged at his friend and headed in the same direction as the constable. His heart thudded out the steps, and the clock tower called out the quarter hour, as they closed in on the cluster of townspeople buzzing around an area near the tree line of Witch's Woods. Darby looked at him, shaking his head. Roderick wasn't sure what to make of it all.

Parting, the crowd murmured around him, whispering behind cupped hands, their voices frantic, eyes accusing. He stepped closer as the constable turned back toward him.

"This is indeed the woman from last night is it not?" he asked loudly.

The crowd grew quiet, which only let the weight of the moment seem heavier to him. Roderick looked down at the woman and felt a shudder move through him as his eyes took her in. His stomach lurched as he realized that the shards of whatever he had seen the night before pushing against her skin now jutted through. It was not just on her face though, it was all over her arms and presumably everywhere else as well. And yet, despite that, there was no blood on her body or across the nearby ground surrounding her.

"My God," Darby managed, the back of his hand against his clenched mouth.

"I'll ask only once Roderick."

"Sir?" he asked, finally pulling his eyes from the woman's shredded face.

A terrible thought rose through his mind that she looked like she had been stretched around a porcelain vase that someone had then crushed inside her, skin drawn flat, with the sharp pieces jutting through.

"Did you see her again after last night?"

Shaking his head he said, "No, I did not."

The constable frowned, looking down at her before saying, "I honestly don't believe you did this, I truly don't, but I have to carry this through. I mean what kind of tool would a man use to do this to someone? Can you answer that?"

He couldn't, and was about to say as much, when someone called out from the back, "Serves her right the witch."

"Wasn't a witch," someone else countered.

He wasn't able to see who it was, the voices coming from all sides.

"She surely was practicing the dark arts. The woman said so herself!"

"Made me a potion or two, she knew the ways."

"Not a witch! Not a witch, I say. They wouldn't even take her into the coven. Working in the ways of the devil mayhap, a trollop, but not a witch! In league with Satan I say!"

The constable stood up and demanded, "Who said that? Who is it?"

"The dark arts at work. Just look at her!"

"Never been a witch in this town."

"That's a bloody lie!" shouted someone from the group. "They took my sister into the woods, they did!"

"Can hear chants sometimes coming from Witch's Woods."

"Burn them all!"

The constable seemed a bit unsteady and unsure as he stood, "Now good people. Certainly no need for shouting. We will get to the bottom of this."

"Not likely," someone mentioned quietly.

"They're bloody witches. Let them burn, every last one!"

Darby tugged at his sleeve drawing him closer. The look in his eyes was completely alien to Roderick. In all the time he had known Darby, he had never seen the kind of fear that lurked there now. It struck something in his chest, making it hard to breathe for a moment. He had never seen his friend once shy away from any encounter.

"Roderick, we should go," Darby whispered nodding away from the crowd.

"Now ladies and gentleman, please understand this is an official matter. We are making all the proper inquiries and speaking to all associated parties."

He nodded to his friend.

The pair left the group as quickly as they could, the constable too busy trying to restore order with the growing mob, failing to register their disappearance. After the melee grew distant to their ears, he asked Darby, "Exactly what purpose does this serve?"

Finally releasing Roderick's sleeve, his friend said, "There's no hope for the constable to solve this. You already know this. Something is very wrong about all of this."

He thought about it as they continued around another corner, heading toward the eastern most section of town. "Where are we going?"

"Roderick, please trust me. This is the only way."

"I fail to understand how running from the authorities helps me in any capacity."

"The constable told me where she lived when he came by this morning. Rose Everson. That's her name. She lives on Cobbler's Way. I ran into her outside the pub sometime last week myself. I think it's quite possible we might find something at her home that would exonerate you. If we can prove your innocence, then we can put this to bed, constable or not."

They continued on, Roderick feeling more and more uncertain of what he was seeing around him. His head was reeling with the events of the last twenty-four hours. He simply couldn't grasp how things had become so convoluted. *How on earth had so much transpired in so little time? How had he become so entrenched in something he had so little control over?*

As the streets grew darker and darker, the eyes watching them growing more and more predatory, they continued into the seedy part of Salem. There was so little familiar around him, he was almost certain that he had never been so far from what he called home. Filth was underfoot with each step, the stench a wall of an indescribable collage of foulness.

Leering from windows and doorways were women in all state of undress, displaying their pliable wares for the eyes that sought them. Men pawed at them, dirt smudged faces and stained hands roaming their pale curves. He watched as one young girl wagged her tongue at him and pouted her lips, while rubbing between her legs. Not even Ms. Hannigan's ladies were this vile or forward.

"This is it Roderick."

He looked up at the doorway before them, the structure leaning, missing bricks scattered across its weathered face like broken teeth. A lone gas lamp sputtered despite the daylight, its color peculiar.

"Are you quite certain this is what we should be doing?"

"You're not?"

He could think of nothing else to say and so stepped up to the door and opened it. The smells that wafted up across his face were malleable and for the briefest of moments he thought that if he perhaps concentrated hard enough, he might be able to touch those scents, holding them in his grasp. It passed however as he stepped into the dimly lit entry hall.

"I found a lamp," Darby said, lighting it neatly and holding it aloft.

The flickering light pushed back the shadows a bit, but not quite as efficiently as he would've hoped. There were pots of all sorts along one wall, resting on a sagging shelf. Lumpy remains of candles lurked on the mantel and shelves, long strands of spent wax frozen in waterfall of finger-like shapes hanging down from the edges. He noted lengths of cloth draped over some of the furniture, as well as what looked to be a half dozen dress forms, some with sections of gowns on them.

"I think we should leave," Roderick said, the hairs at the base of his neck standing upright.

"We shouldn't be here. There's something not right here."

"What do you mean?"

"The boots are off somehow, and I am certain there's something decidedly not right about the fabric. Please, bring the lamp nearer," he said, leaning over a length of fabric, his hand dipping behind it to lift it toward the light.

He dropped it almost immediately realizing that it wasn't truly linen, at least not in the traditional sense. Roderick wasn't certain it was even fabric. Again, his hand touched it.

"Curious looking isn't it?" a voice asked from the dark corner of the front room.

Startled, both Roderick and Darby recoiled, the lamp raised to try and cast more light about their surroundings. It was merely a whisper in the shadowy sea of the room.

"Who's there?" Roderick asked, recognizing some motion from the far side of the room.

His eyes picked up other objects too in the dim light; a standing bird cage gleamed, the edges of worn furniture, and books stacked below a shelf. That's when his blood ran cold, choked full of icy bits. Blinking several times, his mind not quite registering what he was seeing, hoping that he was mistaken, the chuckle that spilled through the room was filled with shards of fear tipped with dread, needling his heart with each tone.

It couldn't be.

But, there it was none the less.

The crooked, battered top hat was on top of the stack of books. Hands, aged beyond belief with chipped, yellowed nails plucked it from its perch. Tugging it down by the brim, the form looked up, and he realized it was Weatherby, though the guise of the man they knew was all but gone, instead a hideous likeness of something to be feared, something to be loathed, something not of this earth, was now in its place.

"Roderick, my lad, why did you feel it necessary to go prodding where you weren't welcome? What are we to do now?"

"Weatherby, this is not what it seems," Darby started to say, his voice shaky.

"That is quite enough," Weatherby said, his voice guttural and animalistic. "I mentioned you were touched did I not? Your friend is as well from his encounter with Rose last week."

Roderick looked at Darby and noticed he was rubbing his wrist just as he had following Rose's touch.

"Certainly you don't think you're here of your own volition? Oh definitely not. I could see you were quite taken by Rose's work. She is quite extraordinary. I've never been able to walk amongst the world of man as easily as I have since my persuasion of Rose to help me."

Roderick's mouth was dry, his eyes taking in the strange Weatherby creature before him, bits of skin still clinging to the terrifying visage beneath, the gnarled, rutted surface chilling to behold. The fingers ended in talons, revealed through rips in the skin about the man's hands.

"As you can see, with this likeness, I would not be welcomed into most homes," he said, gesturing over his features with a diseased looking hand. "That's why I needed her unparalleled skills. This is all skin, human skin," he said, nodding toward the stretched out material Roderick and first thought to be linen.

"It takes quite a skilled set of hands to stretch it and cure it in way as to stay pliable when is drawn over my body. 'At work with the devil' someone said while staring at her, and they were correct. A devil's seamstress she was, and a fine one at that," he chuckled saying this, "How curious their shouts of outrage were correct on that point. Indeed, she made me the skin suits, perfectly tailored so that I might continue to do my work and tempt mankind. Rose was truly an artist with that needle."

He sighed heavily before continuing, "She tired of me however and tried to leave my..." pausing for a moment before settling on the right word, "employ. I punished her severely as you saw in the alley. I had hoped that would cull her of any further attempts, but indeed this very morning she tried once again, and I could have it no more."

Roderick could only nod, his knees watery, his mind reeling. He turned to look at the doorway behind him, but it seemed impossibly far away. The light seemed to dim with each word Weatherby uttered.

"I'm sure you noticed what was around you, the closer you came to my doorstep. Despair, lust, fear, gluttony, all of it my best handiwork on full display, but it is such a difficult task at times," he lamented. "I need certain things so I can continue, yes, certainly I do. One of those things is a new seamstress. You can see that I wear through these suits so easily," he said, comically flexing his fingers, bits of skin flailing away from the form

131

beneath.

"So yes, I need a new seamstress and, as you know, a seamstress most assuredly needs material, yes, she certainly does. You look to be about the right size, and, gentlemen, I'd like to thank you for your donation. Yes, quite," Weatherby spewed, his bleating laughter becoming intermingled with the screams, as his rage consumed them both.

IT'S A WONDERFUL DEATH
Mike Carey

A cool October night breeze lazily wandered across Salem Commons, dancing its way across the faces of grand old Victorians. The houses had all seen far better days, but still, they stood as elegant sentinels over the cobblestone streets. The breeze turned down a side-street lined with decidedly less impressive homes, and seemed to cease when it reached the door of a small studio apartment; perhaps sensing something within, far colder than itself.

Opening the veins had hurt more than she expected, even with the razor blade being new and so sharp. Now the cuts along her wrists burned with a pain that was, gladly, numbed by the amount of alcohol and pills she had taken beforehand. She slid back into the warm water and waited for death.

She felt stoned. Really, really stoned. Her thoughts began to wander and blur. Why was she in the tub? She didn't know. She just knew that's what people did when they slit their wrists in movies and on TV. She wasn't sure if the water was supposed to be warm or cold, but she knew she didn't want to climb into a tub of cold water.

She looked down at her soaked jeans and shirt. *So weird to be in the tub with clothes on*, she thought. It briefly crossed her mind how funny it was that she didn't mind people finding her dead, but she didn't want them to find her naked.

A fresh wave of depression washed over her as she wondered how and when she'd be found.

Jennifer did not talk to her family; she hadn't in years. She was unemployed. The few people she considered friends were all busy with their own lives to bother with her. The week before, she had dropped off of Facebook for several days just to see if anyone would notice and check on her. No one did.

She didn't feel an overwhelming urge to die, she just did not see the

133

point in continuing a miserable life.

She resigned herself to the fact that she probably wouldn't be found until someone noticed the smell (how long would that take?) or until Mr. Mahoney, the asshole landlord came in looking for his rent.

Jennifer was getting cold. The water in the tub had turned red. She could feel herself dying.

At that moment, something happened. The water near the drain began silently swirling. Jennifer wondered if she had somehow kicked the drain open, but she didn't remember doing so.

Then, something began to rise. Jennifer squinted and tried to un-blur her vision. It was as if a small hill made of the red water was rising on the other end of the tub.

Jennifer stared at it curiously. She wasn't scared, but she was confused by the strange occurrence. Finally, somewhere within her rapidly fading mind, she realized what it must be, a hallucination. It made perfect sense that she'd be hallucinating at this point.

She grinned and relaxed, staring with amusement at the hallucination at the end of the tub.

The hallucination opened its eyes and stared back.

Startled, Jennifer pushed herself back against the wall, a brief burst of adrenaline momentarily clearing both her mind and eyes.

It was not just a hill made of red water. It was a face, Jennifer's face, made of shimmering water.

The hallucination, if that's what it was, rose up a bit more until red head, neck, and shoulders all appeared above the water. With each passing second, it seemed to grow more and more detailed.

Jennifer watched silently, still convinced it was some final trick of her mind, but transfixed by what she was seeing.

The thing at the end of the tub tilted its head, first to the left and then to the right, considering Jennifer in a manner not unlike a curious cat.

Jennifer's head spun violently, everything in her stomach violently leaving her body all at once. The corners of Jennifer's vision went black. The blackness rapidly began swallowing the light.

"This is it," she thought, with no small measure of relief.

A red shimmering hand rose from the water and a voice nearly identical to Jennifer's spoke.

"Wait."

One simple word.

Jennifer felt herself pulled back from the abyss. The light returned, and her eyes and mind cleared.

She rubbed her eyes and stared at the thing in the other end of the tub, no longer sure that it was a hallucination.

"Did you say something?" Jennifer whispered, and hoped that it would not respond.

The question went unanswered, but the thing did respond.

"Why…" it began, its mouth moving awkwardly, "why you killing you?"

Jennifer stared back. The hallucination, or whatever it was, wanted her to explain herself?

"Why you killing you?" it repeated.

Jennifer closed her eyes.

"This is messed up," she said to herself.

"WHY?" it demanded, annoyance beginning to be apparent in its voice.

"Because," Jennifer yelled back at her red shimmering double, "I want to! Okay?"

A confused look crossed the red face.

"Why you want death?" it asked, its English slowly improving.

Jennifer felt foolish having this conversation with the thing, but continued. This strange being was the only one who seemed to want to know what she was going through. It felt good to tell someone, even if that someone was just a trick of a quickly dying mind.

"I don't want death, I just don't want to live. I've got nothing to live for," she explained.

"Human life precious," it countered, "there are many dead things that wish for life."

Jennifer snickered.

"They can have mine. I don't want it."

"Fool," the thing disdainfully murmured.

"I have *nothing*! I have *nobody*!" Jennifer cried, feeling stupid for trying to justify herself to this thing, "Every day is the same. I watch everybody having great lives, getting married, having kids, going on vacations. Doing fun stuff I can't afford to do. *And I've got nothing!*"

"You have a future!" the thing argued, "or you had. A future is everything. A future can be anything. Every day is same when dead. The dead have nothing."

"I don't care," Jennifer sighed, "I've heard all that before. I've got nothing to look forward to. My future would be looking for a job so I can survive long enough to die old and alone. Why go through the hell of working every day of my life, just to make the hell last longer?"

The thing closed its eyes and seemed to think for a moment.

"I can show you," it whispered.

"Show me? What?"

"The future you were meant to have," the thing smiled, showing its perfectly formed white teeth, "What you're so anxious to give up."

Jennifer didn't fail to notice that the thing had stopped talking like Yoda.

"O-okay," Jennifer hesitantly replied, "I guess. Show me."

With amazing speed, the red figure lunged toward her. Before Jennifer could even react, the thing was pressing its lips against hers. Its mouth was hot, almost painful to the touch. Jennifer tried to push it away from her, but her mind was swirling. She felt as if she was plummeting through space.

The plummeting stopped, and she found herself somewhere else. She could not see herself but everything else was vivid and clear. She felt like a ghost, and she thought perhaps she was.

She saw herself; a slightly older, happier version, but still herself.

Jennifer watched the older version of herself for what felt like days.

She watched as the older her worked at an office, and made friends with co-workers.

She watched as she took a painting class and discovered a new talent.

She watched as a handsome man in the class glanced at her and smiled.

She watched the entire span of a relationship. There was love, there were laughs, there were fights, and in time, there was a wedding, and in a little more time, there was a child.

She watched as she had the first of many gallery showings of her paintings.

She watched holiday family gatherings with children and grandchildren and dear friends.

And finally, she watched as an elderly version of herself peacefully passed from this existence while surrounded by loving family.

It was a wonderful life.

Suddenly, Jennifer found herself back in the bathtub. She felt the hot lips of her doppelganger parting from her own. Jennifer realized that she was crying.

"Oh my God," Jennifer sobbed, "That's all I wanted. That's all I have ever wanted. A- a soul mate. A family. A job I liked. It's all I've ever wanted; to have what other people have."

The tears were running out of control. She could barely speak through her sobbing.

The thing at the other end of the tub stood up. Unlike Jennifer, it was naked and seemed somehow more solid, although it was still covered in shimmering red.

"Can you help me?" Jennifer implored, holding up her damaged wrists, "I don't want this anymore. I want my future!"

The thing looked down and smiled warmly; then it reached behind itself and turned on the shower. As the hot water shot out onto them, the thing spun gracefully beneath the spray. Red streamed off of its body while red water splashed in Jennifer's face.

It only took a few moments for the red to wash completely from the thing's body. It stood there, glistening, now perfectly identical to Jennifer, in every visible way.

But Jennifer was looking different now. Her face was streaked with a combination of red water and tears. Red covered her hair, and her shoulders.

"My future?" Jennifer cried.

"Now you understand," it said, warmly looking down at her.

"Yes. I do. Life is everything. I understand now!" Jennifer cried.

"Too late," the thing hissed.

Redness dripped into Jennifer's eye. She watched as the thing stepped out of the tub and began to towel off.

"As I said," it continued, "there are many dead things that wish they had life, and sometimes one of us figures out how."

Jennifer felt strange; stranger than she had during any part of this night that came before.

It was, perhaps, a mercy that Jennifer had no mirror to look into. She was spared the sight of her features slowly melting away, her body growing smaller.

In the end, she melted like ice cream on a hot day, and became one with the red liquid that still filled the tub. How long her consciousness remained, no one can say.

The thing bent over and opened the tub drain. It stood and watched until the liquid was gone. A red stain covered the tub.

It whistled as it retrieved a bottle of bathroom cleaner from the hall closet.

"I am Jennifer," it said with pride, "and this is the first day of the rest of my life."

It smiled and whistled as it scrubbed the last traces of the girl named Jennifer off the sides of the tub.

Somewhere, inside what was left of her mind, Jennifer was screaming.

* * *

The morning sun was shining brightly overhead, seeming to search out every reflective surface to glare blindingly from. At the small studio apartment, it opened the door and looked outside. Its eyes squinted tightly, as if they had never seen the sun before today, and in fact, these eyes had not.

It briefly felt the urge to retreat back into the safety of the dark apartment, and then scoffed at the idea of fearing the sunlight.

"What a foolish thought," it said, "I am Jennifer Marie Hawthorne."

It strode proudly out onto the Salem streets, blending easily with the morning crowds on their way to their various jobs, and knowing that it would not be long until it crossed paths with more of its own kind.

THE THING IN THE GRAVEYARD
R. C. Mulhare

"I don't know, Amanda, on Halloween, I just like to chill with some horror flicks and man the bribe bowl," I said, cradling the phone against my shoulder as I emptied a bag of mini Hershey bars into a large, black plastic bowl decorated with orange bats.

Then came five words that an introvert most dreads hearing from the person they like: "Come on, it'll be fun." My inborn people-pleasing tendencies made it hard for me to say no to Amanda when she used that wheedling voice, asking me to come along with her and her pack of friends.

I drew in a breath. "Yeah, all right."

"Okay, see you at the T station in Salem about seven!" she chirped.

I started to remark on the horrors of the MBTA and the repellant state of the cars on the commuter rail, but she hung up before I could get the words out. I sighed before hanging up and went to hunt up a witch hat from last Halloween, popping that on over what I had on, a long sleeved black Court of Thorns t-shirt, black jeans, and black motorcycle boots, before finding my black leather jacket and hauling it on. *Keys, wallet, phone*, shoving them into my pockets before calling out to Dannie, my cousin and roommate, that she'd have to man the candy bowl tonight, since Amanda had invited me along on a jaunt to Salem.

"You're going to Salem on Halloween night?" Dannie asked me, her head around the bedroom door.

"Amanda can be hard to resist when she really turns on the wheedle," I said.

An hour later, I stepped off the commuter train packed with other Haunted Happenings goers, some in costume, some pulling the hurried throw-something-on thing I had done, some families, including a few with wee kids in adorable costumes: pumpkins and princesses, ickle skeletons, and superheroes. We poured out onto the platform, with even more people disembarking who'd had the same idea. Thank the stars that Halloween fell

138

on a weeknight, otherwise even more people would have taken the T. Amanda, at the furthest edge of the crowd on the platform, with a colorful kerchief on her head, started jumping up and down, waving to me, the huge hoop earrings on her ears bobbing. She'd opted for a Viennese operetta Gypsy costume this year, after several Halloweens as various witches, enchantresses, and Renaissance ladies.

"Shay! Shay, over here!" She'd dragged along Tamika and Gary, the former dressed as a pixy faerie, though she'd had the foresight to make it a cold-weather faerie, with thick arm warmers and gossamer wings over several layered pastel t-shirts, the latter had made about the same amount of effort that I had, only with a pirate hat and an eye patch over a black shirt and black jeans.

"Planning to drink enough rum to keep warm?" I asked Gary when I had made my way through the crowd to join them. I'd thought to button my jacket over my chest, against whatever chill came in off the ocean.

"If I get the chance to," he said, with a grin.

Tamika looked up and down at Amanda in her gypsy get-up. "Really? You realize the Romani people are a culture, not a costume, and they don't actually dress like that, except maybe if they're on the carnie circuit, because it's what the crowd expects."

"Grandma always said we had some Gypsy blood on her side," Amanda said, airily, twirling to set her colorful skirts swirling as she ignored Tamika's concern.

"Says the girl dressed like a pixie," Gary said, looking at Tamika. "Do all pixies dress like that?"

"Pixies are fantasy creatures, they're hardly the same as a real world ethnic group," Tamika replied, hands on hips.

"It's actually a sanitized version of the original pixie faery. They started out as troublemakers and not particularly cute ones," I said.

"Someone needs to dress as *that* kind of faery," Gary said, with the kind of grin that he meant to look sinister, but which only looked goofy. Chalk it up to Gary's red hair and pasty Irish freckle face.

"So are we gonna go to the movies, or are we gonna talk about costumes and social theory?" Amanda said.

"I think the general consensus was we were going to the movies," Gary said.

We took the long walk down Washington Street to the Essex Street Pedestrian Mall and then to Cinema Salem for back to back Universal monster movies as part of a marathon. Nothing really frightening by today's standards, but certainly eerie. I can see why that old gent from Providence who wrote horror didn't find them especially terror-inducing. Once Gary started getting hungry for something other than popcorn, and the rest of us had gotten restless, we headed out, Amanda leading the way past the rock fountain in the middle of Museum Place and into the costumed throng on the Pedestrian Mall: several zombies, some with convincing gore makeup, some with not so convincing ragbag reject clothes and cheap green face makeup, slutty fairy-tale characters, and a big guy in a gorilla suit towed along on a chain by a girl dressed like Fay Wray. Someone was wearing a Cthulhu mask and squamous green latex hand pieces over a business suit with a huge "Vote for Cthulhu: Why Settle for a Lesser Evil?" button pinned to the lapel. Gotta love the stuff people come up with during election years; totally edges out the people in candidate caricature masks. There was also any number of slutty witches, to Amanda's annoyance. I very nearly collided with a very real-looking Lon Chaney-esque Wolf Man, who growled at me in a very not-real way. Not wanting to let the guy down, I reared back, letting out a stage yelp.

Coming the other way, we met a ghost tour with a woman in 1600's garb and a hooded cloak leading the way, carrying a lantern before her, with a group of obvious tourists trailing behind her, carrying candles of their own, hanging on the guide's every word said in an eerie stage hush.

We landed at Rockafella's, Amanda's favorite haunt (pardon the pun) in Salem, for drinks and appetizers. No cheap bars for her, and with her picking up the tab, I certainly couldn't complain.

"No vampire ball this year?" Tamika asked, once we had settled at a table on the patio, the better to watch the costumed passers-by.

"I thought it was the Vampire and Witches Ball?" I asked.

"No, they aren't having one this year," Amanda said, with a sigh.

"Any reason why?" I asked.

"Puritan fathers objecting to the shameless displays of wantonness and the pagan music?" Gary said.

Amanda poked him under the table with her foot. "No, they had problems getting funding."

"The bane of every fun event's existence," Tamika grumbled, with resignation.

"But back to that thing about the costumes earlier: isn't dressing at Halloween supposed to help you hide from whatever ghosts and goblins might have slipped across the veil?" I asked.

"Says the person who just threw on a witch hat over their regular stuff," said Amanda.

"I was in a hurry because someone called me on short notice," I said.

Someone behind me cleared their throat. "I always took the wearing of costumes to be a means of hiding in plain sight through showing a part of the true self that we hide from everyone, perhaps even ourselves," said a gruff voice behind me. I looked over my shoulder and spotted, sitting at the next table, a very tall, very thin guy with a long, sharp-featured face, his lank hair low on his forehead and his eyes hooded, so deep it made it hard to see them easily. Something about his face gave him a vaguely feral look, as if he had a set of costume fangs covering his teeth, but he didn't lisp when he talked. Likely a vampire or werewolf lifestyler who'd had a set of high quality veneers put in by a dentist. I took him for an actor on break from one of the little theatres or ghost walks in town, or the story telling at the Witch House, given the nineteenth century frock coat he wore and the top hat sitting in front of him on his table.

"See that," Amanda said to Tamika, with an *I told you so* smirk.

"Arrrh, that makes me inner self a pirate," Gary growled. I would have shaken my head, but with my own lame attempt at costuming, I couldn't really throw those metaphoric stones.

Tamika ignored them both, but I could see her face tighten a bit. "So how does that explain people dressing as zombies or werewolves or something like this? Besides them being horror fankids."

"It might reflect the monster that lurks in every one of us, even the so-called best of us," the tall guy said.

"So, does that make your inner self a guy in a Jane Austen movie?" Gary asked.

The guy gave him a quiet smile, but that somehow didn't make his face look any less unsettling. "It's a reflection of who I might have been, in another life."

"So, you're one of those past life people?" Tamika asked, darting a look across the street, to a psychic's sidewalk booth, draped in dark fabric covered in glow in the dark stars and moons.

"Perhaps not past lives, but perhaps an alternate route I could have taken, or one I might be taking now. I believe that parts of our personalities, fragments drifting from our souls, like some kind of psychic answer to the body shedding spent cells, linger in the mortal world and attach themselves to new lives beginning their journey," the tall guy said. "If life is a form of energy and the energy in this world cannot be created or destroyed but rather transformed, then it would make sense for some of the personality to become energy at the end of one life and return to the aether from which it came."

"Whoa… that's pretty deep," Amanda said.

"I don't think I've had enough to drink to really buy into that," Gary said, looking at his beer.

"Then allow me to buy you another round to help open the portals of your mind a little wider," the guy said, signaling to a passing waitress to refill our drinks, which she did.

"Thanks, but I'm good," I said, looking to my vodka and cranberry juice, more cranberry juice than vodka. When I looked up, true to the archetype, the guy had gone.

"Where'd that dude in the Jane Austen coat get to?" Gary asked.

"Probably had to get back to the event he was involved in and left quick," Tamika said.

The night wore on and toward midnight, the crowds of passersby had thinned, some likely attending the closing ceremonies on the town common, others going home.

"Come on, let's go to the cemetery," Amanda said. She had that *let's take a risk that isn't too risky* look in her eye that she often got when she'd had a few.

"Which cemetery?" Gary asked, raising an eyebrow, clearly game for whatever scheme she had in mind.

"Is that really a wise thing to do?" I asked. "I bet a lot of people have the same idea." Someone had to supplement Amanda's voice of reason when hers got impaired.

"The one behind the Peabody Essex Museum, the Old Burying Point, of course," she said.

She had to pick the one right in the middle of everything, I thought. It dawned on me, though, that if she had to pick one for her hare-brained midnight romp, she'd made a wise choice: with it smack in the middle of the downtown area more or less, that gave us fewer chances for something stupid to happen. With more people around us, maybe a cop or two, to say nothing of other people with the same idea, we'd have some amount of safety in numbers in case something should go horribly wrong. Not that I believed something nasty would come out of the stonework, but that one malicious or disturbed person could turn up to do things you shouldn't do anywhere, least of all in a graveyard.

Sure enough, when we arrived, we realized we hadn't come up with the most original plan. Someone had put out rows of candles along with flowers and food offerings on the stone benches set into the wall that make up the Witch Trial Memorial. A short, slight figure in a long black coat paced around one stone in a slow circle, sprinkling something around it, while a few others moved among the stones and the box tombs by the Charter Street entrance.

"Oh no, zombies," Amanda said dramatically, moving in closer and clinging to Gary's arm.

Gary pointed toward the one grave that the small, dark figure had circled. "Let's check out that one grave. Wonder why someone was moving around it?"

"Trying to raise the ghost of the person buried under it?" Tamika asked as we made our way over there. "They shouldn't play around with that. The dead should be left alone, and for that matter, if you try and call up a dead person, you might call up something nasty that's taking advantage of your curiosity."

"Aww! So no séances in the graveyard?" Gary asked, with a pout in his voice.

"She's got a point. It's not a good idea, especially on Halloween, when the veil is thin," I said.

Gary turned to look at Tamika. "You really believe that stuff? How much did you have to drink, 'cause that doesn't sound like you and your skeptical mouth."

"I wouldn't want to take chances," Tamika said, her wings rustling in a shrug.

By now, we'd come close to that one grave, a stone with a rounded top and narrow shoulders, cased in newer stone. Clearly someone had broken the original stone off at the base at one point, and the historical preservation organizations had restored it. Gary took out his phone and hit the flashlight app, shining light on the face of the stone.

"Here lyes interred ye body of Colo John Hathorne Esqr Aged 76 years who died May ye 10 1717"

"Oh no, the hanging judge," Amanda whimpered, taking a step back and tracing a pentagram in the air before her. I kid you not: her folks raised her Catholic, so she does this instead of making the Sign of the Cross like her Irish grandmother does when something weird or upsetting happens. Some habits just evolve rather than fade away.

"Amanda, he's gone, he's been gone since the 1700's. He can't hurt you," Tamika said, putting a reassuring hand on her shoulder.

"Well, that would explain why someone would pour salt around his grave: put a ring of salt, preferably blessed, around it, and if he tries to rise, he'll be contained," I said.

"That is, if he'd rise from here. Ghosts usually don't stick around their graves, or so I've heard," Tamika said. Then dryly, she added, "Wonder what he think if he came back to Salem today."

"For starters, he'd probably be scandalized by all the psychic studios and occult bookshops," I said.

"Aren't there some of his victims buried here?" Tamika asked. "Bet he'd be really burned up, knowing his body is lying in the same ground with them."

"I think Giles Corey is around here somewhere, and some of the Pickman family members are," I said, looking around.

"Most of the hanging victims didn't get the dignity of a proper burial, their bodies got dumped in a pit on Gallows Hill like so much garbage," Amanda said, bitter-toned. I didn't blame her, and I squeezed her shoulder again, letting her know she had me for company in that feeling.

Gary spread his hands, making what I can best call ooga-booga gestures, for lack of a better description. "John Hathorne, I command thee to arise!" he said in a deep, too goofy to sound creepy voice.

"Oooh, so scary," I drawled, not convinced in the least. "And you just asked about séances in the graveyard."

"John Hathorne, I command thee to arise!" Gary intoned again, ignoring me and still making those stupid fake magical gestures.

"Gary, this isn't a game," Tamika warned. "Knock it off."

Gary only ignored us. "John Hathorne, I command thee to arise!" he called out.

"Gary, knock it off, or so help me, we are never going to Salem you and me together, ever again!" Amanda snapped.

Gary lowered his hands. Then a breeze arose, rattling the dry leaves of an oak tree overhead, stripping a cascade of leaves from the swaying branches and tumbling them over us.

"Now you've done it," Amanda growled, looking up at Gary. "Now he's going to haunt us. He'll have a field day with me because I'm a witch."

Gary plucked a leaf from under his shirt collar and reached for the neck of her peasant blouse, trying to pull another out, but she pulled away. "Yeah, he's going to stuff leaves down our shirts."

Another gust arose, scattering the fallen leaves about our feet and sending a cold draft up under my jacket. The timing with Gary's fake invocation, plus the late hour, the holiday, and the number of drinks we had had, made it all the more unsettling.

"We're down near the ocean, it gets windy," Tamika said, trying to sound flat voiced.

The candle flames on one memorial nearby flattened, guttered, and then went out, casting our surroundings in shadow.

"Dark..." Gary muttered. I almost said "stating the obvious", but the back of my neck had started to prickle.

A tall shape loomed up from the darkness, making its way between and among the tombstones. It was the man with the top hat whom we had spoken to in the sidewalk café, though something about the way he walked sent a skin-prickling sensation along the backs of my limbs and down my spine, as if he was slightly out of sync with the rest of the landscape, if not the rest of the world.

"What's he doing here?" Amanda whispered.

"Maybe here for some event or to pay his respects to someone?" I asked, hoping that alone had brought him to this graveyard.

"Why are we whispering?" Tamika asked, but the wobble in her own already lowered voice answered that question. She felt it too, for all her reasonableness.

The figure approached a tomb at a near distance from us, a stone close to the ground either by accident or design, given the way he stooped down over it. He slid his hands under it, the way someone would slip their hands under the edge of the lid on a trunk, and lifted it, like it moved on hinges. A greenish flickering light shone from under the stone, as if the slab covered the entrance to some underground vault where someone had lit a fire or torches. Chanting, in deep, guttural voices rose up from the depths, punctuated by a slow beating drum and the atonal skrilling of a flute. Without so much as a glance around, the figure stepped into the cavity underneath, descending as if down a staircase below, leaving the stone raised.

"Let's get out of here, now," Tamika said, trying not to whimper, but I felt her edge toward me, trying not to get singled out.

"Anyone want to check that out?" Gary said, taking a step toward the open vault. "Bet there's a bitchin' party going on down there."

"No, and you'd better not, either," Amanda warned, starting toward the Liberty Street entrance, but pausing to look back at him.

"Well, more fun for me," Gary said, walking toward the vault.

A shadow moved within the vault and a head reared up, vaguely canine in profile, the hair mangy and fur-like over the forehead, but longer and lank over the shoulders, dog hair melding into human. A grin crossed its face, uncovering fangs that didn't belong in a human's mouth.

Gary howled, panicking and stumbling back, turning to run, but the thing clamped a hand onto his left ankle.

"Come join the festival," the thing rasped. Gary screamed again and fought to wrench himself loose.

I broke loose from standing with the girls and lunged forward, grabbing Gary by the shoulders, knocking the pirate hat off his head, and hauling him away from that thing. I dragged him, stumbling, between the stones, heading back through the Witch Trial Memorial, Tamika and Amanda yelling at our heels, as we bolted for Liberty Street, into a crowd threading its way out toward Derby Street.

We didn't stop until Gary's ankle buckled under him, and he collapsed, pulling me down with him. People in the crowd pulled away, some staring, one guy chuckling and commenting on the "awesome make-up", but his sexy witch companion scolded him.

"What was that thing?" Tamika said, panting and looking back.

"No idea. Weren't there stories of people in the Witch Trials meeting dog-things out in the woods? Or turning into black dogs?" I ask.

"I thought that happened in Dogtown?" Amanda asked.

"Maybe the dog-things ended up there after the Witch Hysteria?" I said.

"I can't feel my foot," Gary moaned. I looked down to check for injuries. Not only had the thing peeled off his shoe and sock, it had also raked the skin, de-gloving half his foot.

"You kids all right?" asked an older gent in a top hat with steampunk goggles perched on it, over a Victorian suit bedecked with rivets along the seams.

"No, no, a... a dog came out of nowhere and bit our friend in the foot,"

Amanda babbled.

"Someone call 911!" I yelled, peeling off my jacket and wrapping it around Gary's foot, pressing on it to try and stop the bleeding.

"There's a first aid station nearby," the sexy witch said, coming forward to help me lift Gary from the pavement.

We carried him to the first aid station, but the EMTs there could only do so much on the spot. The four of us piled into an ambulance, Tamika and I riding in the back, while Amanda huddled in the front with the driver, a blanket around her shoulders.

"I'm gonna die, I'm gonna die..." Gary muttered under his oxygen mask.

"You're doing fine," the EMT kneeling over him said, looking him in the eye to keep him focused.

We didn't get out of Salem until daybreak, when the trains started running again, after we'd spent the night sacked out on chairs in the waiting area of the North Shore Medical Center, waiting to hear from the doctors about Gary's condition. Amanda thought to call Gary's parents, and his dad arrived shortly, jeans thrown on over pajamas, asking us what had happened.

"Someone's pitbull got loose and attacked him in the graveyard," Amanda said, speaking for the group, telling him what he'd believe. If we said anything else, if we told him what we had seen, he'd never believe us. He'd think we had too many drinks or someone messed with them, or we'd done drugs in that graveyard, got some bad stuff and had a collective psychotic break.

Maybe we had, but I think I can see why people saw strange things in Salem back in the day.

I had class later that morning and had to leave so I didn't miss it, plus, I had to bring a doctor's note along with me on Gary's behalf. No way the doctors would let him out of the hospital with his foot torn up, plus they had him under observation in case he'd contracted rabies. Gary's mom came later, and according to Amanda, started yelling threats to sue the event planners for not keeping the downtown area more secure, as if they could foresee errant loose dogs, much less errant dog-person-things living in a vault under the graveyard.

The police later investigated, even taking a look around the slab where we'd said the dog had appeared. The slab lay partly lifted the next day, which the media described as "the result of vandalism", but they found nothing else. No sign of a vault, much less something a dog could come out of, either due to shoddy detective work, or maybe because the thing cleared out overnight. Of course, they never found the dog that matched the description we gave, to wit, a huge black pitbull mix, though they did find a Yorkie mix that had gotten loose from a nearby apartment. A veterinarian kept it in case the dog also showed signs of rabies, but none of us in our group believed for minute they'd caught the culprit. I later went back to the burying ground and got a look at the slab, which bore the name *Pickman*. That hit a little too close for comfort, since I'd seen the name in a history of local art. He was an artist back in the twenties who'd gotten obsessed with painting dog-like monsters before he vanished in Boston, under strange circumstances.

Meantime, Amanda broke up with Gary, at least romantically. She decided she couldn't put that kind of trust in a guy who'd stick his nose where it didn't belong, particularly a graveyard vault. At least they've stayed friends. Given the amount of therapy, physical and psychological, he has ahead of him, he needs all the friendship he can get.

He's gotten back to drawing again, and not the kind of curvaceous bodacious fantasy babes he used to draw, but ghoulish things, like the thing that attacked him. His therapists seem to think it will help him get past the trauma of the attack, but I think they've put an optimistic slant on it.

You see, a lot of the ghouls he draws look too much like himself.

THE BEAST OUTSIDE
Mary Jo Fox

Thankful Warren sat next to the warmth and light of the hearth as she read from the Bible. The young Puritan bride was alone in the small two-story house. Her husband was away in Boston and not due to return for two days. All she had for protection were a musket next to the hearth and a heavy wooden bar on the door.

Her husband had reassured her all was safe in Salem Village and she had little to fear. He had said he would not leave her alone otherwise.

But Thankful had heard her whole life about this wild land across the sea from her native England. It was a place full of hostile savages, strange beasts, and rumors of witchcraft. It was said devils lived in the woods encircling the villages and outposts. Even though she felt safe enough with her beloved John in the house with her, with him gone all of those nightmarish tales replayed in her mind even as she sought comfort in her Bible.

She had only come to Massachusetts Colony a few years beforehand with her family and was betrothed shortly thereafter to John. Life here was difficult, harsh, and unforgiving. Hard work and God's favor meant survival. Failure meant death. So she worked as hard as she could tending the garden and keeping house, prayed frequently, and never missed church. She was as good a wife John could ever hope to have; soon she hoped to bear him children.

She also stayed in at night and never went into the woods alone.

The sharp snap of branches outside startled Thankful as she began to doze off in her chair. Her heart pounding, she listened for any other noises. But all she heard was the crackle of the hearth fire.

"It is only an animal outside," Thankful told herself as she set the Bible on a table and rose from her chair. She lit a candle and went up the stairs to the bedroom where she knelt next to the bed to say her prayers, then got into bed, blew out the candle, and pulled a quilt over her body. She closed her eyes and just as she was drifting off to sleep, she heard a low growl outside.

"It's only the wind," Thankful whispered to herself, but the usual

148

whistling through the trees was noticeably absent. Never mind it didn't sound like any breeze she had ever heard in her life. Thankful drifted off to sleep again and another growl, this time closer to the house, woke her. Reluctantly she got out of the bed and went to the window to peer outside. It was a moonless night and a low fog had settled over the land, so it was pitch black outside barring the distant twinkle of stars high above wisps of fog. She could not see anything.

Her common sense told her it was likely an animal of some sort, a nocturnal creature out for prey. The door was barred so there was no way for it to get inside. Sighing, Thankful returned to her bed.

An hour later, she awoke to the sounds of growling and pacing around the house. The pacing sounded more like human feet rather than a four-legged animal like a dog, a wolf, or a bear. Thankful went to the window again and still could not make out a figure.

Thankful began to worry that what she was hearing wasn't an animal at all but a savage. Could it be a group of them was about to attack the house? The thought of it terrified the young woman. She'd heard the stories of these men carrying off women and girls with them, never to be seen again, or entire families being scalped. How could this happen while John was away? Did they wait until he left for their opportunity?

Thankful knew that even these wild men would need light to see their way. It was foggy, there was no moonlight, and there were clearly no torches. Still, any trespasser was potentially dangerous. Thankful decided to go back downstairs to fetch the musket and keep guard. She relit the candle and went down the stairs as the growling and pacing continued.

Back in the main room, the hearth was still alight, heating the house. Thankful set down her candle and picked up the musket next to the hearth. She quickly loaded gunpowder and a lead ball bearing into the chamber, just as John had taught her. Carrying the musket, she checked the windows and again saw nothing outside, even as the growls seemed to come mere yards from the house. She settled into her chair with the musket cradled in her lap, tired but too afraid to fall asleep.

Thankful heard scratching on the clapboard outside. Gasping, she ran to the window but the scratching came from the side of the house, which she could not see. It sounded like a claw running along the wood rather than that of a dog indicating it wanted to go inside or outside. It chilled her to her bones. She dared not go outside to investigate, but in her home, she felt trapped and helpless. All she could do was pray whatever it was outside would simply go away.

The scratching ceased. Thankful held her breath and looked around warily, holding up the musket. Then a crash shook the house from the back, as though a heavy boulder was thrown against it. The windows rattled.

Thankful jumped and screamed. She was now terrified whatever was out there was going to burst its way into the house. Should she hide in the root cellar? Should she run?

Perhaps she could make it to the Jasper house half a mile away.

Crash! Scratch! Scratch!

No, running outside would be foolish. She was safest here with the bar on the door. She aimed the musket at the front door, terrified but ready should the beast attempt toget in.

After what seemed like hours, Thankful heard it growl again outside the front of the house. Thankful's shaking hands struggled to take control of the musket. Then something rammed at the door again and again. The windows rattled and Thankful shrieked, but the heavy bar on the door held and the would-be intruder howled with frustration.

Then, Thankful saw it at last in the window, peering in at her. An unearthly muscled thing with glowing red eyes, sharp teeth and long claws, and the face of an old hag. Thankful shrieked and aimed her musket at the window. "Be gone you demon! Or I will send you back to hell from whence you came!" It was no boast or show of bravado, Thankful trembled uncontrollably as tears streamed down her cheek.

The hideous face vanished as suddenly as it had appeared, and Thankful heard running feet leading away from the house. She immediately pushed furniture up against the door and spent the rest of that night hiding in the root cellar, praying for dawn to come.

The next gray morning she went outside with the musket and saw the long deep claw marks on the clapboards, as well as damage to the wood on the front door and on the back of the house. She fled to the Jaspers' house and remained there until John returned from Boston. She showed him the damage to their house and tearfully recounted her tale of terror. He vowed never to leave her alone again.

"John, I'm sure what I saw was a witch in league with the devil. I've heard the stories," Thankful said. "That was no man or animal."

"We will go to the village magistrate," John said. "There is something bedeviling us here in Salem Village, and it must be stopped."

THE FAMILY HOME
P. L. McMillan

"Here we are," Mr. Althaus said, pulling into the short cracked driveway.

Mrs. Althaus looked through the windshield at the tiny cottage that sat nestled in the woods at the edge of the Forest River Conservation Area on Pickman Road. The cottage was a single story, built of logs and covered in patchy red shingles. The front door was pitted wood, and the windows were small and narrow. A massive chimney dominated the left side of the cottage, built from rounded river stones. The front yard was plain, patchy with yellowed grass that was wilted in the autumn chill.

"It's been in the family for centuries. The Althaus family moved to Salem from Germany in the 1670s, if I remember correctly."

"It's quaint," Mrs. Althaus said, thinking with a wistful bitterness of the studio apartment they'd left behind in Columbus.

Mr. Althaus turned off the engine of his car and opened his car door. A sharp gust of wind chose that moment to blast through the trees, showering the car and its occupants with fragrant and wet leaves from the nearby maple and oak trees. Mrs. Althaus hated the naked look of those trees. Their twisted branches curled upwards in cruel angles, scratching at the cloudy sky. And even the sky seemed different. Paler, washed out, cold. Mrs. Althaus shivered and followed her husband up the pebbly walkway to the front door.

"This is the original door. My ancestors carved it from the tree that originally stood on this spot," Mr. Althaus placed a hand on the door and smiled at his wife.

"So it's like a tombstone."

He frowned. She frowned at the door. He turned away from her and fumbled the heavy iron key from his pocket. He slid it into the lock, and she heard the tumbler clunk.

151

"There's only one key, unfortunately. We'll have to be careful not to lose it."

He opened the door and stepped inside.

Mrs. Althaus followed Mr. Althaus into the small, cramped house and looked around. The layout was simple, a large common room that became an open kitchen at the end opposite to the giant fireplace. Two doors offered a small bedroom and a bathroom. Ms. Althaus went over into the kitchen area. The appliances weren't prehistoric, but they were close. The hospital green fridge hummed angrily, the stove only had two rusty elements, and there was no dishwasher.

"We'll have to pay to have our stove and fridge shipped here, that will be expensive," Mrs. Althaus said.

Her husband shrugged.

"Do we really need those stainless steel monsters? My family's made do with those, I am sure we can. Especially since you lost your job and all, we can't afford the shipping costs."

She ignored him, as she often did, as she often felt she had to. She poked her head into the bedroom. It was full of dust, cobwebs, and a sagging queen sized bed that had probably seen more than a few at-home births if the stains were what she thought they were. The bathroom was all rust and water stains. She looked into the tiny tub with a sinking despair. There was not enough CLR in the world to fix the rust coating in there. She flushed the toilet and listened to the violent rattling of century old piping struggling to suck away the toilet water and only half succeeding.

Mr. Althaus was still in the main room, fondly caressing the rough stones that made up the top of the fireplace's mantle. She heard a persistent whistle.

"Do you hear that?" she asked him.

He shrugged again.

"That whistling?" she said.

She walked around the main room, cocking her head, listening at the windows and doors. The sound led her to the fireplace. Her husband watched her with a pained look.

"It's here. Look," she pointed up to where the chimney exited the house, stretching up into the sky.

The house and the chimney weren't flush. Instead a gap of about an inch separated the two, leaving a significant space for the autumn wind to blow in.

"No wonder it is so cold in here!" Mrs. Althaus scolded. "You need to call someone, get this chimney torn down. I am sure we can get this place fixed up with proper central heating for a fair price, it's so small after all."

"It is big enough for the two of us. Why should we need three bedrooms and two bathrooms? Our kids are grown and gone, we don't

have any pets. It's time to face facts, dear. You aren't going to find a job –
not at your age. I am lucky to have found one here, and that only happened
because of my family's connections here in Salem."

"So you'll have me cook on an eighty year old stove and live among
drafts and dust?" Mrs. Althaus asked.

"Would you rather we be out on the streets in Columbus? The chimney
stays. It's part of the home, and it serviced my family fine for all the years
we've lived in this house," Mr. Althaus replied.

Mrs. Althaus opened her mouth to say that, yes, it worked fine when her
husband was a child happy to play in the dirt but she was a grown woman
and wanted better – but there was a knock at the door. Her husband looked
more than happy to turn away from her and open it. A group of men and
women, six couples in total, flooded in. The house seemed even more
cramped with all these strangers, and Mrs. Althaus wanted to scream at
them to get out. *Get out!*

The three women were slightly younger than her, though that could
have been the expensive perms they all seemed to sport and the
professional makeup application on their faces. They each held a casserole
dish, each that wafted its own column of steam and savory scent. The
husbands were well dressed and grinning. They clapped her husband on the
shoulder, surrounding him in companionable jokes and welcomes.

The women surrounded Mrs. Althaus, but their welcome was chillier,
full of judgment. They looked at her scuffed sneakers and her ripped jeans
splattered with house paint from when she'd had to repaint their old
apartment for subletting. They examined her flyaway hair and cast a pitying
eye on her wrinkled face bare of concealer or blush.

Then they were past her, with 'oohs and 'ahs' at the "quaintness" and
"vintage feel" of the house. They clustered in the kitchen, comparing dishes
before placing them in the ugly mint fridge. They floated into the bedroom
and bathroom, before finally settling into a cluster in front of the fireplace.

"Fran."

She looked to her husband. He stood among his friends, a semi-circle in
front of the drafty fireplace.

"These are my cousins: Paul, Brian, and Ken," he said.

Each man nodded when his name was called. Like her husband, their
hair was gray and balding in the middle of their scalps. They each shared the
same brown eyes, the same thin lips, and underdeveloped chins. The only
thing that varied was the amount of fat they carried around their bellies, of
that her husband was the winner.

"And their wives: Carrie, Darla, and Mona."

The Stepford wives smiled thinly.

"Glad you're finally back, man!" said one cousin. Mrs. Althaus had
already forgotten who was who.

"You're so lucky to have gotten this family treasure!" said a wife.

"The old family home! We have so many good memories of this place!" nodded another cousin.

"And the low maintenance cottage style is so fashionable right now," added in a different wife.

"Yes, but of course, the fireplace will need to be removed," Mrs. Althaus said, crossing her arms.

Her husband glared at her. The cousins and wives looked at him, then back at her. They looked as stupid as cows watching a car pass their field. Mrs. Althaus had to resist a smirk.

"I am sure you've all noticed how drafty it is in here. I guess, what with the house being so old, the beams separated from the fireplace and now there is a gap," she said.

"Drafty? I don't feel anything," said one cousin.

"Remove the fireplace? It's one of the main selling features, you'd be destroying the center point of the room!" said a wife, stamping her heeled foot on the floor.

"A little plaster would go a long way," said another cousin.

"We discussed this. I won't allow it," said her husband.

The wives smirked. The cousins nodded. Her husband stared at her, his arms crossed and his face red.

"I don't understand why this shoddy fireplace is so important to you," she said.

"Oh look! The moving truck," said a wife loudly.

"Great timing! We can all help bring in the furniture and then we can all go out for dinner," said a cousin, opening the front door.

"Our treat, of course! Think of it as your official welcome to Salem," said the woman who followed him out the door.

One by one, the cousins filed out followed by their respective wives. Then Mrs. Althaus was alone with her husband.

"The chimney is a nuisance, and I am calling a contractor on Monday," she said.

Mr. Althaus shook his head and left. Mrs. Althaus did not join them. She watched the seven of them unpack the U-Haul, carrying the sparse amount of furniture the Althaus' could afford to bring with them. She watched the cousins struggle to squeeze the king size mattress into the bedroom after removing the stained queen at her insistence. Mr. Althaus laughed and called out to them as they carried in boxes of dishes and cutlery. The wives chatted out by their cars, smoking and looking back at the house through their cigarette smoke.

It only took a few hours for the four men to bring everything in. Now dozens of boxes were stacked on the stove, against the walls, and in the bedroom. The couch and armchair were placed in front of the fireplace, and the table shoved against a wall beneath the kitchen window, its three matching chairs surrounding it and burdened with boxes. The bed was set up, only one of the two bedside tables next to it since the bedroom was too small for both. The heavy oak dresser had been left in the main room, along with the china cabinet and TV unit. The TV, a flat screen meant to be mounted on a wall, was leaning against the wall next to the bathroom door, looking highly out of place in such a humble abode.

The men were sweaty and jostling each other. They called for beers and piled into their cars with their wives. Mr. and Mrs. Althaus were left to lock up. The two stood next to each other, in front of the front door, staring around their new home, which looked even smaller with the modern furnishings.

"It looks good," Mr. Althaus said. "It looks like home."

"Like a home," Mrs. Althaus said, looking at the cramped kitchen area, the dimly lit main room, and that damned fireplace.

They left the lights on, flickering floor lamps plugged into dusty sockets, and Mr. Althaus locked the door behind them. Outside, the sun had already set and the moon was rising above the tops of the old trees that surrounded the property. Mrs. Althaus listened to the susurration that was the wind in the branches and the sound of dead leaves skipping over the driveway. From the front step, she could see the road, paved and modern. The streetlamps didn't illuminate the yard, the trees were too thick.

The yard was thrown into sharp relief as Mr. Althaus started their car and turned on the headlights. She walked down the path and opened the passenger side, getting into a silent car. Mr. Althaus already knew the way to the restaurant. It was an old family favorite, owned by one of the wives' sisters, a pizzeria as small and cramped as the family home. It was filled with the type of people that only ever went to the same restaurant every Friday night and ate the same thing with the same wine. Old couples with leathery faces sat at tables neighboring middle aged mothers and fathers, fat with laziness, cooing at red faced bawling babies.

A table was reserved at the back for them, near the kitchen. A pimply faced kid, another family member of one of the wives, took their order with a sullen indifference. Mrs. Althaus had been maneuvered into a chair in the very corner, two seats away from her husband, and pinned between two wives.

"Has your husband told you his family history?" said the wife to her left.

"You know the Althaus family has lived in Salem since the 1670s?" said the one to the right.

"Old blood they're called."

"Beautiful heritage, really. Think of all that history in that house!"

The two giggled at each other. Giggling was not attractive in women that age, Mrs. Althaus thought, but she forced a smile.

155

"That chimney was not part of the original house, of course," said left wife.

"The original family home was just the one room, it burnt down in the 1690s," said the right wife.

"Oh yes. They rebuilt it larger and with that lovely chimney. The family was bigger by that time. There were four brothers. The eldest owned the house you live in now. He was the one who rebuilt it. His three brothers built other houses around Salem. Of course, all that witch nastiness was happening around then. You'd think as German immigrants, the Althaus family would have been subject to some of the accusations but it never happened," said lefty.

"You married into a lucky family!" said righty.

"Well," tittered the third wife, from across the table, "Lucky for the brothers. Their wives weren't as lucky."

The third wife's face was flushed, her lips stained red from wine. She grinned and ignored her husband's hand on her arm.

"They married sisters. It was a huge affair. Four brothers marrying four sisters, like a fairy tale. The girls came from a poor family. They must have been so excited to get married and move into these new houses being built."

"Oh stop! She doesn't want to hear that old story," said the wife on the right.

"Wives' tales!" said the wife on the left, taking a sip of wine.

The husbands stared at their wives. They glanced at Mr. Althaus, who shrugged and leaned his head on his fist.

"They had one big wedding. There wasn't any dancing or music, of course. Not with all that witch hunting going around, no one wanted to be accused of being Satan's bitch!"

The wives laughed and raised their glasses to those at the other tables who looked over at them.

"Their husbands hadn't quite finished their homes yet. Only three walls were up and the chimneys half finished. But the wives were eager to get to their new homes. Then the next morning, the morning after their wedding, the sisters were gone!" said the third wife.

The wives sipped from their wine. The cousins shook their heads, picking up the last slices of pizza and taking bites.

"What happened to them?" Mrs. Althaus asked.

The wives looked at Mr. Althaus.

"No one knows. There was uproar for a while. Slight suspicion on the brothers, but the Althaus luck prevailed. The case was dismissed, and they remarried and had kids, and that was that," he said and signaled the sullen waiter for their check.

The three cousins and their three wives invited themselves in, having followed Mr. and Mrs. Althaus back to the old family home. Mrs. Althaus protested. There weren't enough comfortable seats for everyone, the house was still unpacked, but she was ignored. The women took the couch, the cousins and her husband took over the single armchair and three kitchen chairs. Mrs. Althaus stood by the fireplace, staring down at the stones that made up its base.

"Lovely, lovely house!" said the wife sitting in the middle.

"You know, our houses still have the original chimneys too?"

Mrs. Althaus tried to look interested.

"Yes, we built an additional wing attached to the original building. We use the main fireplace room as a gathering place," said the middle wife.

"We did the same," nodded the one on the left.

"My husband and I tore down the original walls and built around the chimney, because you just can't get rid of history like that," said the third and last one, on the right.

"The chimneys are good luck!" said the wife on the right.

"What do you mean?" Mrs. Althaus looked up at the gap by the chimney that allowed numbing gusts of wind to run wild in the house.

"Nonsense," said one of the paunchier cousins.

"It's true!" protested the wife on the left.

"What do you mean?" asked Mrs. Althaus again.

"Well, when those Althaus brothers built these original chimneys, their luck changed completely. Their businesses thrived--" said the wife on the right.

"One owned the town bakery, the other owned a farm, and the last two shared ownership of a clothing store," added the wife on the left.

"They even survived the witch hunting frenzy without any kind of ill fortune," said the middle wife.

"But their wives disappeared," said Mrs. Althaus.

"Yes, well," said the wives.

"They married again," said a cousin.

Mrs. Althaus frowned.

Over her head, she heard the wind whistling through the gap again. The cold autumn wind caused a shiver to run down her spine, casting goosebumps across her arms and neck. The older woman wrapped her thin arms around herself and shifted away from the fireplace.

The wives chattered on about decorating and renovating the family home. The cousins cracked open beers they'd brought along with them, leaving empty cans on the floor. It was only at half past midnight that the six stood and made their excuses to go.

Mrs. Althaus cleaned up the lipstick blotted tissues and beer cans while her husband said good night to his family. She looked out the front window onto the yard and watched her husband hug each cousin and bestow a kiss on each wife's cheek. Then he watched and waved as each of the three cars pulled out onto the street and drove away. Mrs. Althaus went and poured herself some wine, sitting at the kitchen table, and waited.

Her husband didn't immediately come in. She began to wonder, halfway through her large glass of wine, where he could have gone. The house was quiet except for the persistent whistling of the constant draft that slipped in through the fireplace gap. Mrs. Althaus tried to tune it out. She thought of going outside to find her husband. The whistling continued but there was also another sound, a mournful cry, like that of a weeping woman trying to sob as silently as possible. It was a thin, wet intake of breath followed by a low throbbing keen.

Mrs. Althaus strained to hear the sound over the drafty whistle. She stood, hand at her wrinkled throat, and peered about the room. Of course it was empty. She'd been facing the door to watch for her husband and would have noticed a weeping woman sneaking in. Mrs. Althaus checked the bedroom and bathroom again despite this and found nothing. She noticed that the sound was the loudest by the fireplace.

"One of the neighbors," she said to herself.

The front door crashed open, causing her to jump. Mr. Althaus lumbered in with an armful of dead branches and brush that he'd apparently collected from around the property.

"Close the door," he said, dropping the wood into the wide mouth of the fireplace.

"Can you hear that?" she asked.

"Close the damn door! You're letting the heat out," he replied.

Mrs. Althaus wanted to ask, *what heat?* She closed the door and sat back down at the kitchen table, fingering the stem of her wine glass.

"Can you hear that?" she asked again.

Mr. Althaus piled the sticks and brush carefully, forming a cone of kindling. He took a small bottle of lighter fluid from his pocket, dousing the pile before lighting it with matches he'd taken from the restaurant. The lighter fluid caught immediately, flaring up, and filling the house with an acrid stench. Mrs. Althaus wrinkled her nose in distaste. The branches and dead leaves caught easily, soon there was a large fire burning cheerfully in the stone fireplace. The crackling of the bright flames among the dead things drowned out the draft, and the crying. She didn't bother to repeat her question.

"See, isn't that nice?" her husband said.

He scooted the green armchair closer to the fire and sat down in it, stretching out his legs and offering his feet up to the warmth.

"I'll call someone in the morning about that crack that's letting in all those drafts," she said, trying to get a rise out of him.

"Honey, you know why these fireplaces are so important?" he replied, in a calm and even manner.

She shrugged.

"I don't really care. It's a nuisance, I feel like I am living in the dark ages. I can even hear the neighbors! There's no insulation at all!"

"It's a Germanic tradition, stemming back hundreds of years. I guess you wouldn't understand that kind of thing."

Mrs. Althaus knocked back her wine in such an unladylike way that her husband scowled. She got up and refilled her glass. Mr. Althaus went to bed, slamming the ill-fitting bedroom door behind him. The reverberation caused the light bulb hanging over the kitchen table to flicker and go out. Only the lively fire in the fireplace gave any light to the home now.

The tired woman slumped in the kitchen chair, burying her face against her hands. She wept in silent, throbbing shudders. She thought about the things she'd lost. Her job, her home, and now her husband seemed to be drifting away as well. She felt helpless. Mrs. Althaus cried until she felt empty and had no more tears to shed. Wiping her eyes and nose on her sleeves, she drank half the glass she'd poured in one gulp.

By now she was feeling numb, and pleasantly so. She began to feel tired, wearier than in all the days of her mundane life. Mrs. Althaus stared into her wine glass. The white wine inside swirled and rippled, mesmerizing her tired eyes. It was like a crystal ball, pulling her back into her own mind. Instead of showing her the future, however, it brought her back into her memories.

She'd met Mr. Althaus at a business conference in Las Vegas in 1991. She'd been twenty-one, he'd been twenty-six. He looked handsome, strong, all muscle and gelled hair. She'd been flattered by his attention, although male attention wasn't something she wasn't used to. She'd held her own with her long, slender legs, sun kissed skin, and naturally blond hair that hung down to the perky tips of her breasts. He'd taken her out for dinner that very night after the conference ended. They'd made love on a scratchy hotel comforter and drank scotch until the sun rose.

She didn't know the man who slept in the other room. He'd become a stranger. A cold, unforgiving stranger who flinched away from her touch and yelled when he got angry. He was not that beautiful man who had literally swept her off her feet on their wedding night, knocking her head against the door frame and kissing it better as they lay on the bed.

The man who slept in the bedroom wasn't the man she married. Mrs. Althaus never felt so alone. At least at the old apartment, their two children, now fully grown with busy families of their own, had been able to stop by and visit. They wouldn't bring their families here, not to this run down dump of a house. It was embarrassing.

Her lip began to tremble again, a warning sign of tears to come. Mrs. Althaus pinched her nose and bit her lip, a trick she'd learned to stave off the tears. The urge to sob passed, leaving her with another bout of deep hopelessness. It was then she heard that mournful crying. This time, it sounded more urgent, more stricken, as though the woman were afraid.

Mrs. Althaus stood, crossed the large room, and opened the door. The night was cold and silent. She heard nothing but the whisper of leaves and wind, the creaking of bare branches. The crying was coming from behind her, from inside the house.

She turned, back to the open doorway, and stared about the room. It was impossible that a woman should have gotten in. The house only had three rooms. The L shaped main room, the bathroom, and the bedroom where her husband currently slept. Nevertheless, Mrs. Althaus crept to the partially closed bathroom door and peeked in. Empty. Now suspicious, Mrs. Althaus pressed the side of her head to the bedroom door and listened for any tell-tale sounds that Mr. Althaus might be entertaining a female guest without her knowledge. Silence.

The crying continued, still behind her. She turned and saw the fireplace. The sobbing grew more insistent. Mrs. Althaus approached it. With each step, the crying woman moaned as though warning her. Standing before the stone fireplace, Mrs. Althaus tilted an ear up towards the gap. The sound wasn't coming from above. It was coming from below. She clenched her fists and stared at the large white stones that made up the base of the fireplace. The crying rose up in a fever pitch before subsiding into silence.

Mrs. Althaus knelt and placed a hand on the largest stone. It was smooth, polished, and still warm from the dying fire. The primitive mix that had been used to cement the stones together had dried up and was crumbling. Absentmindedly, Mrs. Althaus scratched her left index finger between two of the stones, examining the sediment under her nail. She placed both palms on either end of the largest stone and pressed down with one and then the other.

The stone shifted. Mrs. Althaus froze. She looked over her shoulder, where she'd thought she'd heard a floorboard creak. The bedroom door was still closed. She got up, picked the grit from beneath her nail while staring at the stone. She didn't think about why she was digging out a butter knife from a box on the floor. Only that it was important.

Using the knife, she scoured and scraped the binding agent out from around the largest stone. It was quick work as most had dried to dust, and flaked away under her labored breath.

The crying hadn't resumed but she could hear it echoing in her head. That plaintive and helpless sobbing of a woman trapped and alone, like she was now. Had the woman crawled under the house and gotten stuck? Was she a robber that had come, thinking to plunder while the owners were away at dinner?

The stone began to wiggle and shift under her prying. The gap between it and the other stones was too small for her to get her fingers in for a good purchase, so she rooted around in the boxes until she found her husband's largest wrench. She jammed the handle into the space she'd made and leaned her right hip against it, levering her body weight down onto it. The stone refused to move, but then with a jerk, it popped up and to the right. It thumped to the floor on its polished side, exposing the heavily scratched and muddy bottom.

Mrs. Althaus fell onto the wrench and gasped as it dug into her leg. She rolled off it and got back onto her knees in front of the exposed dirt that had lain beneath the stone. She listened for a moment. Had that been another creak of a floor board? Mr. Althaus had always been a light sleeper, but she heard no movement from the bedroom.

She examined the dirt. It was perfectly smooth from where the stone had rested. She pushed the fingertips of her left hand in. As her fingers disappeared up to the first knuckle, she felt a smooth hardness. A part of her knew. Deep down inside, she knew what was there and it screamed at her to put the stone back and to go to bed.

Mrs. Althaus swallowed down her rising wine soured gorge, and began to sweep the dirt away with her hands. She tossed handfuls of the dry soil behind her, it thudded and slid softly on the hardwood. She unearthed the ribcage first. Next came the left arm, broken just above the elbow and shoved behind the skeleton's back. She found the hip. The left leg. Finally, she worked up the courage to scrape the dirt and dust off the small, delicate skull. The woman – it had to be a woman – was curled in a tight fetal position with her arms pulled behind her back and rough, rotting twine still discernable around the wrists. The tattered remains of clothing, now colorless and shapeless, lay in the dirt around the skeleton.

"Meddlesome bitch."

Mrs. Althaus spun, tripping over her own legs and landing akimbo, her back to the fire. Her heart thundered at the scare. Her husband stood above her, wrench in hand.

"The luck's gone out now. Don't you know anything about tradition? Goddamn bitch," he said, raising the wrench above his head.

Mrs. Althaus raised an arm up and felt it break under the heavy blow. She tumbled to the side, clutching her arm to her chest. She whimpered and kicked at the ground, sliding herself mere inches. Mr. Althaus kicked her legs aside and reached into the hole she'd made. He flung the bones out, not caring where they landed. He dug out handfuls of dirt, muttering under his breath. Mrs. Althaus rolled onto her ample stomach, crying out from the pain of lying on her broken arm. She clawed and kicked at the floor, crawling towards the front door.

The floor creaked as Mr. Althaus stepped over her to one of the half empty boxes next to the front door. He pulled out a roll of packing tape. It squealed as he pulled an arm's length from it.

"No! Please!" Mrs. Althaus cried.

His face was stony, cold, and unfeeling. His face was not that of the man she had married. Mr. Althaus reached down and wrenched her good arm back, pinning it to her back, and then he pulled her broken arm out from under her. She cried out, kicked her feet, and struggled to roll away. The blinding pain made her weak. He knelt on the backs of her knees, grinding them cruelly into the floor. He soon had her wrists taped together.

"Stop it! Oh, stop it, what are you doing?"

He dragged her body to the fireplace. Mrs. Althaus stretched out her legs, forced her back straight against the pain of her arm. He kicked her in the stomach, and she felt the bile spew from her lips. She felt herself pushed and kicked into the new hole. Her legs were jammed back and crushed against a stone. Mr. Althaus tossed the excavated dirt onto her. She tried to scream but choked on it.

The dirt blinded her but she heard the grinding of the large stone on the floor. Mrs. Althaus rocked on her side, trying to get her legs free, trying to roll up out of the shallow hole. She squinted up, craning her neck, in time to see Mr. Althaus roll the stone on top of her.

It fell. She felt the enormous weight. She felt several cracks inside her body as the thing settled. She grew deaf, blind, and buried in the dark. She tried to cry out but her lungs couldn't pull in anything but dirt. So, Mrs. Althaus did the only thing she could.

She began to cry.

DEAD HORSE BEACH
Amber Newberry

"No way," Georgie said back to his cousin in disbelief.

"Is too!" Jenny replied, tossing an old baseball back to him.

She wiped her arm across her forehead, removing beads of sweat. It should've been cooler that close to the ocean, but the wind had been absent for days, just like the clouds, causing the summer sun to beat down harder. The year was 1922, and the salty summer humidity was the hottest Salem had seen for years.

"No way. No how," Georgie said, and threw the ball back, hard. Jenny, ever the tomboy, caught the hard throw without hesitation or trouble.

"I'm tellin' ya. It ain't called Dead Horse Beach for nothin'!" Jenny spat back, her thick North Shore accent especially hung on the word *horse*.

"Well... how do *you* know?"

"Aunt Sadie told me a story, she wouldn't lie. When you get as old as her, you can't lie anymore or they won't let ya into heaven," Jenny said matter-of-factly.

"What story?" Georgie asked.

"She and your granddaddy was up at Dead Horse Beach when they was kids. Got caught in the rain," she threw the ball back to her cousin, "They tried to wait under the willows for it to let up, but it didn't, so they took off down the beach. It was pourin' and Aunt Sadie said she had to leave her boots on the porch for a month to dry--"

"I don't care about the boots, get to the part about the horses," he tossed the ball back at her.

"So, they was runnin' along the beach, tryin' to get home when Aunt Sadie spots some kinda sticks juttin' up outta the sand. 'Cept they ain't sticks."

"What was it?" Georgie asked, catching the ball and holding it, suddenly enthralled with an old family story.

"Legs! Four of 'em, sticking straight up outta the ground."

"Gross! Horse's legs?!"

"Yeah, ya dope! Horse legs! What else?"

"I thought it was baloney, people burying their dead horses out there."

"Why else would they call it Dead Horse Beach?" Jenny laughed.

"Anyway… get on with the story," Georgie urged, throwing the ball back at Jenny.

"So I guess someone buried that horse too shallow, because them legs was sticking straight up. Aunt Sadie dared grandpa to go up and pull on one of the legs, and get this, *he did it*!" Jenny said, astounded.

" 'Course he did! Ain't nothin' that scares Granddad!' "

"Anyway… so he goes up and pulls on one of them legs… well, I guess that horse had been there rottin' a while 'cause the whole thing come right off 'a that dead horse! Granddaddy fell backwards, still holding that leg and Aunt Sadie took off screaming, Granddad runnin' along after her."

Georgie stood there, mouth gaping, disgusted at the thought of jerking a leg right off a rotting animal.

" What a bunch of hooey!" Georgie asserted, breaking the silence.

"Oh sure, you're just sayin' that 'cause it creeps you out," Jennie snorted, shaking her short, boyish hair out of her face.

"Oh yeah? I bet I could scare the piss right outta ya, little girl," Georgie boasted, knowing that calling his cousin a 'little girl' would really get her riled up.

"Sure, let's hear it, then," Jennie asked, skeptical.

"Ya know that kid Mickey Walsh, the one that lives out there on Chestnut?"

"Sorta, yeah, what about him?" Jennie pulled the old ball glove off her hand, which was plenty dirty from a day of playing outside. Georgie fell into step beside her as they made their way up to the porch on Great Aunt Sadie's old colonial, set back from the water on Juniper Point.

"His brother went missing a few nights ago. Rudy Kelly said he overheard that crazy old guy who cleans up at the Willows, what's that fella's name, again?"

"Henry? He ain't crazy, he's just a little odd. Aunt Sadie called him 'feebleminded' or somethin' like that…"

"Yeah, well… anyway, Rudy heard Henry tellin' some fella' that they saw a guy bury a body out at Dead Horse--"

"Nuh-uh, Georgie, you just made that up to try and top the story about the horse!" Jennie punched Goergie in the arm, which made him wince, but he tried not to show it had really hurt and refrained from rubbing the spot.

"I'm tellin' ya, the cops even went up there to investigate, but they didn't find nuthin'—"Jenny cut him off again.

"So a hogwash story about a dead body that wasn't even there is supposed to scare me?" Jenny asked as she climbed the four stairs onto the porch.

"Nah, see, they didn't find a body, but they found a pair 'a shoes that looked like they might a' belonged to Mickey's brother."

"What's a pair a' shoes got to do with a whole body?"

"Will you stop and let me tell the story?"

"Sure," Jenny replied in exaggerated boredom, following up under her breath with, "shoes got nothin' to do with a body, that's what."

"So the cops told Mickey's mom that maybe he went for a swim and the rip tide got him, or he got a cramp and drowned."

"Well, that's a sad story, alright, but I ain't wet my pants, yet, cuz," Jenny joked.

"Yeah, it's sad alright… but not as sad as if he was murdered," Georgie asserted, finally climbing the steps and standing next to his cousin, who suddenly perked up.

"Murder? Here in Salem? I heard they don't do that no more, ever since all that stuff with the witches way back when," Jenny teased, still interested in the prospect of a local unsolved murder.

"Go ahead and make jokes, but they found some kid beat to death out there in the woods over by Dead Horse Beach a few weeks back. He weren't buried or nothin', just lyin' there bloodied and broken. July eighteenth, it happened, I bet Aunt Sadie still has the newspaper somewhere 'round the house." Georgie spoke proudly, knowing that he actually could find proof about this particular murder. Jenny was finally silent, accepting this story as truth.

"Why didn't I hear nothin' about it, then?" Jenny finally asked.

"You only been here two days, people don't like to talk about that stuff around kids, they wouldn't want to scare us, ya know?" Georgie was the one doing the teasing, now.

"Children, come along for lemonade!" Aunt Sadie called from inside the house. The doors and windows were wide open in hopes that a summer breeze might eventually find its way in.

Jenny begged Aunt Sadie to rehash the Dead Horse Beach story for Georgie, and after some coaxing she relented and told the story again. She was likely resistant knowing about the recent disappearance from the beach, but she did not mention it as a reason for not wanting to tell the tale. Nothing made her quite as happy as telling a bit of ancient history, especially if it was from her own childhood.

"Now that's enough about horses," Aunt Sadie said, dabbing a wet cloth across her neck, her grey curls stuck to her forehead and temples, wet with sweat. "Goodness, it's hot as a Boston bean pot."

"Can we go down to the bathing beach?" Jenny asked, fanning herself with her hand.

"Oh, I don't know, children, there's been some news…" Aunt Sadie paused before mentioning a possible drowning on Dead Horse Beach, which was only a short walk from her house, an even shorter walk from the Kiddies Bathing Beach, where the cousins wanted to go to cool off.

"What news?" Georgie questioned, knowing she was talking about the missing Walsh boy.

"Oh, nothing for you to be concerned with; I'd rather you waited until your daddy comes back from downtown so he could take you to swim," Aunt Sadie told the children.

"We went out on our own last year, Auntie," Jenny offered.

"Yeah, and there's always tons of people, and a lifeguard," Georgie urged.

Aunt Sadie was uneasy about sending the children alone, but she felt sorry for them, cooped up on a sweltering August afternoon with their seventy-year-old Great Aunt. She looked from face to face and saw the sweat drip down Georgie's temple.

"Well then, I suppose if you went on your own last year it would be just fine." The children smiled one to the other. "Please be careful, and stay where your feet touch the sand, don't go out too far."

"We won't, we'll be extra safe, Auntie!" Jenny said, jolting up from her seat, Georgie did the same and downed the last of his lemonade.

"You two be back here before dinner or it'll be your last dip on the bathing beach alone!" Aunt Sadie called after the children, but they were already up the stairs, changing into their bathing suits.

Seconds later, their steps rumbled back down the stairs, as though a herd of elephants had suddenly appeared within the house. They each donned a black tank top body suit that cut just above the knees into shorts. Jenny's had a skirt piece, but both suits had a white belt around the waist. Aunt Sadie had made the children matching swimsuits since they were big enough to wade in the water. Each summer, she would order a new pair of beach slippers for her nieces and nephews to match their homemade swimwear. Georgie's had arrived a little large for his feet, but he had grown out of last year's pair so he'd have to make do with the new pair, because there were jagged rocks to step across before reaching the beach.

"Come and have a nickel, each of you! I don't expect you'll be able to pass E.W. Hobbs without stopping for a bit of popcorn," Aunt Sadie smiled as she placed a shiny coin in the hand of each child. Georgie had no pockets on his swimsuit, so he handed his to Jenny for safe keeping in her skirt pocket.

"Thank you, Auntie," the children echoed in jubilant unison before taking off out the door and down the steps onto the green lawn that stretched out toward the dirt road that would take them to the beach. Aunt Sadie vaguely heard a challenge to race in the distance as she took a seat in her rocking chair on the porch and watched the two disappear on their way to cool off.

When the cousins arrived beach-side, Jenny unquestionably the winner of the race, they stopped short at the wall, admiring the sand and water. Families were scattered about, blankets strewn across the beach while folks waded and swam.

"Race ya to the shore?" Jenny asked, ready to bolt when Georgie accepted the challenge.

"I think I want popcorn, first," Georgie suggested.

"Yeah, okay," Jenny agreed, and the two walked toward the amusement park, where the smell of popcorn filled the humid air. The scent of salt and butter made the children's mouths water as they got closer.

"Hey, ya know what? If we combine our money, we can get popcorn and a coke!" Georgie offered as they transitioned from the harsh summer sun to the shade beneath the willow trees.

"I guess, or we could just get ice cream instead--" Jenny began, but paused when she heard the tinkling music playing from the old carousel that had graced Salem Willows since the 1880's. When the two reached the wide open entry-way into Hobbs, they were overcome with the midsummer joy of a Salem tradition.

Lines of people waited to be served popcorn, sodas, and ice cream cones. A small crowd stood gazing at the spinning carousel animals who jaunted their passengers round and round to the tune of some forgotten folk song. Jenny admired the delicate paintings that lined the top as they passed, one by one. There were portraits of presidents long passed, and American scenery among the white, gold, and red adornments on the round circus-like top. The paintings were a detail she was sure most people didn't notice as they were entranced by the lovely and elaborate menagerie of animals. There were giraffes, camels, and lions, none of which the children had ever seen in real life. There were also dogs large enough for children to climb atop and ride round and round, as well as carriages led by beautifully carved horses of every color. The horses were Jenny's favorite of all, and when she spotted her favorite horse, a white stallion with a dark red saddle, passing by on its way around, she knew her nickel would not be for popcorn that day.

"I'm gonna ride the carousel," Jenny said, as if she were telling herself to do so.

"What about popcorn?" Georgie asked as Jenny dragged him toward the line for the merry-go-round.

"We can get that another time."

"We can ride the carousel another time," Georgie replied.

"You can get your popcorn, but I'm goin' for a ride," Jenny insisted, and Georgie relented, as he often did with his assertive tom-boy cousin.

The wait was a long one, The Willows being such a popular tourist destination in the summer. The carousel line was much longer than the one with people awaiting treats. The children followed the queue as it snaked around the building, all the way round the amusement they were waiting patiently to ride. After a long while, Georgie finally became antsy, as a child might in terrible heat and such a long queue.

"We've only made it halfway up there and it's already been a long time, let's just get ice cream and go swim," Georgie urged.

"No way! I'm not getting' outta line after waiting so long!" Jenny insisted. Georgie huffed and crossed his arms over his chest, knowing he wasn't going to get her to budge.

"Fine then," he said, "You can ride by yourself, I'm getting' ice cream and goin' to swim."

"Don't leave me here alone! You waited all this time!" Jenny snapped at him.

"This is silly, we've been waitin' forever! It's gonna be dark by the time we get our ride."

"So what?" Jenny said, "We'll be late for dinner. Aunt Sadie will give us a good scolding, big whoop!"

"I'm not afraid of getting' in trouble, I'm just hungry," Georgie lied. It was too hot for a big meal, anyway. He just wanted to get a swim in before it was too late and they had to get home.

"If we get outta line now, we wasted all that time. Don't be dumb," Jenny said, frustration apparent in her voice.

"Fine. I'll stay if you come with me to Dead Horse Beach after our ride," Georgie said, a smirk on his face. He knew his cousin talked like she was brave, but after his story about murders and drowning, she'd likely want to pass up on the deal and settle for ice cream instead of the ride on her favorite carved horse.

"Fine!" Jenny huffed, her nose pointed upward, knowing what Georgie was up to. She turned away from him and moved up in the line. Georgie was dumbfounded, knowing he'd tacked on a later return home. Now he was getting worried about that scolding.

By the time we get our ride, the sun will be setting and Auntie will be putting food on the table, Georgie thought. She usually served an early dinner, but this time of year, she waited until late in the day to cook dinner as the evening got cooler.

The two stood at the back wall waiting their turn, and by Georgie's calculations, that would be either the very next ride, or the one right after. He tapped his foot nervously, hoping they would be next. Jenny turned away from the carousel as a breeze swept in through the back door way, carrying with it the smell of fresh paint that had something off about it. The back door was open and she could see an old man dressed in blue jean overalls painting one of the carved dogs from the carousel. She could see where the paint had chipped in places, and instead of painting over the chips, he was painting over the whole seat. It was a grey-hound painted a cheery pale blue with the same dark red saddle color that was on her favorite horse. The old man's gnarly fingers worked the brush effortlessly, covering the saddle in wet paint. She saw the paint dried over the edge of the bucket, especially brownish red in contrast to the bright burgundy it was while it was wet. It seemed he'd mixed the color too dark, and she hoped he wouldn't touch her perfect stallion.

Her gaze moved to a dark horse leaned up against a tree, the blood-red paint drying into a weird brownish red. The old man picked up a large tub of thin, red liquid, probably a paint he'd thinned out too much in an effort to save a dime. As the old man went to pour it into the bucket of burgundy, a gust of wind picked up and swept the scent of the liquid toward Jenny. When she caught the smell, it reminded her of something but she couldn't quite place it, like water on tin, a sort of metallic scent. The smell reminded her of Aunt Sadie's old cast iron skillet. The old man caught her staring as he poured the liquid in, and he parted his lips in a grin that was missing more than a few teeth.

"C'mon, it's our turn!" Georgie said, passing her and grabbing her by the wrist, not wanting to waste another second. The children hurried toward the carousel and Jenny ran for her horse, getting it just as a younger boy was coming at it from behind the horse. She grabbed the reigns and jumped on before the boy could do the same. He stuck his tongue out in his defeat and rushed toward the next nearest animal, a lion.

Jenny looked down at her white stallion and hugged it around the neck whispering 'gotcha' in his ear, as though it were alive. She ran her fingers down the length of the horse's neck, admiring the golden paint that, up close, did appear to be chipped and weathered.

"Remember me?" she whispered in the horse's wooden ear.

"Don't be stupid, it's not real," Georgie grunted from the horse next to her, an equally weathered black stallion with a gold seat that was worn enough that you could see the waves in the wood through the paint.

"Shut up, it's starting!" Jenny snapped, wanting to enjoy the ride, regardless of Georgie's ever-growing grumpiness.

In her mind, Jenny was on that carousel alone, and the horse broke free from the confines of the golden bar and galloped away down to the beach. Jenny felt the salt air whipping at her hair as she rode a living replica of her carved white stallion, a chiseled horse she was certain would be named Thunder. For such a long wait, the ride seemed to be over in a matter of seconds, and Georgie immediately interrupted Jenny's fantasy telling her it was time to go before the carousel even slowed all the way to a stop. She slid down off her horse and looked into its charming blue eye, and she swore it looked back at her, like it had a spirit of its own.

"Let's go, Jenny! They're letting other people in!" Georgie insisted, and he tugged at her arm, getting her to finally let go of Thunder and leave the Hobbs' building. As they exited, Jenny looked back over her shoulder and saw that the old painter had disappeared and the back door was now shut.

When the children stepped back outside beneath the willow trees, the sun was setting ,and the sky was scattered with flat-looking clouds in hues of tangerine and coral. It was dim under the trees and the encroaching evening sent the sun quickly down, soon it would disappear behind the houses across the water in Beverly.

"We should probably just head back," Jenny said, acknowledging the sunset. The hour was late and it would likely be eight o'clock before the children got home.

"I knew you'd chicken out of going to Dead Horse!" Georgie spat at his cousin, triumphant.

"I'm not chickening out, it's getting late. We can go tomorrow," Jenny said. It was the logical answer, to avoid further scolding from Aunt Sadie, but Georgie wasn't having it.

"You agreed to it when I stayed in line with you, so unless you're chicken, let's get going!" Georgie was smug, expecting her to insist on going home.

"Race ya there!" Jenny said, and she took off running in the direction of Professor Kenerson's Casino, which was opposite the way they'd need to take to get to Aunt Sadie's.

"Hey, no fair!" Georgie called after his cousin, but it didn't stop him from jolting after her, trying to catch up.

Before long, Georgie was gaining on his cousin. As he got closer, he noticed sorry Old Henry picking up rubbish left behind by the tourists. Jenny wasn't paying attention, and this was his chance to pick up the pace and pass her for the win. As he expected, his cousin ran smack into Henry, both of them tumbling backward. *This is it, old boy*, Georgie thought, *this time I beat her.*

Jenny had fallen backward onto her rear end, and she shook her head to steady her vision. She followed the blue overalls up, half expecting to see the old man who'd been painting the carousel horses standing before her, but she found an unnerving sight when her eyes met one pale blue eye, the other covered with a black eye patch. Old Henry might have been 'short of mind' as her father had once put it, but he looked fearsome in his dirty work overalls. His head was misshapen, as though he'd been in some freak accident, but Aunt Sadie had informed Jenny that he was born that way; deformed, and with only one eye.

Old Henry cracked his mouth into what he hoped would be a gentle smile, but his jagged, yellow, and unkempt teeth only made him appear more monstrous, and Jenny was up and running away before he could offer his large and twisted hand to help the child up. Henry stared after her until she disappeared over the knoll and behind the curtain of a willow, as she ran to Dead Horse Beach to catch up to her cousin.

Somewhere between Hobbs and Dead Horse, the sky had gone from twilight to nearly dusk. When Jenny's feet reached the sand, she stopped to catch her breath. She hunched over and placed her hands on her knees while she sucked in the sea air.

"Don't think this means I'm going to lose next time, Georgie," Jenny said between huffs, still looking down. She expected him to gloat right away, but there was no answer.

She raised her head and waited for her eyes to fully adjust as it grew darker.

"Georgie?" she asked, but it remained silent, save for the sound of the water lapping against the shore and the sound of people in the distance, back at the Willows. Music began to play from Professor Kenerson's Dance Hall at the Casino, and it drifted down to Jenny's ears, giving her pause as she listened for Georgie to move and give away his hiding place. She looked down the length of the beach, it was very dark, but she could see the high stones at the other end of the beach, and there appeared to be no figure between her and the rocks.

"Alright, you won, Georgie, and now we gotta get back or Aunt Sadie will have our hides!" Jenny called out. She waited for an answer and grew angry with herself for allowing him to get at her nerves. The wind tumbled in from the water, cooling Jenny's skin and raising goosebumps up and down her arms and legs. She turned to look behind her and was comforted by the light of the Casino behind in the distance, casting a glow over the park.

A fish splashing in the water startled her, and she jumped, turning around to stare back at the dark and empty beach.

"That's enough, Georgie, you come out right now!" Jenny shouted, her voice echoed back to her, bouncing off the rocks across the beach. She sighed and stepped forward, hoping she'd find him hiding at the other end of the sand. The large rocks had deep crevices and she was certain he'd be hiding among them.

A stalling motor car sent out a loud pop and caused Jenny to jump again, she was growing angry in her nervousness. Fear made her walk faster until she tripped over something and fell onto her knees, catching herself on her palms. Leaning back onto her heels, she brushed her hands together, removing sharp shells and rocks that hurt, but had not punctured her skin. She looked down at what she had tripped over, and recognized the matching beach slippers Aunt Sadie had ordered from a mail away catalogue for each of the children.

Tears welled up in Jenny's eyes as she recalled the story her cousin had told her just a few hours before about the Walsh boy, and all they'd found of him when he had disappeared. Trembling, Jenny ran from the beach and called for help. Tears stung her cheek as they rolled down her face, as she ran toward the casino screaming for help. The hanging curtain of a willow tree whipped at her face and arms as she ran through them toward the green and white building, where light, music, and laughter tumbled from the windows, in contrast to her own terror.

Two gentlemen who were walking with young women on their arms heard the child's screams and jogged toward her to see what was the matter with the hysterical little girl.

"My cousin is missing, I was following him down to the beach," Jenny sobbed, barely getting the words out. "Georgie, he might be drowning," she gasped between her cries. The two men took off toward the beach, while the ladies who had followed their gentleman companions arrived and tried to comfort Jenny. Upon hearing what had happened, one of the women went back toward the casino building to ask for more help. Several men ran by, two carrying lanterns to help in the search for Georgie.

After a while, some of the men returned and asked Jenny questions, and the police were called to the scene. They asked many questions, wanting to know where she and her cousin had been and for how long. They wanted to know if she'd noticed anything strange or if she'd seen anything out of the ordinary. Why were they on the beach? Why were they alone? Why were they out alone after dark? Had she seen anyone else?

"I ran into Old Henry, I only saw him," Jenny whimpered. She began to cry, again, and tried to explain that it was all her fault for asking Georgie to race. If she'd been paying attention, they both would have made it to the beach at the same time.

"If I hadn't run into Old Henry," Jenny sobbed into a towel someone had wrapped around her.

Some of the men were sent to find Old Henry, to ask him questions about what he'd seen. The rest formed a search party and they combed the area around Salem Willows, Dead Horse Beach, and out on Juniper Point. When Jenny's father arrived, he held her in a tight embrace and assured himself that she was not hurt. The two nice ladies who had been with the gentlemen who heard her screams offered to bring Jenny back to Aunt Sadie's house, so her father could join the search party.

When they arrived, Aunt Sadie's eyes were red from tears of worry. "We've sent for your uncle. Georgie's parents will be on their way up from Boston immediately," Aunt Sadie said, rocking the little girl in her arms. She held Jenny tight and told her they would find him, trying hard to reassure herself, as well as her niece.

* * *

Weeks passed, and on the day Jenny and her father were to return to Boston, Salem Willows was winding down the busy summer season. The two would take a boat back into the city right from The Willows, and as they rounded the corner at Hobbs, the familiar tinkling music of the carousel drifted out of the building and into the ears of passers-by, luring them in for the final ride of the season. While many of the businesses had already closed down for the coming autumn months, one or two places remained open for the last of the tourists, and Hobbs was one.

The familiar scent of salty butter and popcorn mingled with the bittersweet ocean air, the humidity gone. Jenny stared into the building, nearly empty, apart from a few couples getting the last popcorn of the season. The carousel stood in all its glory, empty of riders. She watched the animals stampeding round and round, and at first it made her smile, but it inevitably made her think of Georgie. The family had resigned themselves to the loss, knowing he would've probably returned by then if he were coming back. The Walsh boy had also never resurfaced, and it was another indication that Jenny's cousin might be lost forever beneath the water.

Deep in thought, Jenny felt herself drawn to one of the last places she saw her cousin alive, and she walked toward the carousel, her father not noticing that she'd left his side as he looked out toward the willow trees, his thoughts also on his nephew. When she got close, she could see that the entirety of the ride had been repainted, the white and gold was fresh, as though it had been done within the week. She looked for Thunder and when she caught sight of him, she noticed that each of the horses now had the odd dark brown, burgundy paint on the saddles.

"Care for a go 'round, miss?" A ragged voice asked. Jenny looked up to see the old man she'd seen painting the horses the day she'd lost Georgie.

"No thank you, sir, I haven't a nickel," Jenny replied softly.

"This one's on the house," he said, opening the gate to let the little girl in.

"Go on, Jenny, if you'd like," her father said, he'd come up behind her.

"Okay, then…" Jenny said, it might have been cheerful if she hadn't felt such sadness at the absence of her cousin.

She stepped up onto the platform and felt it quiver, even with her little weight. Her feet tapped the wood as she went toward Thunder. She lifted a leg to the stirrup, but before she lifted herself up, she felt as though the black horse was calling for her. She turned toward it and pressed a hand against the formerly gold saddle, now with a fresh coat of brownish red paint; the strange iron-like scent of the coating still lingered. Jenny looked into the eye of the horse and saw that it matched the dark details of the harness and saddle, and, for some reason, Jenny suddenly felt cold. It was September, and being that close to the water, perhaps the wind had chilled a little.

"Need a hand up, Jenny?" her father asked.

"No, I got it," she replied, and climbed up onto the horse that Georgie had ridden a few weeks before.

The music began to play that familiar tinkling melody, and the carved animals whipped into a gallop. The motion swept up Jenny's short hair and made her even colder. She felt a smile touch her lips for the first time since the night she'd lost Georgie, and suddenly she felt the warmth of two arms around her waist and a body pressed against her from behind. She closed her eyes and the horse was as real as Thunder had been on that day several weeks before, and so was Georgie, sitting behind her on their black stallion. It was like he was there, forever, trapped in the wood, in the music, in the paint.

When the carousel slowed, Jenny held on tightly to the horse's neck, as though she were holding onto Georgie, as though, if she let go, she would be letting go of him. Tears stung her cheeks and she held her eyes closed tight, still feeling Georgie's arms wrapped around her waist, trying just as hard to hold onto her. It was like he wanted to pull her into limbo so they could be together.

Finally, her father came onto the platform and detached her grasp from the black stallion and replaced them around his own neck. When they passed the old man who was running the ride, Jenny saw something in his eyes that said he knew what had happened to her beloved cousin, and she stared at him through her tears until she couldn't see him anymore. The poor child sobbed all the way home to Boston.

It was years before Jenny returned to visit her Great Aunt Sadie out on Juniper Point in Salem. In 1930, the year that Jenny was sixteen, she returned to spend a summer with her Auntie. On her first day, she'd gone down to where the carousel was to look for Georgie and their horse, but they were gone, and so was the old man who'd offered her that final ride. When she enquired at Hobbs about the missing horses, they told her they had been sold to a well-known department store in New York City for a window display.

That summer was also the first anyone had told her that Henry had been blamed for the disappearances of three local boys. He had been the only person seen near Dead Horse Beach the night Georgie went missing. Old Henry was never tried, and was quickly hanged the winter of '22. Only Jenny knew that he'd been wrongfully accused, certain the old man at the carousel was responsible.

Jenny rode the carousel for the last time that summer, but she knew Georgie was gone, just as the horse with the blood red paint was gone. Both were lost to her forever.

ABOUT THE WRITERS

-P.L. McMillan is an avid fan of all literature- horrid, horrible, and horrifying - that's why she does her part to bring a little horror into the world one story at a time. She has previously published two creepy tales in Sanitarium and Neat Magazine.

-M.R. DeLuca's writing, running the gamut from book reviews to short stories, has placed in various national writing contests. In addition to the beauty of words, M.R. enjoys numbers, speleothems, and homemade whoopie pies.

-Melissa McArthur teaches college writing, works as a freelance editor at Clicking Keys, writes twice monthly for Magical Words, and tells stories. Melissa is utterly fascinated by books; she believes that there's something magical about holding them in your hand and watching as the words disappear and the story unfolds before your eyes. She hopes that she can do that for readers both as an editor and a writer—create stories that engulf you, change you, scare you, bewilder you, make you laugh, make you cry, and through stories, reveal deeper truths about life. www.melissamcarthur.net

-A professional writer since 1983, Nancy Brewka-Clark lives in Beverly, which was part of Salem until 1668. In a neat twist of fate, her husband Tom Clark, a direct descendant of Susanna Martin, one of the 19 hanged 'witches,' was a court reporter for The Salem News for many years. For more on her published fiction, nonfiction, poetry, and drama please visit nancybrewkaclark.com.

-Amber Newberry is the editor and proprietor of FunDead Publications in Salem, MA; a lover of all things spooky, she spends her time reading and writing stories macabre in nature. Amber has published a gothic romance novel called Walls of Ash, a novella called The Widow's Blessing, and has been a featured writer on BloodyDisgusting.com. She has a follow-up to Walls of Ash in the writing stages, as well as two YA novels in the works. www.AuthorAmberNewberry.com

-Born in Massachusetts, R.C. Mulhare has felt at home in Salem since she was a wee thing listening to her mum reading Grimm's Faery Tales and quoting Edgar Allen Poe, as well as her Irish storyteller dad's tales of oddballs and their antics. Later, she learned that the inspiration for H.P. Lovecraft's "witch-haunted Arkham" literally was home to some of her family, as she has ancestors on her mother's side who arrived from England and settled there a few years before the Witch Hysteria of 1692.
Her writing blog and other goodies can be found at www.goodreads.com/matrixrefugee

-Laurie Moran is a lover of the macabre, quirky, and cute, and wishes it were Halloween every day. When she isn't reading or editing Amber Newberry's writing, she likes to make costumes, cupcakes, and tiny cemeteries. Laurie lives in Lynn, Massachusetts, and works and plays in Salem, Massachusetts.

- Fueled by imagination, and the relative quiet unknown of his hometown, Cincinnati native David J. Gibbs looks for the lost threads of stories wherever they might be. Never losing touch with the wonder and terror of childhood, he continues to push the limits of imagination with stories that will excite, delight, scare and, most of all, surprise his readers. Details about his work, which has appeared in dozens of magazines and anthologies, can be found at www.davidjgibbs.com

-Patrick Cooper likes ginger ale and his work has appeared in Thuglit, Shotgun Honey, Akashic Books, Out of the Gutter, Spinetingler, and other shady places. He's allegedly a film critic for Bloody Disgusting and Collider. A Salem State graduate and proud as hell of it. Dig: patrickgcooper.com

-Alec Anthony Firicano hails from the peculiar city of Malden, Massachusetts. When not attempting to purge his mind of strange tales, he is occupied with efforts to finish various musical and artistic projects. He will be posting news about his various exploits as well as new novel excerpts, stories, opinion pieces and poetry at www.Facebook.com/AlecAnthonyFiricano

-Mary Jo Fox lives in San Diego, CA, where she toils as a paper pusher while trying to finally get her writing career off of the ground. Another one of her stories will appear in "Deadhead Miles Volume 2," due out from FOF Publishing August 2016. When not writing, she is spending her time reading, watching endless hours of true crime and paranormal TV shows, and putting together that perfect geek girl outfit for the next convention.

-Richard Farren Barber was born in Nottingham, England. After studying in London he returned to the East Midlands. He lives with his wife and son and works as a manager for a local university. His first novella "The Power of Nothing" was published in September 2013. His second novella "The Sleeping Dead" was published by DarkFuse in August 2014. His third novella "Odette" was published in July 2016 in the anthology "Darker Battlefields". His website iswww.richardfarrenbarber.co.uk

-Brian Malachy Quinn currently teaches Physics at the University of Akron and in his free time writes and creates art. He is the author of "Astronomy: A Computational Approach" Van-Griner 2010 and ghost writer of a book on wealth management. His gold standard for short story horror is Poe's "Fall of the House of Usher" and he enjoys writing specifically historic horror in which he has to learn about a certain by-gone period. His art can be found at: www.brianquinnstudio.com

-Fort Worth writer Jonathan Shipley creates in the genres of fantasy, science fiction, and horror and has published (or has pending) over seventy short stories, including seven in the Sword & Sorceress fantasy series, and one in the After Death anthology that won the 2014 Bram Stoker award. Old houses are a major part of his life and although Redridge House where "Love and Oil" takes place is fictional, it represents all the actual old houses that come with built-in creaks and bumps in the night. Jonathan maintains a web presence at www.shipleyscifi.com where you can find a full list of his short fiction.

-A lifelong fan or horror and the macabre, since he was traumatized by an episode of 'Alfred Hitchcock Presents' as a child, Mike Carey is a wee bit twisted. He's spent his years doing cool stuff, lame stuff, and all the stuff in between. He's lived his entire life in the Salem area, and plans to have his entire death there, as well. www.SalemUncommons.SmackJeeves.com

-Born in Pennsylvania, Salinda Tyson lived a long time in Northern California, and now lives in North Carolina. Always a fan of Fractured Fairytales, fantasy and science fiction, she's a bookworm and former tree-climber, as well as a history buff.

-Kathleen Halecki possesses a B.A. and M.A. in history, and a doctoral degree in interdisciplinary studies with a focus on early modern Scotland. Although born in New York, she now lives in Salem and teaches humanities courses at a local college.

-Bill Dale Grizzle, or just Dale to all who know him, was born and raised in rural Northwest Georgia; he resides there still and almost all of his writings are heavily influenced by his folk surroundings. Dale has a soft spot in his heart for Christmas stories and just last year released, 'Mandy the Mischievous Elf', a 100-page chapter book from Mirror Publishing. A sequel is in the works along with a collection of Christmas stories from around the country. Dale's latest novel, 'Millie McCray', is in the process of being edited for publication and the second installment of what will become a trilogy is well under way. 'Inspection Connection' is Dale's first attempt at spooky stories and is honored that it was selected by FunDead Publications to appear in 'Shadows of Salem'. He hopes you enjoy the story and welcomes your feedback on Facebook or at billdalegrizzle@aol.com.

-Jonathan D. Nichols has been writing for seven years, and has always been huge into horror. Jonathan was in the military and spent over a year stationed away from this family, where he began writing and hasn't been able to stop since. Jonathan has previous published works in Tome Magazine, Blood Moon Rising Magazine, and has been featured in several anthologies.

ABOUT FUNDEAD PUBLICATIONS

FunDead Publications initially began as a satirical blog offering advice to the undead and those interested in the undead. The site picked up a little steam answering write-in's 'Dear Abby' style, and eventually resulted in a series of amusing self-help pamphlets geared toward those wishing to date the undead. We still use some of these pamphlets as marketing material, featuring a different artist in each one, sharing the promotion for both the illustrator and the writers, as well as FunDead Publications.

Later, as FunDead creator, Amber Newberry, began writing serious projects, she soon discovered a love for helping others in the development of their work. Having a background in sales team management and marketing proved to be a great asset in the gathering of submissions, and in the promotion of her own work, as well as of others. Because of her love for Salem, MA (her current hometown) she wanted to pay homage in the best way she knew how: by writing, and thought it would be the perfect opportunity to invite others to do the same.

The result of months of work is a collection of macabre short stories that read a little like a love letter to Salem and its darker side. Amber couldn't have hoped for a better outcome, and she hopes to produce more collections set in her favorite town.

Shadows in Salem is the first official release for FunDead Publications, and the submission process has been as much a learning experience, as it was a huge success. This first anthology has already inspired a series of other spooky anthologies based in other locations around the US that are considered hotbeds for ghosts and the macabre. Future plans for spooky short story collections include Savannah, Gettysburg, and New Orleans. (Just to name a few, because why would we stop there?)

Currently, FunDead Publications also has a similar style of anthology in the reading process called 'Night in New Orleans', as well as building the foundation for a collection of chilling Christmas tales. FunDead also has a few poetry anthologies slowly coming together, and Amber hopes to have those available to the public by fall 2017.

Dear Reader,

Thank you for purchasing this copy of Shadows in Salem, it has been a labor of love, and a true joy to work on. The interest in this project has been overwhelming and only reassures us that a second volume should come in the near future.

We'd also like to thank you for supporting a local and independent small publisher. We may be the little guys, but we do this for love, with the hope that we might help keep the art of story-telling alive and well, and a little on the spooky side.

With Gratitude,
Amber Newberry
Editor-in-Chief
FunDead Publications